"VIVID CHARACTERS...DOMINATE THIS CHARMING MYSTERY."

—*Publishers Weekly*

———————— ★ ————————

"...A SERIES BEGINNING WORTHY OF FURTHER ATTENTION."

—*Murder ad lib*

———————— ★ ————————

"...A TRADITIONAL COZY...POPULATED WITH VIABLE CHARACTERS..."

—*Mystery News*

———————— ★ ————————

"A PERMANENT RETIREMENT HAS ALL THE ELEMENTS OF A GOOD MYSTERY."

—Worcester, MA *The News*

———————— ★ ————————

"I HOPE LAURA AND AARON WILL BE BACK FOR MORE ADVENTURES."

—Ruth Robinson, *The Chatanooga Times*

Forthcoming from Worldwide Mystery by
JOHN MILES

MURDER IN RETIREMENT
A MOST DEADLY RETIREMENT

A PERMANENT RETIREMENT

JOHN MILES

W🌐RLDWIDE®

TORONTO • NEW YORK • LONDON
AMSTERDAM • PARIS • SYDNEY • HAMBURG
STOCKHOLM • ATHENS • TOKYO • MILAN
MADRID • WARSAW • BUDAPEST • AUCKLAND

A PERMANENT RETIREMENT

A Worldwide Mystery/February 1997

This edition is reprinted by arrangement with Walker and Company.

ISBN 0-373-26228-0

Printed in U.S.A.

A PERMANENT RETIREMENT

ONE

A RESTLESS, HOT NIGHT wind faintly stirred the scrub oaks and sycamores scattered over the shallow rural hills a dozen miles south of Oklahoma City. There was no moon, but the vast dry sky teemed with stars. A car hummed down a dirt road, leaving a faint plume of pink dust as it passed a distant structure nestled into the side of a hill; in the building, light shone warmly from a hundred windows. Here in the remote countryside, it was as unexpected as a giant alien spaceship, landed from another universe.

Inside the Timberdale Retirement Center, the vast central atrium on the main floor stood quiet, deserted except for a young woman behind the reception desk, lazily turning pages of a college textbook. No one else could be seen; it was past 11:00 p.m., and all the residents of the Timberdale Retirement Center had toddled off to their rooms.

The girl at the desk, Stacy Miller, turned another page of the botany book and yawned. Without turning her head, she rummaged with her right hand into the wreckage of a pizza brought with her from Norman earlier in the evening. Blindly finding a piece, Stacy bit into cold dough, congealed provolone, and leathery pepperoni. Yum.

Stacy hoped she could stay awake all night. She had her days and nights rather well-turned around this summer, and usually didn't feel so sleepy. But she had been off Sunday and last night, and had played hard both days, missing her daytime winks.

Stacy wondered why Timberdale's big boss, the formidable Mrs. Judith Epperman, was such a fanatic about night staff staying awake anyway. Timberdale was tomblike from midnight to six in the morning. Nothing ever happened. Sometimes Stacy wondered how the old people here kept from going straight through the ceiling, it was all so *dull*. Honestly, what kept them going? Stacy knew she'd die from boredom if she ever had to live like Timberdale's residents did, day in, day out. Did any of them—she wondered suddenly now—ever really do much of *anything?*

Stacy would have been surprised.

Many of the hundred-plus retirees living in the Timberdale complex were already asleep. Some restlessly watched TV, or read, because old age and loneliness are sleep-robbers. Most, despite outward appearances, carried secrets.

In their apartment on the second floor, Julius Pfeister, seventy, and his wife, Dot, sixty-six, were ready to turn in. Standing on opposite sides of their big canopy bed, they carefully turned down the peach brocaded cover and white skirt-sheet beneath it. Tall, bulky, with bearlike shoulders and rounded belly, he wore military-cut pale blue cotton pajamas, ironed without a wrinkle, and gleaming brown leather houseshoes. She had already removed her floor-length ivory peignoir, and stood tiny in her matching night-gown, sleeveless, as elegant and flawless as her husband's pajamas.

They crawled into bed from opposite sides, turned off the lamps on either bedstand, and moved close to each other. He sighed heavily.

"Tired?" she murmured.

"Big day," he rumbled. "Bigger one tomorrow."

Dot Pfeister said nothing. Her chest tightened.

"Heavy stock trading tomorrow," her husband told her. "Inevitable, after today's rally. Must be up early, stay on top of it. Keep that old computer humming, eh, dear?"

She said nothing, but held his great, dearly familiar bulk closer against her.

Sometimes she thought her heart would break.

On another floor, artist Ellen Smith paced the floor, devoured by her hurt and anger. Anger had been central to her life for so long now that she didn't remember feeling otherwise. But the latest affront had shocked her, made everything worse.

Ellen was a charter resident at Timberdale, here almost five years. Moving here had been galling to her. She had always prided herself on her independence. But what did you do after Charlie was gone and *twice* the burglars had broken in, and your heart and lungs acted up so that you had to be in a place where you could summon nearby, immediate help?

Timberdale was a beautiful and expensive retirement center. Not so bad, really, Ellen told herself for the thousandth time. Visitors sometimes said Timberdale reminded them of a vacation resort. "It's not bad," Ellen always said in response. *Not bad for a place where you go to die,* she wanted to add, but never did.

She had lived much of her life with simmering hate—of people who refused to take her seriously, of real or imagined slights, of her own ability to be the artist she knew she could be if she could *just once* make her hands portray what she saw and felt in her heart.

The latest cruelty was very, very hard to take. Ellen was going to get even.

On Two East, Maude Thuringer finished putting Oil of Olay on her face, and deftly placed the hairnet over her thinning gray hair. Maude ached—the rheumatism again—and it would be a long time before she slept. Going into the tiny living room, every wall choked with bookcases of mystery novels, she eased herself into her BarcaLounger and picked up the latest Carolyn G. Hart off her end table. It was a grand story so far, but as usual Maude thought she had guessed whodunit. Maude saw mysteries in everything, and knew many of the hidden stories about people at Timberdale. She loved to snoop—admitted it.

Thinking about one of the latest delicious little secrets she had learned about a certain someone, Maude found she was unable to concentrate on her book. Tossing it aside, she got to her feet and began walking restlessly from room to room in her apartment, whispering to herself. Sleep was not going to come. When she began thinking of the secrets at times like this, gloating over how much she knew and how well she kept her own secret thoughts and actions, she often stayed awake most of the night. Her latest project was fascinating and a little frightening.

Others were awake behind locked oak doors. A retired army colonel scowled over gun oil, cloths, and rods, cleaning a Colt .45 automatic. A former vice president of a bank labored over another letter to her son, fighting the palsied tremor of her fingers on the fountain pen, knowing the letter would not be answered and wondering why. A married couple well into their sixties sat close together on their couch, watching the wild, explicit sexual exploits of their most recently obtained X-rated videotape. An old man strained his eyes to read the files of a court case. Another man, younger but also alone, feverishly did push-ups, trying to burn some of the aching desire out of his body so he might be able to sleep.

Thirty minutes passed and Timberdale remained quiet. At her desk, Stacy Miller dozed.

At 11:40 p.m., a door opened somewhere and the killer left a room and took a deserted hallway to the rear stairs, footsteps muted by the dense rose-colored carpet. Reaching the second-floor landing, the shadowy figure entered another hallway that had solid oak doors regularly spaced along its length.

In her apartment on Two, the victim was already dressed for bed. In gown, robe, and slippers, she had been watching some late TV, but had just gotten out of her recliner chair to turn the set off. Channel 13, the Oklahoma City outlet for PBS, was closing for the night, a signal that it was time for bed. She hadn't flicked the switch yet when a soft tap sounded on her door.

A visitor so late was extraordinary. Timberdale's halls were always empty at this hour.

Ignoring the now-continual sharp pain in her chest and stomach, the victim moved unsteadily to the door of her apartment and peered out through the peephole. Instantly recognizing the face on the other side, she opened the deadbolt and swung her door open.

"Oh, that is so sweet of you," she said, deeply touched. "Come in. Please. I was just turning off the TV, but I'm not at all sleepy. We can have tea."

The killer entered the apartment. Babbling happily about how pleased she was to have this late-night call, the old woman limped into the kitchen to prepare tea. Tea was such a friendly thing, she believed, and she felt so happy; wonderful friends always took her mind off the pain for a little while.

TWO

DRIVING TO WORK, Laura Michaels glanced at the digital clock on the panel of her little Honda sedan. It read 7:16, which meant she was right on time. Even at this hour, however, summer heat had begun to build. The car's air conditioner was already working overtime, and haze blued the sparsely wooded hills southeast of Oklahoma City.

Laura had dropped her daughter, Trissie, off at the day-care center promptly at seven, then had taken State 77 north out of Norman, headed for Timberdale Retirement Center. It wasn't far away. Wednesday was one of her busiest days at Timberdale, but she would have time to prepare for everything: check the schedule of events, deal with any overnight problems, shuffle paperwork, and review her notes before going in to meet the residents who formed her Wednesday group, which some of them wryly called "the breakfast club."

Everything normal, and no premonition of trouble.

Reaching a familiar intersection, Laura turned off the state highway onto a narrow blacktop county road leading east. A small sign said *TIMBERDALE 3 MI*. About a mile later, she met a dirty, white county dump truck coming from the other direction. The driver looked down at her as he passed, and apparently got a glimpse of her long tan legs through the Honda window. The admiring blast of his airhorn threatened to blow the Honda's windows out. Grinning to herself, Laura tugged at the hem of her ivory linen dress, which didn't accomplish much.

Soon she reached another intersection, this one with a red dirt section-line road. Beyond it, her road became well-smoothed gravel. She downshifted and drove on, reaching Timberdale property on her left.

The location was impressive—the side of a gentle, grass-covered hill looking down on landscaped grounds replete with small poplars, sycamores, silver maples, and Russian olives, a brushy creek meandering along the far edge of the property, with dense wild brush, mostly native blackjacks, beyond. The higher ground above the center was more natural and broken by a scattering of firs and scrub oak. Curvilinear concrete parking lots flanked the broad sweep of the entry road, with graceful light towers and carefully tended flowerbeds all around. Laura drove in.

Timberdale was five years old. Its main building was a handsome, buff brick, three-story structure. It looked contemporary, but there was something vaguely Edwardian in its rounded window treatments and shallow wood balconies for most apartments. Built in the form of a great block letter H, it dominated the hillside yet did not overwhelm it. It looked like a nice place to live, which it was.

A retirement center, as distinguished from a nursing home, Timberdale more nearly resembled a condominium development. But it offered many services that the usual condominium did not: health services, transportation, planned social activities, maid service, a recreational program, and good meals served in a community dining room. For an extra fee, the ill could have meals delivered to their suite, and each unit also had a completely equipped kitchen for those who preferred to prepare their own food. For all the extra services and amenities, however, Timberdale was far from a nursing facility; it was possible to live quite independently there and to maintain privacy. Residents liked that.

Although the median age of residents hovered around seventy, everyone was quick to point out that people who lived here were lucky: in relatively good health, and fairly well off. Timberdale's smallest unit, an efficiency, rented for $950 a month on an annual-lease basis, including all meals and normal services, while the larger two-bedroom suites started at $1,300. Unlike some retirement developments, this one did not require residents to invest life savings or sign a death bequest to a church or corporation in order to live there.

Laura had worked at Timberdale for less than a year. There were problems, but she felt lucky to have the job. It paid enough to help her make ends meet, and the academic credit she was getting from the School of Social Work for her volunteer counseling work was terrific. She worked normal hours and confined her classwork to the weekend program at the university, which ordinarily allowed her to take Trissie to school or day care and then get home in time to pick her up at the sitter's early in the evening, Monday through Friday, with some semblance of normalcy. Both of them needed a sense of normalcy after the divorce.

Dr. Barnett Hodges, Laura's faculty adviser, had had misgivings about it at first. "You'll kill yourself with that schedule."

"I'll be fine," Laura said blithely.

Hodges clamped his jaw on his ugly, smelly pipe and scowled. "Might not work. You're the first student we've ever placed out there. No precedents…no established procedures. You've got to break your own ground."

"I know," Laura said cheerfully.

"Wearing two hats will make it harder."

"I know," Laura repeated.

Hodges scowled worse. "So?"

"It'll be great," Laura assured him.

"I wish you luck. You're going to need it."

Mrs. Judith Epperman, Timberdale's manager, had put it a bit differently, of course.

"It's fine with me, dear, if you want to volunteer free

time to provide a service that some of these sweet old dar-
lings might want to try out. I never thought talk therapy
was much use, personally. I mean, isn't it all sort of silly,
really? *I* certainly don't need it. Of course, not everyone is
as strong as I am. I must admit, however, that I do have
some misgivings about the program. I feel compelled to
warn you that this sort of thing must *never* be allowed to
interfere with the administrative work we pay you to do.
You understand that, don't you?''

"Yes, Mrs. Epperman," Laura said meekly.

Mrs. Epperman retrieved her eyeglasses from the end of
a thin gold chain somewhere in the depths of her massive
bosom. Clamping them on her nose, she gave Laura a long,
thoughtful look. "I mean, Laura, you do have a good job
here. I certainly am not threatening you, but we do have a
long list of *highly* qualified people waiting to take it over
if you slip up. Right?''

"Right, Mrs. Epperman.''

Judith Epperman was a good administrator, a George
Patton in orthopedic shoes. She looked about forty-five. No
one knew for sure. She was married, but no one had ever
met her husband. When not wearing her glasses, she bore
an uncanny resemblance to Babe Ruth. She could be sentimental. While manipulating schedules, budgets, room
assignments, and people with the cold, penny-pinching cal-
culation of an Ebenezer Scrooge, she could summon up
genuine tears by the gusher if one of her "darling residents" so much as got a head cold. She was capable of
screaming bloody murder if someone smoked in the dining
room, but Laura had seen the packs of Silva Thins hidden
in her desk. Such contradictions interested Laura as a student of human psychology.

It also interested Laura that Mrs. Epperman was in regular psychic contact with Cleopatra and someone she
thought might be Queen Victoria. These visions or voices—

she was very vague about the precise nature of the psychic channel—usually came in the middle of the night, although once she had almost made contact while soaking in the Timberdale Jacuzzi.

"Is it scary at all?" Laura once had the temerity to inquire.

Mrs. Epperman let her pince-nez drop to her breast at the end of their thin gold chain. "Scary? What do you mean?"

Laura already wished she hadn't asked. But she persisted. "When you hear these voices?"

"That's personal," Mrs. Epperman snapped. "It's unwise to get too personal when you have an employer-employee relationship like we do. Ask me after you quit working here, or get fired. We can talk about it then."

"Yes, Mrs. Epperman."

It was 7:28. Circling the flag terrace in front of the building, Laura drove to the west parking area and her usual slot. When she opened her door, the air that swept into the car was steamy. Fooey, the hottest day yet.

Carrying a battered attaché case heavy with class and case notes, she hurried along the pristine sidewalk toward the front of the complex, passing curved flowerbeds filled with ground-hugging junipers and clumps of petunias and periwinkles. The determination of her stride riffled the hemline of her pretty summer dress, which discreetly bared her arms and just a bit of her creamy tan shoulders. A yard man standing nearby leaned on his shovel for a moment, admiring her. Dark-haired, with wide brown eyes and even, intelligent features, she wore only a trace of makeup, a touch of pale pink lipstick, and a suggestion of eyeliner. Her ringlet hair, shoulder-length, bobbed as she walked. The yard man had a few fervent thoughts.

Laura reached the sidewalk corner near Timberdale's main entrance. As she started around it, she heard a series of sharp little *spritz!*ing sounds start in the flowerbeds. Alerted just in time, she hopped nimbly into the driveway. Even as she did, sprinkler heads started popping up from hiding in the flowerbed woodchips to start spraying pavement and flowers alike. One tiny bit of cold spray caught Laura's left leg before she was entirely safe, but no harm done. She strode under the winglike shade of the great pale blue canopy, and headed along the tile toward the front doors.

A tall, ungainly figure emerged from the shrubs near the entrance. Well over six feet tall, wearing faded bib overalls and a straw hat that would have looked better on a scarecrow, Still Bill Mills was dragging a heavy green garden hose and didn't see Laura until they had almost collided.

"Wow!" he grunted in surprise. "Almost run you over!" Sixtyish, he had bright blue eyes that didn't quite track together. A soggy cigarette hung from the corner of his mouth. "How you doing, Miz Michaels?"

"Fine, Bill. You?"

"Great, just great." He removed the disintegrating straw hat to reveal a shaggy head of gray hair, pulled a red bandanna out of his hip pocket, and mopped his face, knocking his dead cigarette to the ground in the process. "Them sprinklers didn't get you when they came on, I hope?"

"I dodged in time."

"That's good." His eyes momentarily got in sync as he gave her a raking one-second glance, head to toe. "Shame to get that pretty dress wet, Miz Michaels."

Laura smiled. She liked him. "It's Laura, remember? The 'Miz' business makes me feel a hundred years old."

Still Bill Mills took a deep breath and stuffed his bandanna away. "Well, maybe so, but you can imagine what kind of a constabulary Mrs. Epperman would throw if I forgot and called her by *her* first name. So I just make it a habit to call everybody formal. I mean, I have never been one to proliferate, it's just the way I am.''

"Okay, Bill." Laura sighed. She turned toward the door. "Guess you'll have to be doing a lot of watering from now on, huh?''

He nodded. "It's ninety-two already. Just the kind of weather that can really make you feel like it's hot.''

Laura walked on to Timberdale's heavy, etched glass front doors, tugged one of them open, and entered the welcome chill of the air-conditioned building. Going through the small entry foyer, she removed her sunglasses. Inside, the light was filtered and soft. It always felt nice here, quiet and sheltered.

The building's core area, a central atrium, stood open a full three floors to a silvery skylight roof. White metal railings encircled the area on the upper floors. Open hallways up there gave access to some of the suites that faced in. The feeling was one of cool vastness.

The ground floor of the atrium, rose-carpeted with conservative traditional living-room furniture scattered in conversational groupings, provided the center's social focus. Offices and activity rooms, along with the center's post office, library, and sundries shop, opened off the lower level. To the rear was the main dining room, together with doorways leading to elevators, staircases, and wings of the building containing most of the suites and many of the services. At this hour, however, everything stood quiet and deserted. Breakfast service began at eight-thirty, and residents seldom came down much before that time. The only sign of life at the moment was at the long, curving white reception desk in front of the office area to the left, where Laura spied Stacy Miller, the night girl, at her usual station.

Laura walked over and thankfully put down her heavy briefcase. "Morning, Stacy.''

Stacy Miller looked up, sleepily startled. "Oh. Hi,

Laura." She was a pretty little college girl, plump, with strawberry hair and root beer eyes. She got slowly to her feet and started collecting fast-food wrappers and Diet Coke cans for the concealed trash bin. "Hot outside?"

"Yep. What's been going on here overnight?"

"Um, not much, I guess. Ms. Abercrombie called, said her air conditioner was too loud. Ms. Smith is *real* mad about something, but she wouldn't tell me, she said she wants to talk to you about it. The colonel, he came down a while ago, he says he wants to complain again, why don't we serve breakfast before eight o'clock."

"Good old Colonel Rodgers." Laura sighed. "Anything else?"

Stacy glanced at the incident report pad. "Guess that's about all." She slapdashed a paper towel over the remains of her overnight pizza wreckage. "Can I go now?"

"Go, Stacy."

Stacy Miller yawned again. "Okey dokey. No problem." She ambled out, shapeless flats kerplopping on the tile of the foyer. She paused at the door and produced a thin black cheroot. She touched the flame of a Bic to it and swung the door back to start home.

Laura stifled another sigh. Stacy was twenty, only ten years younger than she. But they might as well have been born on different planets.

Well, maybe it figured. Stacy was working at Timberdale as a summer job. In another six or seven weeks her parents would infuse her life with another large dose of money, and she would go back to college, where she evidently planned to spend much of her adult life, no problem.

Laura, on the other hand, only faced a heavier schedule when classes resumed late in August. Not exactly "no problem." Two years out of a failed marriage, not quite a hundred percent over it, still teetering on the edge of financial disaster all the time, still with Trissie having to alternate between school and day care, still not a hundred percent sure that working for her master's in social work—which still looked to be a century in the future—was the right thing to be doing anyway.

Not to brood, my dear. You'll get wrinkles, and you couldn't be like Stacy anyhow. You compulsive types never can be.

So she started getting down to the day's business.

These few minutes at the beginning of her day were her favorite time. The dining room remained dim and vacant, although she could hear the distant sounds of voices in the kitchen beyond, and the occasional clink of a pot or pan as breakfast was readied. The vast, carpeted sitting area remained unoccupied. There was no foot traffic on the upstairs halls. Everything was quiet.

She checked the weekly schedule of events. This was Wednesday, a shopping day, and also a day when residents needing to visit their own doctor could get transportation to do so. Still Bill Mills, handyman-gardener-chauffeur and volunteer philosopher, would have the small blue GMC bus parked under the canopy in front at ten-thirty, right after Laura's group. A dozen residents' spidery handwriting adorned the sign-up roster for transportation to doctors' offices starting at that time. Still Bill would get them there and have them back in time for late lunch. Then at two-thirty he would have the bus ready to roll again, this time for stops at the Homeland grocery, WalMart, Jefferson Drug, and anyplace else in Norman that someone signed up to be taken. In the meantime, here in the retirement center, there would be visitors, gossiping in the atrium, good business in the clinic, and the usual games in the card room. Nothing spectacular or unusual.

Squaring her shoulders, Laura rearranged the memo pads and tablets, moved the telephone where she liked it, straightened the VISITORS sign on the top level of the desk, scanned Stacy Miller's notes, called maintenance, and stole a few precious minutes to review her notes about the "breakfast club."

She had known back in the winter that forming therapy groups or lining up individual clients in a place like Timberdale might meet with resistance. Older people tended to mistrust talk therapy even more than younger ones. But her job in the center had helped a bit—residents already knew and seemed to like her—and now she had two weekly small groups and a half-dozen or so individual clients she saw regularly.

The breakfast club was the oldest group. It consisted of five regulars, although occasionally some other resident would drift in and take part for an hour or two. Laura had learned a lot in working with them, and knew she had done some good work with some of them, those who had dared to open up, talk about things that really scared or angered them. Those had been the good days, the ones during which Laura worked hard, too, and invested her own feelings along with the hard thinking.

Now, given a few minutes, she dug her notebooks out of the attaché case. A slender, blue-jacketed book came out with them, reminding her of the telephone call she had received last night just after getting home.

"Laura?" the thin, energetic voice had piped up when she answered. "Hey, this is Cora Chandler." Then the old woman added with her customary irony, "Over at the *home.*"

Laura had grinned into the phone. "I recognized your voice, Cora. What's up?"

"Hey, didn't you say you had a copy of that Stephen Hawking book, the one about time and all?"

"*A Brief History of Time?* Sure. It's right here on my coffee table, where I gave up trying to get through it."

"Well, hey, how about letting me borrow it? I just

watched this thing on educational TV and they tried to explain relativity and all, and they had these colored Ping-Pong balls rolling around on a warped billiard table. I couldn't make heads or tails of it. Maybe that book will straighten me out.''

Laura had imagined Cora—five feet one, about ninety pounds, thinning gray hair, and eyes as sharp and canny as they had ever been—trying to figure out relativity. There was no one sharper at Timberdale. But the Hawking book was something else.

She tried to explain. ''Cora, I'll bring it, but I haven't found anyone yet who could get through it and understand everything he says in there.''

''Well, hey, that's okay. I need to exercise the old brain cells. I mean, I can't just watch *Sesame Street* and old movies all the time, right? They've got something on there right now with Phil Harris. Yuck.''

''I'll bring the book tomorrow, Cora. I'll put it in my attaché case right now.''

''Hey, dynamite. I'll get downstairs early, and by the time the group meets, I'll be a genius. Thanks, Laura. Ta ta.''

Remembering, Laura glanced toward the elevators, expecting Cora any minute. Not seeing her yet, she went ahead and glanced over the few notes she had made during the last session. Wouldn't it be grand, she thought, if they were all as bright-eyed and bushy-tailed as Cora, even with her unspecified chronic illness.

Finishing the note review, Laura hurried down the office hallway behind the desk, going into the dusty Xerox room long enough to unlock her filing cabinet and pull out another folder where she kept additional materials relating to the breakfast club regulars. When she got back to the desk, it was 7:47, but still quiet.

A few minutes later, the first resident showed up. It

wasn't Cora. Up on the third level, a residence door opened. Seventy-year-old Julius Pfeister came out on the landing. A bulky, round-shouldered old man with a cane, Pfeister was pink and bald, and wore metal-rimmed eyeglasses. He liked to dress up, and usually looked like a million dollars. Today's outfit consisted of pale lemon slacks, a mint-colored sport coat, a white shirt open at the collar, with an ascot that matched his slacks, and white wing-tip shoes. From past experience Laura knew he would be enveloped in a gentle cloud of Old Spice cologne.

As Laura watched, Dot Pfeister came out in the hall with her husband. Tiny beside her husband, she did not reach his shoulder in height, and looked lost in her wispy, floral silk dress. A stray beam from the skylight blazed blue off one of her rings as she put her hand on Pfeister's arm. They started for the elevators, she a feather, he lurching heavily from side to side, depending on his cane.

It was almost as if everyone else had been waiting for someone to go first. More signs of activity appeared at once. From the west hallway came a heavyset, elderly woman with bluish, beehive hair and a dark brown summer dress straight out of the twenties. Davilla Rose, Timberdale's reigning poet, had pictures of Gertrude Stein in her apartment; and always dressed this way. Almost at the same time, from the east wing hallway, came more residents: Mr. and Mrs. Stoney Castle, seventyish, wearing matching blue sweats and Nike walking shoes. Right behind them bounded Ken Keen, one of the center's youngest at sixty-two, blond and ruddy and grinning in his Levi's and Sooners T-shirt.

At first, Keen had been the object of fervent speculation by most of Timberdale's widows, until it became apparent that his body might look fifty, but his memory didn't work at all. He tended to repeat the same leering insinuations over and over, and any female in sight was fair game. Laura had been shocked the first time he tried to back her into a corner of the elevator and slip his hand under her skirt, then had learned that he had tried the same thing with almost every female in the county.

"The old fart," Davilla Rose had snapped when Laura happened to mention it. "You slap his face and five minutes later he's forgotten the whole thing and tries it all over again."

"Doesn't matter," another of the ladies retorted. "He tries to grab everybody, but beyond the irritation I think he's probably all talk and no action anyhow."

By the time the Pfeisters had reached the main level via an elevator, palsied Judge Emil Young, at ninety-one the center's oldest resident, had made his unsteady morning appearance, spoken to Davilla Rose and the Castles, and was already in one of the easy chairs, his head nodding. Ken Keen's voice echoed faintly as he demonstrated his golf backswing to Maude Thuringer, seventy-three, and then tried to pat her on the backside. She jumped a mile and slammed an elbow into his side, almost knocking him to his knees. Colonel Roger Rodgers, seventy, he of the complaint about breakfast hours, strode in to join the conversations, standing at ramrod parade rest and nodding snappishly in agreement with whatever Julius Pfeister was telling him. Milly Kett came in, moving a painful few inches at a time in her chromium walker; well into her eighties, she wasn't at all well, but her bright smile for everyone lit the atrium. Laura had never heard her complain.

As a few more minutes passed, other residents sifted in. The pleasant sound of muted conversation filled the area. A staffer turned the lights on in the dining room, and waitresses began putting out grapefruits, orange juice, and a variety of toasts, rolls, and doughnuts.

Laura still had not caught sight of Cora Chandler, who had promised to be down early to get the book from her. But for the moment she thought nothing about it.

THREE

By 9:25, ALMOST TIME for the breakfast club to convene, Cora Chandler still had not appeared in the atrium. Feeling her first twinge of concern, Laura looked up Mrs. Chandler's telephone number in the residents' directory and dialed it. A busy signal buzzed in response. Laura hung up with a feeling of reassurance.

Across the atrium, four other residents were entering the activity room for the session.

First came Ellen Smith, sixty-five, the center's most notable artist—southwestern landscapes—and resident crab. She was dressed as usual, in a short buckskin skirt and fringed suede blouse, with moccasins and a tinkly variety of large silver necklaces and bracelets. She looked angrier than usual, which was saying a lot.

Close behind her came Milly Kett, struggling along cheerfully in her chromium walker. Picture-of-health Ken Keen bounded along next, leaning over her with a leer to make some remark that turned her pink, then pale. Last in line was nervous, bright-eyed Maude Thuringer, who attended only sometimes.

Laura looked around for the other regular, Mrs. Veronica Jackson, sometimes called "Stonewall" behind her back because of the way she issued orders to everyone. Stonewall was not in sight.

The great walnut grandfather clock in the far corner softly tolled half-past the hour, time for the group to convene.

Stuck alone on the desk, Laura glanced futilely toward the entry foyer, hoping to see Mrs. Epperman arriving. No such luck. Judith Epperman seldom arrived before ten. She loved to stay up late watching cable TV. Sometimes during an old movie she got messages on a channel that the FCC had never heard of.

Somebody, however, had to be in charge at the reception desk if Laura was to meet her group. She made a reluctant decision to ask the only person available.

In the office of the social director next to Mrs. Epperman's down the interior hall, Francie Blake stood model-slim and gorgeous behind her desk, one pretty ear glued to her white telephone. She looked up at Laura's knock and waved a beautiful tan arm ajangle with bracelets.

"Honey?" she cooed into the telephone. "Can you be a real darling and hang on just a sec? You're sweet." She put long, tapering fingers over the mouthpiece. "Hi, Laura. Need something?"

"It's time for my group, Francie, and I need someone to take over the desk so I can get started."

A little frown crossed Francie Blake's perfect porcelain puss, but then she beamed a megawatt smile. "Why, *sure* I'll do it, Laura. Just give me one sec, hon, to get off the phone." She removed her hand from the mouthpiece. "Now what was that you were saying, you naughty boy?" She winked conspiratorially at Laura, listened to what was being said in her ear, wriggled from golden head to bare-toed sandals, and went hot pink all over. "You really *are* a naughty boy to say that!" she purred, dripping southern accents.

Gag reflex stifled, Laura went back out to the desk. Group would start late; it was just a question of how late. If the telephone call had been Timberdale business, she thought, Francie might have terminated it quickly. With a man on the line, it was anybody's guess.

Five minutes later, Francie Blake swished out of the office hallway, gold jewelry discreetly tinkling, killer legs catching glints of reflected light. Her gray-blue sundress, very expensive and stunningly fitted, looked a bit too much for a day at the office, Laura thought. But none of the residents had ever commented, and they were famous for being catty. Perhaps the elderly women saw a wish-fulfillment figure of some kind in the sexy Francie, Laura thought, and perhaps the old men saw the same thing in her that younger men must. Francie Blake must have stirred more male fantasies in her time than any single year's collection of *Playboy,* but Laura didn't hate her for it—she really didn't—she reminded herself daily that she didn't, because that would have been immature.

The problem, which Francie insisted on pretending she was not aware of, was not that she was tall, strikingly blond, model-statuesque, and overwhelmingly sexy. It wasn't that she wiggled when she walked, giggled when she talked, gushed enthusiasm over nothing, and wore expensive dresses to work that would have been more appropriate for a dinner date at the Petroleum Club in downtown Oklahoma City. It wasn't even that her dazzling good cheer sometimes had all the sincerity of a Leona Helmsley. Laura could have dealt with all that.

What bothered Laura was men. Or, rather, Francie and the men of the world.

All of them attracted Francie like a streetlight attracts bugs. And vice versa. It didn't matter whether they were fifteen or seventy.

Francie seemed to view all of them as a challenge: let one walk into view, and she sizzled. She glowed. She *undulated.* And if her first beaming *banzai* charge didn't render the poor wretch a gawking slave, she simply turned up the voltage until the victim was pronounced dead of adoration.

Laura knew it worked, always. Francie collected broken hearts the way a navy wool skirt picked up lint. She had even collected a new male friend that Laura had carelessly led into her gravitational field one Saturday here at Timberdale. Laura had brought the guy in to pick up a folder; he got a gander at Francie, and vanished from Laura's world forever. Laura would never make *that* mistake again…if she ever ran into another man who interested her as much as that poor lost soul might have.

"Okay, hon," Francie said sweetly now, moving behind the reception desk. "You can go to your little meeting."

"Thanks, Francie." Laura picked up her folder.

Francie patted her hair. "No prob, sweetie. You just have a real fun little time and let Francie handle everything. You hear?"

Laura realized that powder from pulverized fillings was about to fill her mouth. She walked away briskly, heading for the activity room.

Her four regulars awaited her. Possibly there had been some conversation before she opened the door, but the room went tomblike with her entry. The only sound as she walked to the front came from the nylon rustle of her own underwear and the tap of her heels on the tile floor.

She pulled one of the occasional chairs around in a half-circle to face the others, arranged in a loose line. Sitting down, she gave them what she hoped was a nice smile. "Good morning."

For a few seconds they faced her in utter silence, four blank faces: Ken Keen on the left, leering at Laura's legs; birdlike Maude Thuringer, clutching a notebook of "secrets" she had collected on everyone; pale Milly Kett; and finally Ellen Smith.

"Cora will be late," Laura told them. "I just tried to call her, and her line was busy."

Ellen Smith's silver bracelets jangled. "Good riddance."

"Why do you say that, Ellen?" Laura asked sweetly.

Smith's rheumy eyes flared spitefully. "Maybe without

Miss Goody Two-Shoes we can get down to some brass tacks in this session!''

"Is Cora Miss Goody Two-Shoes?''

"Are you blind and deaf? Who else would I be talking about?''

"Tell me about it, Ellen.''

"Not on your life!'' Smith snapped, and clamped her jaw.

Ellen Smith tended to dislike everybody, so Laura pressed on. Turning to Ken Keen, she asked, "Ken, how are you today?''

Keen's eyebrows rustled. "Hot and ready, babe. How about you?''

Ellen Smith clucked.

Keen looked over at her. "What was *that* supposed to mean?''

Smith glared. "Nothing. I suppose we should be grateful you're just making dirty remarks and not pawing at us.''

Keen looked sincerely puzzled. "What dirty remarks?''

Ellen turned back to Laura. "I've changed my mind. I want to talk about the pig.''

"What?''

"Her pig,'' Milly Kett said meekly.

"Right!'' Ellen Smith agreed, metal jangling again. "*My* pig—the painting I hung in the second-floor east alcove.''

Laura started to understand. "Your painting, Ellen? The one that's hanging on the second floor?''

"Of course. My pig. How many pigs do you think we have around here?''

Laura elected to dodge that one. Instead she tried peace-making. "I think I mentioned to you, Ellen, how very nice it was of you to allow Timberdale to hang it in the upstairs hallway. I—''

Ellen Smith's lean arm banged on the arm of her chair. "The flowers are gone!''

"Flowers?" Laura started feeling dazed again.

"The glass vase on the table in the alcove under my pig!" Ellen's angry eyes looked alarmingly wet, like she was going to cry. "There's never been anything in that vase since the day it was put on the table more than a year ago. More than a year ago! So *yesterday* I went outside and *personally* cut a lovely little bouquet—three white tea roses, a tiny spray of crepe myrtle, a sprig of nandina, and some snapdragons—and made a bouquet for that vase. I arranged it myself. It looked wonderful. The sweetest thing you ever saw, and right under my pig—well, it was *perfect*."

Ken Keen roused. "Looked real good." He appeared surprised. "I remember it."

"'Looked'?" Laura repeated. "Did something happen to it?"

"Yes!"

"What?"

"That's what I'd like to know!"

"What do you mean?"

"It's gone, that's what I mean."

"The pig?" Laura gasped.

"No, you ninny, not the pig! The bouquet! The flowers! Gone! Just the water left in the vase, and you can see by spots on the table where some nasty person just *ripped* my flowers right out of the water and made off with them!"

Laura paused, gauging how the others were taking this. She couldn't read their expressions. "There must have been some mistake."

"Thieves, is what it was. *Thieves!* Someone jealous, probably, because I had my paintings entered in the show there at the gallery in Norman last month. So they just stole my flowers to spite me, and I'll just bet *someone* is smirking right now, knowing how hurt I am, and them having the flowers in their apartment, hidden from view."

"Oh, Ellen, I think there must be some other—"

"I want an announcement made," the old woman cut in, silver tinkling. "I want some kind of investigation. When the maids clean the apartments this week, I want them to be alert to watch for those flowers." She paused, eyes snapping and loop earrings swaying. "You may think this is a big joke, but it isn't."

"I certainly don't think it's a joke."

"Then stop acting like it. What do you plan to do about it?"

"I'll report it to Mrs. Epperman the moment she arrives this morning. You can be sure we'll look into it right away."

"Well, you'd *better,* that's all I've got to say, young lady." Smith got to her feet and started for the door.

"Ellen?" Laura called after her. "The session is just starting."

Too late. The door slammed behind her and she was gone. There was a profound silence.

Finally Milly Kett sighed. "Bless her heart, she's truly upset."

"She's a picklepuss," Maude Thuringer pronounced. "Do you remember the grandmother in *The Trembling Hills?*—a picklepuss. Just like Ellen. As to the missing flowers, this is a baffling and paradoxical mystery, and you needn't worry, Laura. It's an open-and-shut case."

"Open-and-shut? You know who did it?"

"No. Of course not. But I intend to. All I have to do is find the stolen flowers, and whoever has them is the thief."

"How," Laura inquired, "are you going to find the flowers?"

Maude blinked several times. "Well, I haven't worked that part out yet. But I will. You wait and see."

Ken Keen leaned forward to remove a comb from the

hip pocket of his slacks. He began thoughtfully combing his hair.

Laura turned to him. "Had you heard about the flowers, Ken?"

Keen stopped combing and stared at her. "What flowers?"

"Ellen's. The ones she put in the vase. The ones that were stolen."

"Something got stolen?"

Laura persisted, but she couldn't get anything going. Ken Keen could not seem to focus. Milly Kett fell silent, her watery eyes sad, looking into somewhere else. Laura tried to do some double-chair work with her, but it didn't jell. Maude Thuringer suggested that scent-dogs might trace the flowers, but first she had to inspect the scene of the crime. Without either Ellen Smith or Cora Chandler, the group was really too small, and no one would cooperate.

After forty minutes, Laura quietly gave up.

"Okay," she said with false cheer. "Our time is almost up. Let's break a little early. We'll move on next week, okay?"

Chairs scraped. Ken Keen walked to the door of the room and then stationed himself beside it, smiling sleepily. Laura started gathering her file folders and notes. Milly Kett struggled into the embrace of her metal walker and approached her.

"Laura?"

"Yes?"

"I think you should check on Cora. She really hasn't been feeling well, and this isn't like her."

"I'm going to call again right now, Milly."

"She *never* talks to anyone on the telephone more than a minute. It isn't like her to miss group."

Maude Thuringer fluttered up, her silky, old-fashioned print dress swirling like hummingbird wings. "Milly, you ought to get the rubber tips on that walker replaced. They're looking worn. *You* may not have noticed, but I've trained myself to notice everything."

Laura went on to the door, where Keen waited. "Did you want to say something, Ken?"

Keen reached for her breasts. She danced out of reach just in time. "Stop that!"

"Aw," he gargled. "You know you love it."

She slid through the doorway and escaped another grab.

A little depressed, she crossed the atrium to the reception desk. Francie Blake was not out front. Laura caught a glimpse of her through the windows that separated Reception from the office area; Francie was back in her office again, talking on the telephone.

A UPS deliveryman stood waiting at the counter, three small packages stacked up. Laura hustled around to help him. She signed the delivery sheet. "Sorry about the delay. Somebody is supposed to be here."

"Been waiting more than ten minutes," he said, and turned to hurry off.

Still Bill Mills, mopping his forehead with a bandanna, appeared from the front foyer. "I woulda signed, but I've been told not to."

Laura put her folder under the counter. "That's okay, Bill. No harm done. Have you seen Mrs. Chandler come down?"

"Nope, but I sure saw Ellen Smith. She was ramming around here in a high dungeon."

Laura suppressed a smile. "That's one of the worst kind."

Still Bill's eyes roved the vastness of the atrium as if he were afraid to see Timberdale's resident artist coming after him again. "When she's like that, I stay outta her way, boy."

"Did she say anything to you about her flowers?"

Still Bill recoiled. "Hey. Does a chicken have lips?"

"What do you suppose might have happened to them?"

"I dunno, really."

"Housekeeping couldn't have—"

"No!"

"I hate to think someone took them just to be mean to her."

He sighed and shook his head. "Might be, though. She makes people mad. I mean, when things don't go to suit that girl, she can really get fractional."

Laura thought about it. "Bill, would you mind staying here for a while until I can run an errand?"

"Don't mind if I do. It's getting hotter'n a fruitcake out there."

Laura left the counter and hurried along the side wall into the now-darkened dining room and toward the kitchen beyond. The dishes had been stowed in the big washers, now noisily at work. Two of the kitchen workers were wiping counters, while a third stood near the back doorway smoking a cigarette. The smoker, Mrs. Mullins, gave Laura a friendly smile. "Don't tell on me."

Laura grinned back. "Smoking in the kitchen? Better be careful."

"I usually am, but I was having a nicotine fit." Mrs. Mullins tossed the butt down a drain. "Do you need something, Mrs. Michaels?"

"I just wonder if Mrs. Chandler ever came down for breakfast, or possibly had something sent up?"

"No, we haven't heard a peep out of her."

"Thanks, Sue."

Back at Reception, Francie Blake was on duty and the lights blazed in Mrs. Epperman's office. Laura tried the telephone again and got another busy signal from the Chandler apartment. She hung up and went to the door of Mrs.

Epperman's office, where she found her employer hunched over *The Daily Oklahoman* crossword.

Epperman looked up. "Laura. Good." She glanced down, then up again. "Twenty-two across. 'Echidna's fare.' Four letters, the third letter may be—"

"Ants," Laura said instantly.

"Thanks. That will work." The large woman bent over her pencil.

"Mrs. Chandler hasn't been down this morning," Laura told her. "I'm going to go up and check on her."

Epperman erased something in the puzzle and wrote something else in. "Good," she said absently.

After getting the master key from the security box, Laura rode the elevator to the second floor. Walking silently down the dusky blue carpet into the east wing, she passed the alcove where Mrs. Smith's sad-eyed little pig looked out over a crystal vase containing nothing but slightly greenish water. The Chandler apartment was just beyond.

Reaching the oak door numbered E-244, Laura detected the faint sound of a TV set or radio playing inside the apartment. Laura rapped hard on the door. There was no response. She tried again, getting nothing.

Tightening her lips, she inserted the master key into the heavy brass door lock and turned it. The deadbolt clanked back and the door swung open.

The television set was on, a morning game show. The draperies were drawn so that everything was dark, the TV picture a bright blob of color at the far end of the suite. The set's sound was turned up rather loud. Laura noticed a faint but distinct odor of something like camphor. She turned on the dining-room lights as she went in toward the TV, entering a room filled with bookcases and tasteful, old-fashioned furniture.

"Mrs. Chandler?"

The high back of the leather recliner chair facing the

television set made it impossible to see from the rear if anyone might be sitting in it. Laura took another two steps into the living room to look.

Someone was sitting in it. Cora Chandler, fully dressed in a pretty blue housedress, her hair in rollers, stocking feet extended straight out to the footrest, stared straight ahead with unblinking seriousness, as if the picture on the TV set might be the last thing she would ever see.

It had been.

FOUR

It took Mrs. Epperman less than two minutes to get to Cora Chandler's room in response to Laura's telephone call.

"Well," Mrs. Epperman said gravely, looking down at Cora Chandler, "she's dead, all right. Damn, I hate it! It upsets everybody when something like this happens. It's bad for business."

Laura was shocked. "Is that all you can think about?"

The big woman stared at Laura, then frowned as she understood. "Well, no. Of course not." Her face twisted, and gobby tears appeared in her eyes. "The poor dear. It's so sad. She was such a sweetheart." The tears coursed down Mrs. Epperman's face.

Knocked offstride by the sudden, easy sentimentality, Laura simply went numb for an instant. "I mean," she whispered, "it's a shock. No one ever said Cora was at death's door."

Mrs. Epperman whipped out a large, man-sized handkerchief from a pocket in her military-cut dress. "Of course not. They go fast." The drill sergeant was back in charge, the tears were gone. She reached down to Cora Chandler and pressed her fingers against an inert wrist. "But there's no doubt about it. She's dead." She released the dead woman's wrist and made a face. "Phew. Smell that Ben-Gay? Jar right there on the end table. She had arthritis, among other things, but I would have thought she was smarter than the ones who think patent medicines help. She must have slathered the stuff all over herself not long before she died. Probably got heart pains and thought they were muscular."

Mrs. Epperman walked briskly into the kitchenette, where she vigorously rushed water over her hands before drying them on a dish towel. "Cold, too. Getting stiff. Must have died early last night. Will you turn that TV off, please? Game shows are so disgusting."

Laura went to the set and punched a button. The apartment suddenly seemed very quiet. To her surprise, she felt tears well up in her eyes.

"We have to be strong," Mrs. Epperman told her. "It's sad, but you're supposed to be a professional, and it's not like she was a spring chicken."

"She was only sixty-seven."

"Yes, but she was sick. We all knew that."

"I didn't think she was *that* sick."

"Well, obviously she was."

Laura dabbed at her eyes. "She was one of my favorites, always wonderful in the group. She didn't complain."

"Maybe she should have. Doctor Which might have been able to give her something." Mrs. Epperman heaved another sigh. "I should have known something like this was going to happen. I had a message about imminent difficulty just the other night. 'Be prepared,' the queen said."

For an instant Laura didn't get it. "The who? Oh."

"I'll notify Dr. Which and the sheriff's office. I'm betting they'll want an autopsy."

Laura stared in dismay. "I know we're required to notify the law any time someone dies outside a medical facility. But does that include an autopsy?"

"It will in this case. It looks like she killed herself."

"*What?*"

Mrs. Epperman's eyelids drooped with disgust. "Didn't you notice the pill bottle?"

Laura turned to look where her boss was pointing. On the end table beside the dead woman's chair she saw a small gold clock, an open jar of Ben-Gay, and something she hadn't noticed earlier: partly hidden by the brass base of the lamp, a small glass of water, half empty, and an overturned plastic pill container with no pills left in it.

Without thinking, she picked up the small plastic bottle. DIAZEPAM 5 MG, she read on the label. And below it: 30 TABS.

"You don't think she took all these Valiums!"

"Whatever we think," Mrs. Epperman decreed heavily, "we'll keep it to ourselves. The *last* thing we need is for anyone around here to think a resident got so sick or depressed that she killed herself."

"I knew Cora. She wasn't depressed at all."

"I'll go to the office to notify people," Mrs. Epperman cut in grimly. "You stay here."

"You don't really think—"

Mrs. Epperman paused, hand on the doorknob. "Of course not. And neither do you. She died of natural causes, obviously. The poor dear just slipped away while watching Johnny Carson or something. That's our story and we're sticking by it. I'm sure we can get the authorities to conclude the same thing. Now, you stay here, keep the door locked. Don't let anyone in until the sheriff or Dr. Which arrives. I'm sure Dr. Which will do the coroner's report. We *certainly* don't want anyone else gawking around in here."

"Stay here…with her?" Laura asked.

Mrs. Epperman's eyebrows slanted. "She won't bite, dear. I'll come back as soon as I can." She opened the door, stepped into the hall, and closed the door behind her.

Shit, Laura thought.

The apartment was as quiet as…as a tomb. It didn't feel good. She glanced at her watch—10:45, the digital readout said. It would be at least thirty minutes before anyone from the sheriff's office arrived, perhaps longer. *What am I supposed to do, just sit here?*

Sitting in the living room was out of the question. The sofa and other chair faced Cora Chandler's recliner.

Nervously, Laura turned away from the dead woman's eyes and looked at the other furnishings. Old book club selections and a few reprint classics packed the bookshelves. Brass figurines, candlestick holders, and a handful of Hummels jammed the glassed-in upper portion of the old mahogany secretary against one inside wall. An unused ashtray with a C in the center and a large book of photos of the Rocky Mountains were arranged with mathematical neatness on the glass-topped coffee table. Last night's *Norman Transcript,* neatly refolded, lay on the floor near the TV. On the walls: a small needlepoint Lord's Prayer, a reproduction of a Monet, and a brass four-leaf clover.

The apartment door swung open. Laura turned gratefully. "That was fast. I—"

She got no further. The person who came in, wide-eyed, was not Mrs. Epperman.

"Oh, my gracious," Maude Thuringer breathed, her bright eyes taking in everything at once. "Something terrible has happened, hasn't it?" She closed the door and rushed past Laura into the living room, a fluttery bird of a woman in her bright floral dress, tightly brushed gray hair enmeshed in a hairnet. She stared down at the chair and one hand went to her throat. "Oh, my *gracious.* Yes, something terrible certainly has happened. Oh, dear."

"Maude," Laura said, recovering, "you'd better get out of here."

"The door wasn't locked," Maude replied, bending at the waist to peer closer into Cora Chandler's dead eyes. "Oh, dear. Oh, dear." She snapped upright, eyes alive with curiosity and excitement. "I suppose I should have knocked."

"Yes, you should have. Now, Maude—"

"I'm rather glad I didn't. If I had, you wouldn't have let me in, would you?"

"No, I wouldn't have. You'd better just—"

Maude's eyes swept the room and lit on the overturned pill container. She swooped down on it.

"Don't touch!" Laura cried.

"I know, I know," the wispy little woman chirped. "Evidence. Might be fingerprints, if this is the result of foul play." Her eyes narrowed. "Unless you already picked it up and spoiled everything."

"Would I be that dumb?" Laura asked uncomfortably.

Maude bent closer, squinting to read the label. "Diazepam. Hmm. Empty. Oh, my. Doesn't look good. I knew Cora was taking medication. She was a very sick lady, you know. Or maybe you didn't."

"Maude, I really think you should leave."

Maude again ignored her. She made a fluttery circuit of the living room. "I knew something was amiss when Stonewall Jackson came back from the kitchen a minute ago and said Sue Mullins told her you seemed concerned. Stonewall goes back there and sneaks a smoke with Sue sometimes. Pretends she's perfect, but she can't even kick a filthy habit like that. Just goes and hides like a grade-schooler. Well. Then I saw old Queen Epperman steaming out of her office like a runaway pickup truck, and I *knew* something was up. So I followed her, and here I am. Good thing, too. You don't like this much, do you? Your color is terrible. You look like you're about to faint. Maybe you'd better sit down."

"Maude—"

"Look at that. Phone's off the hook." The tiny woman flew to the end table, pulled a tissue out of her pocket, and draped it over the telephone receiver before picking it up and putting it back on the cradle. "Won't mess up fingerprints that way. I suppose the sheriff or somebody like that will come. They did last year when Jane Hawes was found like this. It never does any good, but it makes them feel good. Fingerprints seldom help solve a case. I read that in *Ellery Queen.*"

"You need to get out of here, Maude. Really. Come on, now."

Maude frowned, scanning the room again and seeming to gauge the distance from the telephone to the recliner chair. "Isn't that funny!"

"Funny? What's funny?"

A thin arm pointed. "Phone over here, off the hook. Cora over *there,* all propped up and comfy. Couldn't reach this telephone from that chair with a ten-foot pole. Doesn't make sense."

"It's been off the hook a long time," Laura said. "I tried to call this morning and got a busy signal. I guess she took it off so she wouldn't be disturbed while she watched TV."

"Or somebody did it for her."

Laura turned to face Maude directly. In this light, bent slightly at the waist with her whole posture screaming *conspiracy,* the elderly woman looked a bit like Helen Hayes in her later years. Helen Hayes hadn't ever looked quite this suspicious, Laura thought.

She said, "Nobody else could have taken the phone off the hook. My God, Maude. Don't start cooking up a crime, here. Things like this happen. It's sad, but there's no mystery about a heart attack or stroke."

Maude silenced her with an index finger, quivering upright. "Never assume anything. The telephone bothers my mind. I read of a case just like it in Perry Mason years ago. I think it was *The Case of the Lucky Legs.* I'll check." Then, before Laura could react, the little woman had darted past her and into the L-shaped corridor that led to the bedroom.

"Maude!"

"My goodness," Maude's voice echoed from the bedroom. "Isn't *this* strange."

Groaning, Laura went after her.

The bed, piled high with pink and lavender lace pillows, had not been slept in. More lace festooned the bed's canopy, with more lace on the curtains, more lace on the coverlet over the bedside chair, more lace around the vanity mirror. The top of the vanity bristled with what looked like a hundred little bottles of perfume and nail polish and polish remover and a battery of creams: face cream, cold cream, night cream, cleansing cream, astringent cream, whitening cream. And there were lipsticks and powders and rouges and mascaras and brushes and combs and more mirrors of all sizes, and a silver crucifix. The bedroom smelled strongly of a sachet, an old-lady smell.

Maude Thuringer stood beside the luxurious old bed. "Do you smell it?"

"The Ben-Gay?"

"No. In here."

Laura sniffed. "The sachet?"

"No, you ninny." Maude inhaled spasmodically, making her nostrils vibrate. "Smell!" she commanded.

Laura smelled. Then she caught it. Cigarette smoke. Definitely, stale cigarette smoke.

"Cora didn't smoke!" Maude announced triumphantly. "She was a fanatic against smoking! She would never have let somebody smoke in here!"

This was getting badly out of hand. Laura went to Maude Thuringer and grasped her firmly by the arm. "I'm sorry, but you've got to leave. Now."

Maude tried to pull away. "This is just getting interesting. Let me look around. I might spot more clues. Did you read *Bonecrack?* He missed a clue just like this in *Bonecrack,* and it almost cost him his life. Will you please let go of me? You could hurt my arm."

"Now look, Maude," Laura said, propelling her toward the apartment door. "It's important for everyone's peace of mind that things don't get blown out of proportion here. Loose talk and rumors—"

"You don't have to worry about me in that regard. If there's something going on here, gossip can only drive the culprit into deeper cover. Remember how that worked in *The Goodbye Look?*" Maude held her finger to her lips. "Not a word from me. I guarantee it. Loose lips sink ships."

"Good," Laura muttered, getting the door open. "I rely on your discretion."

Maude went on tiptoes as a new idea struck. "Another theory—"

Laura pushed her into the hall. "Maude, we *mustn't* draw attention or create excitement. Maybe you'd better go to your apartment for a while and try to calm down."

The little woman suddenly crouched, eyes narrowing in suspicion. "Are you hiding something from me? What are you hiding, and why?"

"Maude, good grief!" Laura swung the door closed and slammed the deadbolt.

She realized that the apartment was deathly quiet again with Maude Thuringer ejected. A chilly, prickly feeling of unease stole back over her. She felt numb. Maude Thuringer, she told herself, was a mystery addict. She could have smelled foul play in a May procession. There was nothing wrong here except the sad death of an old lady. Maude had even confirmed that Cora was seriously ill, something Laura had only suspected. The telephone off the hook, and the smoke in the bedroom, might be explained a jillion ways and meant nothing suspicious.

To confirm this comforting analysis, Laura wandered back into the bedroom. Unfortunately, she could still smell the stale smoke.

In the adjoining bathroom the smoky smell was stronger. The washbasin and tub were immaculate, as she would have expected, a trio of small pill bottles arrayed on top of the commode. Glancing into the toilet bowl, Laura saw a few shards of cigarette tobacco clinging to the white porcelain at the waterline. So somebody had smoked and tossed the butt here, and the flushing had not quite removed everything.

Without thinking about it, Laura flushed again, sending the tobacco fragments down.

Back in the dining room she looked at the family pictures in small frames on the wall behind the dining table. Mrs. Chandler's grandchildren—if that was what they were— looked like angels squirming until the photographer finally released them. Mrs. Chandler's son did not look squirmy. He looked smug. He did not have a pleasant face, Laura decided, but the woman in other pictures—almost certainly his wife—looked like a sweet woman, smiling eagerly to please, with just a hint of fear in her eyes: the kind of woman who somehow invited mistreatment, and took it as her fate in life, a sad confirmation of her life plan.

Laura wandered into the kitchen and turned on the overhead lights. The all-white room gleamed, as perfect as the rest of the apartment. Most women Mrs. Chandler's age were formidable housekeepers, going around after the weekly maid service and redoing everything just to make sure the nest was *perfect*. The double sinks gleamed. Two cups and saucers, tiny circles of tea still in their bottoms, sat in one sink. Two teaspoons lay beside them.

In the bottom of the sink, a few tiny dark fragments of something caught Laura's eye. She bent closer and saw something else—something sticking up an inch or two out of the stainless steel maw of the garbage disposer. It was a pale green flower stem with a single small leaf attached.

Curious, Laura pulled it out. Some more ragged stems

and bits of leaf came up out of the disposer with it, and also a small spatter of wet petal fragments: bits of bright pink crepe myrtle. The far ends of the stems had been chewed up by the whirling blades of the disposer, but it hadn't quite eaten everything.

This was crazy, Laura thought.

Was it possible that she had just found the remains of the missing bouquet, the one that had been stolen right out from under the nose of Mrs. Smith's pig?

FORTY MINUTES LATER, the ring of the telephone startled her.

"Laura?" Mrs. Epperman's voice. "We're on the way up."

With a feeling of relief, Laura went to the apartment door and stood with her hand on the knob, waiting for them to arrive. For the first time, she heard the soft murmur of a voice—then another—somewhere in the hall beyond the door. She hoped word hadn't gotten around.

After another minute or two, someone tapped on the door. Laura opened it. There stood Mrs. Epperman, a tall, slender man in a gray deputy sheriff's uniform, and the familiar, shirtsleeved figure of Dr. Fred Which.

A half-dozen residents stood farther back in the hallway, their eyes like pie plates. Laura spotted Davilla Rose and the Castles. So much for keeping things quiet.

The deputy sheriff, whose nametag said LASSITER, moved quietly into the apartment, removing his wide-brimmed trooper hat. Laura watched him. He was dark and young and awfully good-looking, and very sober. Dr. Which and Mrs. Epperman followed. The good doctor, bony, pale, his youthful face creased in a worried frown, looked more like a high school basketball player than Timberdale's physician-on-call; Laura had sometimes thought Which's medical school—OU—should have had a capstone course called Doctor, How to Look Like One. Or maybe they had, and Which had flunked.

Mrs. Epperman had remembered to get sentimental. Her eyes looked like she had managed to produce a few tears. "Hallway looks like a convention site," she muttered. "If the CIA could get information as fast as our residents, we would rule the world."

Lassiter went into the living room and stared down at Cora Chandler. Forehead wrinkled in concern, he looked like a young John Wayne.

"Dead several hours, it looks like," he said.

Which, a nervous pallor accentuating his bony, youthful earnestness, went in with his medical bag and bent over Mrs. Chandler. Laura turned away, right into Mrs. Epperman's scowl.

"Laura, I'm going downstairs and type up a brief announcement. We'll run it off and put it on the bulletin boards. The ambulance will be here soon to take her away. I've already talked to her son. He'll be here tomorrow. After they've taken her to the funeral home, we'll just lock up here until her son arrives. Then, back to normal, right? Too many gossips in the hall already. We won't encourage any idle speculation. We'll keep a lid on it as much as possible, right?"

Laura nodded. "People may want to talk about it in group."

Mrs. Epperman reeled in her eyeglasses and jammed them on her nose. "Screw group. This is serious." She turned and marched out.

Depressed that she had to stay, Laura hung back in the dining room. While the doctor bent over Cora Chandler and examined her, Deputy Lassiter frowned his way around the apartment and into the bedroom, going out of sight. After a while, Dr. Which finished with his stethoscope and started doing unspeakable things such as looking in Mrs. Chandler's ears with a little flashlight. Laura beat a retreat to the bedroom, where she found the deputy bent over the vanity in order to see himself in the mirror. He was combing his hair.

"Oh," he grunted, seeing her. He straightened up, reddening, and shoved his comb back into the hip pocket of his gray uniform pants.

"I didn't want to watch in there," Laura explained.

Lassiter's frown came back and Laura could read his thoughts: Better get with the program, here. He took a ballpoint and small notebook out of his shirt pocket. As he looked at her, she felt like she was being x-rayed. He said, "Your name is...?"

"Laura Michaels. I'm assistant manager here."

"Home address? Phone?"

Laura provided them. Lassiter wrote.

"You discovered the body?"

"Yes. She didn't come down for breakfast, and she hadn't left a call saying she intended to skip it. So when it started getting late and she still hadn't shown, I came up with the master key. That's standard procedure here."

"You found her just like she is now?"

"Yes."

"She hadn't called for help, anything like that?"

"No. Her emergency call button was never pushed. The telephone was off the hook, but that was halfway across the apartment."

Lassiter's face went dark. "The phone isn't off the hook now."

"I know. Maude Thuringer replaced it."

"Who's Maude Thuringer?"

Laura explained. Lassiter's expression grew more glum. "Anybody else been in here? How many? Maybe the ladies' aid society or the entire Salvation Army?"

Laura's face warmed. "That's all." She had intended to

tell him about the cigarette smoke and the flower fragments, but now he had made her mad. Let him find his own clues, she thought spitefully.

Lassiter looked around at all the lace. "She was, uh, how old was she?"

"Sixty-seven."

Lassiter wrote. "Wow. Jesus."

Irritated, Laura snapped, "That isn't old. Especially not here."

He looked up, repentant. "You're right. That was stupid of me. Tell me. You think she took pills?"

"No."

"Natural causes, you think?"

"How could it be anything else?" Good Epperman answer there, babe.

Lassiter frowned but put his pencil away. Laura went back to the dining room. He followed her.

"People die here very often?" he asked abstractedly.

"I've just been here a few months. This is the first time it's happened to me, Officer Lassiter."

"I see." He frowned. "My, uh, name is Aaron, actually."

She relented slightly. "I'm Laura."

He grimaced. "I'm pleased to meet you. Please excuse it if I sound brusque. I'm fairly new at this."

"That's funny. When you first walked in, your face looked familiar to me."

"Yeah. Well, I used to be a ballplayer. Maybe that's it."

"A football player?"

"Baseball, actually." He made another face. "Not very good, though. I was at Toledo. Triple-A. They wanted to send me down to Double-A ball, and it finally dawned on me—good field, no hit, not even in Triple-A. Damned sliders, fork balls, stuff like that. Give me a fast ball or let me guess right and I'm okay. But left-handers with sliders, forget it. So I had to see the light.''

Laura watched the play of expressions across his face, which was really quite a nice face, with sun wrinkles around the eyes and possibly a touch of gray at the temples of his dark brown hair. ''You mean you quit baseball entirely?''

''Yep. Decided to come back here and finish my degree. In the meantime, this job opened up.''

''You're from around here originally?''

''Albuquerque. But I played for Oklahoma back in what seems like a million years ago.'' The X-rays probed again, briefly. ''You aren't a native Oklahoman.''

''No. I'm from St. Louis.''

''How did you get down here?''

''My husband was an attorney who worked for an oil company.''

''Was?''

''I'm divorced.''

''Is he still around the area, too?''

''He's in Texas. Dallas. But he comes up sometimes.''

''Oh?''

''We have a daughter. She's with me. But he visits her weekends sometimes. His folks live in Oklahoma City and he picks Trissie up and they go up there. That way she gets to visit her grandparents, too.''

''Trissie?''

''Patricia. Trissie is just a pet name that started, and stuck.''

''Cute name for a baby.''

''She's almost nine.''

Lassiter did a double take. ''You don't look old enough.''

Laura grinned at him. ''I am. But thanks.'' *Why am I*

telling him all this? Mrs. Chandler is right over there, dead, and we're—

"Do you like your work here?" Lassiter asked.

"Yes," Laura said firmly. "Oh, it could pay more and I wouldn't complain. But I'm in a part-time program down at OU—social work—and this is great training for that kind of career. I'd like to do counseling with elderly people. I like them. It's a burgeoning field."

"How do you take classes," Lassiter asked, "if this is a full-time job?"

"The part-time program is set up for people like me. There are night classes and weekend seminars, and then, actually, I can get a little practicum credit for my job here. I spend a few hours a week here doing therapy if anyone asks."

Lassiter opened his mouth to speak again, but Fred Which came in from the living room. "I think we're through here right now, Officer."

"How's it look?" Lassiter demanded.

"Stroke, probably."

"What about the pills?"

"I gave her that prescription. It was filled almost two years ago. I know for a fact that she had taken most of them, because she asked me just recently about getting a refill when they ran out. I know having the bottle there looks funny, but she didn't gulp down a bunch because she didn't *have* a bunch."

"Good," Laura breathed.

Lassiter said to her, "I'd like to see this lady's files, personal information, and so on, if you've got such a thing downstairs in your offices someplace."

"Well, we don't have a lot, but we take some personal information."

"May I look?"

"Sure, come on."

On the way down the quiet, carpeted hallway, Lassiter asked how many residents lived full time at Timberdale, what the fees were, how medical problems were handled. Laura answered in monosyllables.

"You're sad," he observed.

"I liked Cora Chandler."

"Nice lady, eh?"

"She could be a little crabby sometimes, but I realize now that she wasn't well. Most of the time she was wonderful, very upbeat."

"Well," Lassiter growled gently, "she had a full life. That's a dumb thing to say, but—"

"It's all you can say."

They reached the elevator and rode down. Laura watched him twirl his stiff-brimmed hat around and around in strong, nervous fingers.

Just as the car was about to stop, he said slowly, "I guess with this job and your daughter and your schooling and all, you're busy twenty-four hours a day, seven days a week."

Laura was puzzled. "Well...I'm pretty busy. Why do you ask?"

"I was thinking...maybe sometime I could call you? We could maybe have lunch or something?"

Surprised, she hesitated. He was coming on too fast for her, and it seemed totally out of character. Had she judged him all wrong? More important, was there a Mrs. Lassiter somewhere, bouncing a baby on her knee?

She didn't get a chance to reply. The elevator doors opened and they stepped out into the atrium. It looked like most of the Timberdale's population had gathered to stare.

"Oh, hell," Laura murmured, looking around. She started toward the office area, Lassiter close beside her.

Maude Thuringer, old-fashioned silky dress swirling, fluttered out of the crowd and hurried up to grasp Laura's arm with thin, chilly fingers. The old woman was pink with excitement.

"Well?" she whispered urgently in Laura's ear. "What's the verdict? Was it murder?"

"Of course not."

Maude's eyes shone. "Isn't this *exciting*? We can crack this case. We'll be written up in *Alfred Hitchcock's Mystery Magazine* and be on TV."

"Oh, Maude." Laura groaned. "Will you try to behave?"

FIVE

DESPITE ALL HER lectures to herself, Laura worried on the way to Timberdale the next morning. She couldn't convince herself that her suspicions of foul play were unwarranted.

She was behind the reception desk a little before nine o'clock when the front doors swung open and Dr. Fred Which rattled in, bag in hand, ready for his regular stint in the clinic. He was dressed up today, very doctorly, in a baggy white dress shirt, flying mallard necktie about four inches wide, and crumpled brown Dockers that betrayed bright red socks over his loafers. Spying Laura, he came straight over and deposited his bag on the counter.

"Well," he told her, "the preliminary findings are in. It looks like death by natural causes—congestive heart failure."

"Thank goodness," Laura breathed. "The Valium bottle?"

"Bloodwork showed no sign of anything like that in her system. She was taking some painkillers—Darvon—that Dr. Matthews had prescribed, and that showed up, but not a heavy dosage."

"But what about the Valium container, then?"

Which looked smug. "The officers noticed a half-dozen straight pins scattered on the carpet. Apparently Cora was keeping them in the old medicine container, and had spilled them on the floor."

"Oh." Laura felt deflated. *Everything else will be explained as simply.* She studied Which's face, looking for undue concern, but didn't see any. The doctor's soaring ears were bright red from the morning heat, and sweat glistened along his receding hairline, but that was all. She said, "Cora was taking painkillers? For what?"

Which scowled more deeply. "Stomach cancer."

"I didn't know that. Are you sure?"

"Of course I'm sure. I've seen all the reports. It was fairly well advanced, too. Stronger medications would have been required soon. If she hadn't been such a stoic, I suspect she would have already been on them." He sighed. "This kind of death might have been a blessing. It couldn't have been too much longer before she would have had to check into a nursing home for terminal management."

"She never gave us a hint, even in group."

"She was a brave lady, all right. I liked her. She was nice, most of the time."

"Most of the time?" Laura echoed.

Which studied her expression. "Well, she was quite a gossip."

"Isn't everyone around here? My God, if it weren't for all the crazy gossip and rumors, I don't know what these people would talk about."

"Cora had a little vicious streak, Laura."

"I find that hard to believe."

"Well, on at least two occasions she came to me with yarns about Mrs. Rose and Ken Keen."

"Everybody talks about Ken Keen."

Which ignored that. "Two years ago, she spread enough rumors about Mrs. Hutchinson that there was talk that the poor old woman might be asked to leave. Vicious stuff, really. Alleged drug use, petty theft—you name it."

"Who's Mrs. Hutchinson?"

"Exactly," Which fired back. "She moved out when people started repeating Cora's stories; she couldn't stand all the sly looks and whispers, is the way she put it to me."

Laura rubbed aching eyes. "But what I hear is that Cora

didn't have an enemy in the world. And Davilla Rose just told me Cora was her best friend.''

Which hefted his bag off the counter. ''The trouble with you, Laura, if I may say so, is your naïvete. Just because these people are old, you don't think they're capable of lying and deception anymore. I'd better get to the clinic. I'm sure I have people waiting.''

''You've sure given me something to think about,'' Laura said ruefully.

Which brightened, and looked crafty. ''Maybe we need to talk more about it. I've got a little time off this weekend. Maybe, ah, we could think about having dinner Saturday night?''

Laura hesitated an instant. She had been out with him once. He was a nice man, very young for his age in many ways, and he wanted desperately to marry someone—anyone. Laura had thought it was sort of sweet at first when he talked so earnestly about marital bliss and sharing the good and the bad. It hadn't been nearly as sweet later in the evening when he became dismayingly energetic in an attempt to play wedding night in the parking lot.

She said, ''Gosh, Fred, I already have plans.''

His shoulders sagged a bit more until he shrugged manfully. ''Off to work, then.''

Watching him go, she wondered if she had made the right decision. Trissie would be with her father over the weekend, and Tom would be spending half the weekend fishing as usual; she wasn't likely to see him again after dinner Friday evening.

On the other hand, she didn't need two out of three falls with Hulk Hogan. She decided she had decided correctly after all.

FRANCIE BLAKE cruised in moments later. Lubricious hips purring, she came behind the counter. She was wearing a new earth-tone shirtdress that should have been a bad color for her, but looked stunning. A tiny diamond necklace and tennis bracelet glittered. Rummaging in her pretty floral purse, she brought out a Bailey Banks & Biddle compact and carefully inspected impeccable makeup. A secret smoker, she smelled faintly of tobacco along with her Shalimar. "Good morning, Laura. What precious little shoes. Are they Rossettis?"

"No," Laura replied. "Sears. Francie—"

"We have to talk about the upcoming schedule of fun events, Laura. This is the weekend I'm leaving for Seattle, remember. I have everything in *perfect* order for the time I'll be gone. But we should confer to make absolutely sure you understand all the details." Francie gave her a long, serious stare of great sincerity. "I'm sure you'll be able to handle it."

"Thank you," Laura managed through gritted teeth.

Francie lovingly applied a dollop of fresh pink paste to her lips, bared perfect white caps for her mirror, then snapped the compact closed. "It's going to be so fun. Honestly, if you could have *seen* Morgan last night, talking about the Alaska cruise and everything. He's such a darling. And so handsome. Sometimes when I look at him I just can't *believe* him. I mean, doesn't he absolutely take your breath away? And he's *so* devoted. Really, it's almost embarrassing sometimes, the way he *watches* me, and positively hangs on my every word. He wants to buy me a new car. Did I tell you that? Isn't that just precious? I've explained to him and *explained* to him that I simply *can't* accept any more gifts from him—I mean, my goodness, I simply am *not* ready to settle down, and taking a *car* would be like...I don't know...practically being *engaged*, you know? But I guess when you're as rich as he is, things just don't have the same value that they have to ordinary little working girls like you and me. Do you know what I mean? It's such a *problem*."

"You know, Francie," Laura replied, "they have counseling services in Norman. You might really want to think about getting professional help with all these problems you seem to have."

Francie blinked several times. Since she didn't get it, she changed the subject. "It's terribly important for our social activities to go well here while I'm gone, Laura. It's so unfortunate when someone dies, isn't it? I mean, it's *depressing*."

"There were teacups in the sink of her apartment, Francie. She had had a visitor. Were you aware of a special close friend who might have visited her regularly?"

"No. Did Cora have any real friends?"

Laura looked at her in dismay. "You, too?"

"She was a sweet old lady, Laura. But there were people who avoided her like the plague. She could have a sharp tongue, you know." Francie paused. "Why are you asking? *You're* not buying into some of this gossip about possible foul play, are you? Heavens!"

"I'm just curious," Laura said quickly. "I mean, she called me at one point in the evening, and sounded just fine."

Francie tossed her hair. "Well, dead is dead, I always say. If you start poking around, Laura, all you can do is get people upset. I suggest you forget it."

"Thanks, Francie. I will."

No one was going to like her asking questions, she thought, heading for the kitchen to check on the day's meal arrangements. If even brainless Francie thought questioning was a bad idea, it must be a really bad idea.

In the kitchen, Mrs. Knott, the head cook, complained about late food deliveries and criticisms from residents.

"Well, I'm sure they don't mean anything, Mrs. Knott."

"Don't mean anything! Like bloody hell they don't mean anything! Some of these people are just *mean*, Laura, that's all they are, just downright nasty. Did you know somebody has started leaving nasty little comments about the meals under the windshield wipers on my car?"

Laura performed another strategic withdrawal. Leaving the dining room, she met Ken Keen hustling out of the hallway that led to the area where the clinic, sauna, and exercise rooms were located. Wearing red Oklahoma Sooners sweats and jogging shoes, Keen looked harried and nervous. Laura spoke to him, but he bustled right past, evidently heading for his apartment, without more than a glance.

Wondering what *that* was all about, Laura continued her morning rounds, heading down the corridor Keen had just come from. Turning a corner, she almost ran headlong into Kay Svendsen, the clinic's full-time LPN. Svendsen, crisp white in her uniform, looked hectic.

"Hey, Kay, good morning. That was close. We almost wrecked."

A tiny brunette who packed more energy into her five-foot frame than most nuclear devices, Svendsen snapped a wild-eyed look past Laura. "Where is he? I'm going to kill him."

"Who?"

Svendsen stamped a white shoe on the carpet, and angry tears bolted out of her bright green eyes. "That old fucker. I'm so sick of it."

"Who? What? Kay, what in the world—"

"That goddamned Ken Keen," Svendsen panted, digging in a starched pocket for a tissue. "Every time. *Every* time. You can't even be in the same building with him. I'm just going to kill him." She failed to find a tissue and stamped her foot again.

Laura quickly produced a Kleenex. "What happened?"

"He's the main reason I'm enrolled in a karate class. Twice in the past week he's cornered me, and it was like wrestling an octopus with excessive nose hair."

"But what happened now?"

"I took a break and went by Cora Chandler's apartment to collect the oxygen generator she had. Just as I was rolling it to the apartment door, somebody pushed the door open from the hall side and knocked me over. I jumped up, of course, but he had already lost his nerve and run for it."

"Ken?"

"Of *course* Ken!"

"You saw him? Coming into Cora's behind you?"

"Hell," Svendsen said, eyes snapping, "he was out of there faster than a speeding bullet. I didn't see *anything* by the time I got up and went into the hallway."

"Then how do you know it was him?" Laura shot back.

"Of course it was him! Who else around here tracks women like Natty Bumpo and tries to trap them in hidden corners?"

Laura wondered. Was she letting paranoia run wild here, or was it just as possible that the intruder had been a killer, returning to the scene for some reason—perhaps to collect the shredded flowers in the sink?

Carefully, she asked, "I just saw Ken steam past here. Did you confront him?"

"Sure, I did!"

"And…?"

"He denied it, of course. The old fart—he's a consummate liar, but his memory is so bad, he could have tried to jump me on Two and *forgotten* it by the time I caught him down here."

"What are you going to do now?"

"Go talk to Mrs. Epperman. Something has to be done about that man."

Laura went on to the clinic, glancing in to see a full house still waiting, and then checked the exercise areas and the sauna. Everything seemed in order. Timberdale's routine—even including Ken Keen's randy behavior—seemed amazingly unaffected by yesterday's death. She wondered why she apparently felt worse about it than anyone else.

When she returned to the office area, Laura found Mrs. Epperman in her office, bent over the morning crossword.

"Mrs. Epperman—"

"Good morning, Laura. Listen to this one: 'Wee; Scots.' Three letters."

"Sma," Laura told her. "Mrs. Epperman—"

Mrs. Epperman wrote it in. "How did you ever get so good at crosswords, Laura? My God."

Laura decided not to tell her about the crazy-time nights after the divorce, when a book of crossword puzzles sometimes seemed like all that stood between her and really, truly losing it. "Mrs. Epperman, was Kay Svendsen by?"

Mrs. Epperman looked up and a smirk tugged at her mouth. "Yes. She spoke to me about Ken Keen. That sly old rascal."

"Do you plan to take any action?"

"Maybe find out what kind of vitamins he's taking. My goodness. Nurse Svendsen. The old boy was really feeling ambitious, wouldn't you say?"

"Mrs. Epperman, somebody might have been hurt up there."

"Oh, I think he's quite harmless, Laura. But you're right. I'll have to speak to him about this."

"Yes," Laura said, and then took the risk. "If we're sure he was the one who bumped Kay with the door."

"Why, of course it was." Mrs. Epperman looked up sharply. "Nurse Svendsen said it was. Who else would it be? Still Bill?"

"I don't know," Laura said lamely.

"Forget it, Laura. This is my responsibility. Now. Have you heard yet from Mrs. Chandler's son?"

"No, but he ought to be here soon."

"Notify me when he arrives. We want to do everything we can to answer any questions he may have and help him clear out the apartment. This is an important part of our public relations and we want to do an excellent job with it. I don't know if there's much he'll want from up there, though. The furniture was old and worn, and even the TV set isn't worth much. Poor Cora. I don't suppose it mattered. All she ever watched was PBS, and sometimes The Discovery Channel."

Laura didn't say anything, but she felt a fresh and distinct shock. The TV set had been on when she walked into Cora Chandler's apartment to find her dead. But it hadn't been tuned to one of the channels Cora "always" watched. It had been tuned to CBS.

SIX

CORA CHANDLER'S PLUMP, unpleasant-looking son arrived in the middle of the afternoon, met with Mrs. Epperman, went with Laura for a cursory inspection of his dead mother's apartment, and said he would be back Monday with movers to clear out her things.

"She was a dear lady," Laura told him as they rode downstairs together in the front elevator.

The perpetual frown on Chandler's face changed briefly to a raised-eyebrow look of astonishment. "She was?"

"Didn't you think so?" Laura asked quickly.

The frown returned and he didn't reply.

A handful of residents watched with no more than mild curiosity as Laura walked him to the front door, where he left without another word.

"They seem to have lost interest," she exclaimed to Judith Epperman.

"Well, of course, dear. Aren't they sweet? So brave. That's another of the things I like about senior citizens. They're good people, of the old school—keep things neat, don't cause trouble, pay their bills on time."

But Laura was puzzled. Had the residents lost interest, or was there some secret about the old woman hidden behind the hints that she had not always been as innocent and harmless as Laura had thought? *There could be something here—a key.*

If she was to have any peace of mind about the flowers, the cigarette smoke, the TV tuned to the wrong channel, and the other peculiarities, she had to risk probing deeper.

She risked it in the Friday morning group.

"Who was Cora's best friend?" she asked, making it sound as casual as possible.

"I was, as I've said before," poet Davilla Rose said, the usual whine in her voice. "I have nothing but bad luck. Losing my best friend. On top of that, of course, I suffer more than the average person because of my artistic temperament. I'm not strong, you know. I've written a poem about it all."

The sweat-suited Castles exchanged glances with bright-eyed Maude Thuringer, and Laura caught the look. She said quickly, "Maybe it would be better for right now, Davilla, if we just talked about it for a while. You might read the poem a little later in the hour."

Davilla Rose straightened up in the chair, massive shoulders sloping. "Why don't people ever sympathize with all my cares? Cora was a fellow poet. She attended poetry club."

Stoney Castle said dubiously, "Well, we come to your poetry group too, Davilla. So does the judge, here."

Laura made rapid notes. "Who else attends?"

Davilla Rose sighed. "Milly Kett, most of the time. And of course Mrs. Hawes was one of our staunchest members before she died last year. But I don't see what that has to do with my wanting to read my poem."

"We've probably heard it," Castle blurted.

"How can you have heard it, you awful man? I just wrote it."

"Well, we heard the one you wrote about Jane Hawes. I figure a death poem is a death poem."

Tears of self-pity welled in Davilla's eyes. "Sometimes I feel like the whole world is against me."

Old Judge Young, who had already been almost dozing over the head of his cane, roused enough to rustle great white eyebrows. "What Stoney may seek to imply, Davilla, is that talk of death, given the circumstances surrounding the present audience, may be an unnecessary adumbration of the overt but manifestly and intrinsically redundant as well.''

Castle blinked. "Don't tempt fate, you mean?''

"No," Mary Castle said, loop earrings bobbing. "He means there's enough death in all of us already; no sense brooding about it.''

"Well, then," Laura said carefully, "I can see why you may not want to hear Davilla's poem right now. But if Cora's sudden death left any of you with bad feelings, this might be the ideal place to talk about it.''

The judge, leaning forward on his hands cupped over the curved top of his cane, again opened gray, shaggy eyes. "When one has attained the plateau of our senescence, Laura, the necessity for discussion is abrogated, and in its stead most of us develop a veritable paradigm of stoic acceptance bordering upon the languorous. Death is death; it's standing on the doorstep of each of us. The wonder for each of us, in a word, is not that we might be found dead some fine morning. The marvel is manifest for each of us, rather, in awakening every day and discovering with shock that we are still alive.''

Despite her great size, Davilla Rose managed to look pitiful and even hurt. "I worked hard on this ode. Cora always loved my readings, if I do say so myself. I think it's terrible of all of you to say I shouldn't read it. Her passing was so sad—so untimely.''

"She was not well," Stoney Castle observed.

"But it was not her time," Davilla murmured.

"Of course it was her time.''

"How can you say that?''

Castle's face reddened. "Because, you dadblamed fool, she *went*.''

"She was not that sick," Davilla shot back with surprising fire.

"What are you suggesting?"

The old woman's lips parted to reply, but then they clamped shut. "Nothing. I'm not saying anything."

"Davilla," Laura pressed gently but firmly, "say what you're thinking."

Davilla Rose shot her a quick glance of anger—and fear. Then she looked as quickly away. "No."

A rare total silence dropped over the group. Laura looked around, feeling a chill on the flesh of her arms. "Let's pursue this."

No one spoke or moved. The feeling in the room was uneasy...tight...more: they were *afraid*. Of what—or who?

Laura forced a smile. "Hey. What's going on here?"

"Nothing," Castle said finally, glowering down at his Nikes. "It's just that you don't like to see somebody die. Especially when you might be next."

"Any of us might be next," his wife added helpfully.

"Why do you say that?" Laura demanded.

Mrs. Castle looked startled. "Because we're *old*, Laura. Why else?"

Laura tried a different tack. "Tell me about Cora's enemies."

"Had none," Castle said instantly.

"I didn't hear it that way."

"You heard wrong."

Maude Thuringer fluttered. "Or maybe not."

"What do you mean by that?" Laura demanded.

"Nothing."

"Maude, let's not BS the troops, here."

Castle added, "Watch your tongue, Maude."

Maude gave him a quick look full of resentment and turned back to Laura, holding up one talonlike finger. "Just remember that things are not always what they seem. Read Margery Allingham. Or Colin Dexter. For heaven's sake, Colin Dexter, by all means. The world is full of people who take everything at face value. But *I* am not one of them."

Davilla Rose looked dazed. "What are you saying?"

"Nothing," Maude snapped.

Laura saw the puzzled expressions and decided she had to press. "What Maude may be referring to," she said very quietly, "is the fact that somebody had been smoking in Cora's apartment. But that certainly—"

"And the telephone was off the hook," Maude added triumphantly.

"And the telephone was off the hook," Laura added. "Thank you, Maude." She smiled around the circle. "Anybody have any ideas? I mean, let's play Maude's game, all right? Had Cora had a fight with anyone lately? Did she have a secret enemy?"

She waited. There was nothing but more blank, secretive stares.

Laura waited. A minute ticked by, then several more. Ordinarily someone in a group always got uncomfortable with such a prolonged silence, and blurted out something. But this was no ordinary group and this was not an ordinary time. These oldsters had practiced a lifetime at holding back when it was to their benefit. Some of them, at least, seemed to be hiding something—some suspicion or memory. But they would not give it up. Laura could not crack them so easily. *So much for playing detective.*

The silence went on and on. Ken Keen's vacant laughter carried in clearly from someplace far beyond the atrium. Laura bent over her notebook, pretending to jot something down while she groped for how to proceed. People like Mrs. Epperman pigeonholed all the residents and had no emotional problems dealing with any of them, she thought. But when their depths suddenly became apparent, superficial sentimentality was not so easy.

AFTER THE SESSION, Maude Thuringer caught up with her in the atrium. The little woman demanded, "Are you really trying to crack this case?"

"What case?" Laura shot back.

Maude waggled a finger under her nose. "Just ask people about Ellen Smith."

"Ellen? Why Ellen? Her paintings—"

"When she hung that picture of a pig, Cora was standing right there and she laughed. Giggled, right out loud."

"That doesn't sound like Cora."

"She couldn't help it. The thing is silly as a loon. All of us wanted to laugh, but Cora just couldn't help herself. And Ellen—well, you know how Ellen is—she was furious, just *furious.*"

"I'm sure that doesn't mean she might have done anything to Cora. That's a terrible thing to say, Maude. I hope you won't repeat it."

"She's only one suspect," Maude said, looking crafty again.

"You have others?"

"Wouldn't you like to know." Maude turned to flutter off.

Laura walked on to the reception desk. Maude's suspicion was nutty, she thought. But she had a very slight chill. Had the flower wreckage in Cora Chandler's sink been the remnants of the stolen bouquet? Had Ellen Smith gone into the Chandler apartment and seen the evidence and flown into some kind of rage?

It seemed unreal.

Laura went to the desk, checked messages, and then got called to the kitchen to answer some menu questions. When she returned to the desk, she reached under the top shelf to retrieve her notebook and file folders from the session.

The notebook wasn't there.

After getting down on her knees to make sure the notebook hadn't fallen behind the counter somewhere, she went into Judith Epperman's office.

"Yes?" Mrs. Epperman said, looking up with a scowl from her crossword.

"Who was around the desk the last few minutes?" Laura asked.

"I didn't see anyone," Mrs. Epperman said. "Why?"

"No reason."

"What's a four-letter word for 'chest'?"

A DARK APARTMENT awaited her that evening. Trissie's father had picked her up at the sitter's, and would have her all weekend. He had said he was taking her to Dallas, and would be back by eight o'clock Sunday night. Tom was due in an hour, and Laura was looking forward to it. Saturday classes would start at eight and continue for almost fourteen hours, and she already felt wrung out after the events of the past few days.

Locking herself in, she showered, towel-dried her hair, and changed into fresh clothes. She was still tugging her hairbrush through moist ringlets when the door chime sounded and it was Tom, neat and cool and lawyerly as always in an expensive dark suit, ready to take her out for dinner.

"You look great," he said, giving her a kiss and a hug.

"Starved, too," she murmured, and grabbed her purse.

Later, in the restaurant in Norman, Tom suddenly stopped saying whatever he had been saying.

"And," she suddenly heard him say, "you aren't listening."

"I'm sorry, I just got distracted for a minute. Those people at the table behind you are having a birthday party. Say it again, okay?"

He frowned, grim and disappointed. Tom was a young

man who liked everything in his life to be orderly, and people to pay attention. "You're preoccupied," he told her.

"Well, maybe a little."

"School? The job? Trissie? What?"

Laura sipped her chardonnay. "No. Hell, I'm just being silly."

"Want to tell me?"

She hesitated. Tom Benson had come into her life around the first of the year and at first she hadn't taken him seriously. He was a year younger, for one thing, and outrageously good-looking, for another. And if anyone had ever said she might get involved with an attorney, she would have laughed in their face and buried them in lawyer jokes. But Tom was different: he didn't boast or manipulate; he wasn't money-crazy; he hadn't rushed her. Now she didn't know where this was going, but that was all right. Where it was right now was fine.

She admitted to him, "I was thinking about the old woman who died out at Timberdale."

"Cora?"

It vaguely pleased her that he remembered the name. He was a dear and he tried his very best to get involved with her life and interests. But sometimes she got this vague feeling that when she talked about things that didn't really interest him, his eyes turned to marbles—glassies—and he went somewhere else inside. "Cora," she told him now. "Yes."

"I guess she was a special lady, huh?"

"Yes. And there were other things today."

His eyes wandered over her head to something happening at the next table. "Um?"

"Yes." Laura told him about it, concluding, "And then, finally, someone took one of my notebooks while I was away from the desk. Nothing like that has ever happened before. It worries me. My gut feeling is that there really is something going on out there, and someone is watching *me*."

Laughter at the next table continued to absorb Tom Benson's attention. Then he seemed to realize that Laura had stopped talking. His eyes came back to her, glassies. "I see," he said. "Gosh. That's interesting."

"Sure," Laura agreed, disappointed.

Tom reached across the table and covered her hand with his. She looked at his hand. It was a nice hand, blunt-fingered, its back lightly touched with downy hair, his college and masonic rings immaculately gleaming.

"I understand, Toots."

He hadn't heard a word she had said. "Tom, I think I've told you how I feel about being called 'Toots.'"

His eyes glazed again. "Oh, yeah. I forgot. Sorry. Now as I was saying about my car."

"Yes?"

"As I said before, maybe it's time to trade it in."

"I guess you could."

"But I can afford a new one."

"Yes, you can, I'm sure."

"On the other hand," he said, frowning again, "it might be better to put any extra cash in T-bonds or something safe right now."

"Yes, that's an option."

"If I got a new car, I was thinking Lincoln. Prestige. You know."

"Well, yes."

Tom heaved a sigh. "It's a big decision, Toots."

Be still, my heart.

BUT A FEW HOURS LATER, lying in the dark of her bed with his furry weight pressed close against her, she felt comfy and warm, secure and safe and satisfied, and she wondered if this represented her future. Maybe he wasn't exciting, but he was a nice man and he loved her.

Were you supposed to want the moon?

She analyzed as best she could, here in the moist cotton cavern of their lovemaking.

Tom Benson was a nice man, a genuinely nice man who cared about her as much as he was capable of caring about anyone. He was not cruel, he was not a blowhard, and he was not a liar, not anything like Richard.

Richard, who had said it was her fault that he cheated, that it was society's fault he got into coke, that it was his boss's fault he got fired. Richard, controlling her with his ferocious helplessness until it finally struck her like a thunderbolt right in the middle of one of his pitiful harangues: *Wait a minute! I'm not responsible for how he feels, this is bullshit.*

Even as clearly as the realization came, however, the next months had been brutal. So many people experienced divorce, she thought, and no one had ever been able to capture just how devastating it was.

But she had begun to climb back. Starting school part time had been a big step, and so had the job at Timberdale. Now Trissie seemed okay, and here was Tom.

Tom was supposed to represent another step. Possibly a permanent reordering of her life. She wanted him to be all that. Was he? He might not be perfect, but he was…nice, wasn't he? And shouldn't that be enough?

There was no answer.

For some reason, memory of that deputy sheriff's face swam into her mind. Aaron Lassiter. It seemed like a nice name. He had seemed like a very nice man. Mrs. Epperman had volunteered the information that people had called him "Salt" Lassiter during his playing days at the university. Laura wondered now why they had called him that.

Was he salty? If you licked his bare shoulder, would he—

Laura didn't permit herself to finish the thought. She rolled over violently, away from Tom's inert form, and buried her face in her pillow. Almost instantly Cora Chandler's dead face filled her memory, and she wished she had been able to continue thinking about Salt Lassiter, even if she did sometimes almost think things that disgusted her with herself.

RICHARD DELIVERED Trissie to Laura's door promptly Sunday evening. Laura exchanged a half-dozen careful words with him, and then relocked the apartment to follow her daughter into her bedroom. Trissie was already piled up on the bed, her small suitcase dumped out to make a memorable mess.

"How was the weekend?" Laura asked.

"Oh, okay, I guess."

"What did you do?"

"Went to Dallas, went to Fort Worth, went to Irving, met Dad's cheerleader."

"Met his what?"

Trissie looked up brightly from her mess. "Daddy's getting married again."

Laura's insides sank a little. "To a cheerleader?"

"Yep. A Dallas Cowboys cheerleader."

Laura sat on the edge of the bed. "And you met her?"

"Yep."

Well, what did you say next? "Is she nice?"

"Yep, pretty nice. She looks like—what's the name of the girl on the poster at the hi-fi shop?"

"Marilyn Monroe?"

"Yep. Like that. Except I think she's bigger in front."

Laura was aware of her breathing. "She sounds very pretty."

"She sure is. Daddy says they're gonna get married and then I'm going to live with him all the time—with both of them—in Dallas. He says it will be a whale of a lot of fun. That's what he called it, a whale of a lot. He says we'll get tickets to all the Dallas Cowboys games and I can go and sit with him and watch her. Her name is Cindy. He says she's going to be an actress and he can pull some strings and help her with her career. Mom?"

"Yes?"

"How come he thinks he'll have me all the time? Didn't the judge say I was supposed to be with *you* most of the time?"

"Yes, honey. That's what the judge said."

"Then why did Daddy say I would be with him?"

"I don't know." Laura swallowed. Her throat felt dry. "I suppose if you *wanted* to be with Daddy all the time, the judge could change things around."

There was a pause. Laura waited, half frightened, to see what her daughter was going to say next. The silence extended.

Laura felt her sense of dread begin to grow. She knew Richard. If he got married again, even to a Dallas teeny-bopper in a Cowboys miniskirt, he would renew the fight for custody of Trissie. He could provide a complete family environment, he would argue, while Laura—unmarried, working full time, and going to school—could not.

"I can give her everything," he would tell the court. *"Laura can't."*

"That's right, you bastard," Laura would counter. *"Because you used every trick in the book to cheat me out of all but the most minimal child support—"*

"Irrelevant, your honor. My ex-wife won't have her social work degree for at least another year and a half. Should this innocent child be subjected to an endless succession of day-care centers and baby-sitters just so her

*mother can work at a low-paying job in a retirement center
and take this endless series of weekend classes to qualify
her for an uncertain professional future?*

*"If it please the court, we can produce testimony indi-
cating that this woman is not emotionally stable. Very recently, when one of the residents of Timberdale Retirement
Center died a peaceful death of natural causes, my ex-wife
apparently hallucinated some sort of wildly improbable
theory of possible foul play in the case—"*

Trissie closed her suitcase, hopped off the bed, and carried it to her closet. "Daddy says after we live in Dallas
awhile and he makes contacts, then Cindy will be a big
movie star and we'll all go to Hollywood and have a swim-
ming pool and meet famous people like Madonna, and in
the winter we'll have a cabin in Colorado and go skiing,
and maybe even have our own jet once the movies start
coming out."

Laura slowly exhaled. "What do you think about all that,
Trissie?"

Trissie sighed. "Mom, don't tell him I said so. But I
think he's lost it."

The telephone rang. Laura hurried to the kitchen to get
it. "Hello?"

There was no response.

"Hello?" Laura repeated.

She could hear breathing. She slammed the phone on the
cradle.

At any other time she would have assumed it was a ran-
dom weirdo or a kid playing some stupid game. But she
instantly thought of her stolen notebook...the other hints
of hidden things.

She was sure the silent caller had wanted to check up on
her...perhaps issue a tacit warning. She felt irrational...and
chilled clear through.

SEVEN

STACY MILLER looked shocked Monday morning. "Wow, you're here really early."

"Yep," Laura said. "Sit tight, Stacy. You're not relieved yet. I've got something to check in the back office."

Looking disappointed, Stacy slumped back amid the pizza wreckage and doughnut crumbs. Laura marched into the inner office wing, snapping on lights as she went.

In the unoccupied office beside Francie Blake's, many of Timberdale's records, mementos, and supplies were stored. The latest large photo album was on top of the stack on a folding metal table. Laura plumped herself down and started leafing back through the most recent paste-ins. Francie was a Polaroid picture freak—Laura shuddered to think what Francie took pictures of during some of her dates— and there were photos of everything around Timberdale: a recent Sunday dinner; a garden tea that hadn't turned out well because the heat wilted everyone; the last talent night.

Laura wanted to find pictures of Cora Chandler and people she was with. It seemed like a faint trail, but it was the only one she could think of. Unfortunately, like some old people, Cora evidently hadn't liked to have her picture taken. In the recent pages there was only one photo of her, and that was at the dinner table, evidently alone.

Laura was still leafing backward when the footsteps startled her. Hurriedly closing the album, she turned to see Judith Epperman looking in with a thundercloud expression.

"Good morning," Laura said, as if prowling through

photo albums was the most natural thing in the world at this hour.

"What are you doing?" Mrs. Epperman demanded.

"Nothing. Gosh, you're really early today. Is anything wrong?"

"Laura, come into my office."

Oh boy. Storm clouds, all right. Laura maintained a calm expression as she followed Mrs. Epperman's orthopedic shoes into the hallway and office beyond.

"Please close the door, Laura."

Laura obeyed.

Mrs. Epperman sank to the swivel chair behind her littered desk, folded thick hands on the newspaper crossword opened before her, and looked up with eyes that resembled gun barrels. "Sit down, Laura."

Laura sat.

"Laura, what in the hell were you doing in there with the photo albums?"

"Just browsing," Laura ad-libbed, feeling more nervous.

An eyebrow shot up. "Browsing?"

"Sometimes it helps to look at candid pictures of the residents. I mean, I might notice something that could help one of them in therapy." Laura paused, then added, "Or something."

"Laura. You know Timberdale is almost to the break-even point financially. The last thing we need right now— the *last* thing we need—is anyone on staff creating any kind of furor, discontent, or unhappiness with unfounded rumormongering of any kind."

"I'm sure that's true."

"Then why," Mrs. Epperman flared, "are you doing this?"

"Doing what?"

"Encouraging all these wild rumors. And don't look at me like that. You know *exactly* what you've been doing. I can't imagine what was in your mind, asking all those questions in your group sessions, encouraging everyone to gossip about poor Cora Chandler and her death. Didn't you realize you were just getting everyone all stirred up over nothing? I explicitly told you to keep a lid on it.''

"They wanted to talk. They needed to look at some feelings.''

"Nonsense! They don't need to talk about their feelings. They're *old*. All you accomplished was a storm of gossip, rumors, speculation—I don't know what all. Maude Thuringer is even running around spreading the idea that there was something *strange* about Cora's death, and now other people are talking about it. And now here you are, poking around in old photo albums. It's ridiculous. Have you lost your mind? Is senility a communicable disease?''

"I'm sorry. I didn't mean to stir up rumors—''

"That's not good enough.'' Mrs. Epperman flipped off her glasses and let them plump to the end of their gold chain. "Laura, the board of directors is counting on all of us to maintain a happy ship here. This kind of rumor and innuendo could make people decide to leave us. It could start stories that might prevent newcomers from joining us. We can't have that. We *won't* have it. Now is that perfectly clear?''

Memory of Trissie's talk about Richard and the cheerleader flitted through Laura's consciousness. Sure as the world, he would try to get custody. *You've got to have this job or he can win.* "I understand, Mrs. Epperman.''

"Good! I would never threaten anyone, Laura, but if you can't keep damaging gossip down around here, I might be forced to find someone who can. I hope I make myself clear.''

Laura swallowed. She wanted to scream and yell, but she couldn't. "I understand.''

Mrs. Epperman sighed and leaned back in the chair. "All

right. Fine. We'll just put it behind us. We have a big week ahead. Later today we must talk about the social activity schedule for the week, especially Cruise Weekend. We seem to be a bit behind on our planning for that, but I know you'll get us back to speed. That's all for now, Laura. I find I'm terribly busy this morning. I'll let you know the first moment I have free.''

Laura got to her feet and started toward the door.

"Laura? One more thing.''

Laura looked back.

Mrs. Epperman had put her glasses back on, and peered at her over the top of the frame. "The clue is 'Cairo skink.' Four letters.''

"Adda,'' Laura said.

"A-d-d-a?''

"Yes.''

Mrs. Epperman wrote it in. "Thanks.''

Laura went out to the reception desk. Still hot with angry embarrassment, she felt suspicion return. Why had Mrs. Epperman come in early? Who had told her about the discussions in group? Who had convinced her that the retirement center was a cauldron of rumor? There might be many things that took Laura by surprise, but she was well enough in tune with the emotional atmosphere to know that most residents were acting like nothing at all had happened. Who had convinced Mrs. Epperman otherwise—and why?

She didn't have time to think more about it just then. Stacy Miller, sleepily gathering up virgin textbooks and well-thumbed scandal magazines, had a routine list of minor complaints and problems. Stacy wandered off, and Laura cleaned up the pizza and doughnut crumbs and set about working through the list.

Ellen Smith, wearing a beige cowgirl outfit with a floral blouse, came out of the elevator and stalked to the desk, eyes glittering with combat. She clumped her elbows onto the counter. Multiple silver bracelets clattered. "Laura, about my luau painting."

Oh, hell. "Luau painting?"

"Luau painting! Luau painting! The painting I've done to hang here in the atrium for Cruise Weekend this Friday and Saturday!" Smith's eyes snapped. "Don't you know anything?"

"I don't know anything about a luau painting, Ellen."

"I worked it all out with Francie."

Laura began to feel dazed. "Francie Blake?"

Smith's false teeth clanged together like cell doors. "Is there any other Francie around this place? Get with it, Laura!"

Laura took a deep breath. "Francie neglected to tell me about this before she left. You have a painting to hang here in the atrium for the Cruise Weekend?"

"Yes, and it's one of my best. Francie said it was darling, just perfect."

"Well, then, I see no reason why we can't—"

"Not so fast. After what happened to my flowers in the hall upstairs last week, I am forced to demand some assurances from you."

"Assurances?"

"Assurances. If I hang my new Cruise Weekend luau painting here in the atrium, what assurances do I have that someone won't make off with it, or the flowers I intend to display around it, just the way they made off with the bouquet in front of my pig?"

"Ellen, don't you really believe the flowers upstairs were some sort of mix-up?"

"Of course they weren't a mix-up! A lot of people around here are jealous of my artistic ability. I know some of the things they whisper behind my back. Cora Chandler was one of the worst offenders. She laughed at me. *Laughed* at me! But just because she's gone, that doesn't mean my troubles are over. Somebody stole my bouquet just to spite me, and you never have done anything at all about that. They'll just do it again, or maybe even take my luau painting.''

There was no sense trying to argue, Laura saw. The small woman's eyes danced with frustrated rage. Laura asked quietly, ''What do you want me to do?''

''I want a table in front of the painting, and some kind of security glass—maybe something electronic.''

''Something electronic?'' Laura repeated. ''What do you have in mind?''

''How do I know what I have in mind? I don't have any idea what I have in mind! That's your problem, you're the management!''

Laura paused, meeting the full fury of the old woman's eyes, and then saw that this might be a golden opportunity, risk or no. ''Ellen, I'm surprised you're still so angry about those flowers.''

''Why shouldn't I be? Why shouldn't I be? It was a *terrible* trick!''

Laura kept her face calm. ''Do you think Cora Chandler had anything to do with it?''

Ellen's face fell. ''Cora is *dead*. Are you crazy?'' She turned and flounced off, buckskin fringes flipping.

So much for fishing for clues with Ellen Smith. Laura watched her walk out of sight, then turned to arrange papers on the credenza behind the desk. That was when she spotted Judith Epperman standing in the back doorway. Behind her, the office corridor was faintly smoky; Cleopatra must have sent an urge for a secret cigarette.

''What was that all about?'' Mrs. Epperman demanded.

''Cruise Weekend,'' Laura said. ''A painting—''

''I thought we could put this off, but I guess not. You'd better come back into my office again.''

Damn Francie Blake, Laura thought, following the big woman back inside.

"It sounds to me, dear," Mrs. Epperman said sweetly, "like you don't quite have your act together this morning. Maybe if you spent less time meddling and stirring things up, you could pay more attention to everyday details around here."

Laura thought of something to say. At the same time she remembered Trissie's cheerleader report. "I'll try to do better."

"Good. Perhaps I neglected to mention the painting that Ellen was so excited about. We're all busy. You'll just have to make allowances. Now, I want this Cruise Weekend to be special. I expect to have some visitors in, possible new tenants. Everything must be *perfect*."

"I'm sure it will be."

"It won't be unless you shape up. I suggest you work it out regarding the painting. Also, double-check with Mrs. Knott in the kitchen. I want to be sure we have enough fresh fruit and flowers and little sandwiches for the luau. Last year we ran out of pineapple punch—it was very popular—and a few residents were *very* unhappy with us about that. Check to make sure we'll have enough this time."

Laura scribbled notes. "About the dance—"

"Also," Mrs. Epperman cut in, "I want someone to watch Colonel Rodgers like a hawk. Like a hawk! If he tries to spike that punch again this year, you'll just have to take him in hand."

Laura looked up from her paper. "How do you suggest I do that?"

"Just stop him from doing it. Be firm with him. The last time he got snockered at one of our parties, he fell asleep with a cigarette in his hand and burned a four-hundred-dollar hole in a couch. Take the vodka from him, if you have to. But be diplomatic, Laura, and don't offend him, for God's sake. Be discreet. If you must take action, do it very quietly."

The colonel, when angered, had a voice like an elk and the disposition of a bull moose in rut. Laura wondered how she was going to be firm and diplomatic with him, but didn't say anything.

"Now," Mrs. Epperman went on, consulting some notes of her own, "Still Bill is in charge of setting up the platform for the ukelele band on the east side, here, with the furniture moved to both ends of the room, and he *must* be careful with the plastic dropcloths before he lets the florist in with the palm fronds. Make sure he has all that properly planned. I want nametags for everyone, and someone at a card table in front to greet and tag the visitors. New copies of our brochure are due from the printer this week. Follow up on that. No later than tomorrow, I want you to get a little announcement in everyone's mailbox, reminding them about the costumes, and that the party Friday night will stop promptly at midnight. I don't want anyone drinking too much punch and making themselves sick. Make the note cute, dear, with some little Hawaiian references and things."

Judith Epperman flipped a page of her steno notebook, frowning down at her large, loopy handwriting. "The program hasn't been finalized yet. Francie intended to do that before she flew out for her cruise, but she simply ran out of time. She was so excited. Isn't she precious? I just love her. Cleopatra does, too. Now. You certainly have to get on that program right away. We'll have the band, of course. And Davilla will want to read some of her poems. Work all that out. When you write the announcements, make sure to stress again that no one is to invite more than two family visitors. We want to make sure we have plenty of space for the potential new tenants. Is the Friday afternoon trip to Jungle Safari all set?"

"I don't know," Laura admitted glumly.

"Well, Francie intended to work on that, but maybe she didn't. Check it out. Jungle Safari is a nice wild-animal park, but it will be a hot drive. We'll want a special air-conditioned bus at the front door by ten. Make sure Kay Svendsen goes along on the bus. Tell her to keep it moving and don't let anyone persuade the driver to make unscheduled stops. The weather forecast says it's going to be beastly hot, and we can't risk any heatstrokes down there. Also, there are a few details to work out about the Saturday flea market and the evening party. I think Francie left some notes in a folder somewhere about that. I can't seem to find them. Take care of it like a dear, all right? I'm leaving in a few minutes for Tulsa. We're having a stockholders' meeting. But I'll be back sometime tomorrow."

Mrs. Epperman paused and frowned. "Laura, I'm sure you realize this, but let me emphasize it—Cruise Weekend is *very* important this year. Of course, all our special events are important. But we'll have a number of visitors, and if just a few of them would be persuaded to join our happy family here at Timberdale, we could finally turn the corner and start making this a paying proposition. My goodness, dear. In the short time Timberdale has been in operation, we've made gigantic strides. Perfectly gigantic strides. This, as you know, is a very big operation. A huge operation. I mean, it's no secret that our operating budget is set up at well over two million dollars per year. Our projected shortfall for fiscal ninety-two, at the present level of expense and registration, is less than two hundred thousand dollars. We are oh so close to breaking even, Laura. All we need to do is lease a few more of our vacant suites and we're in the black. The stockholders know that, and of course our primary purpose is to provide a lovely, dignified independent life for all our precious residents, bless their hearts, every one of them, but our stock-holders are *inves-*

tors, don't you know, and there's nothing wrong with their wanting to start seeing a return on their investment. So Cruise Weekend really needs to go well. I'm counting on you and the rest of the staff to make it the best yet—the weekend we'll always remember as the time we finally became a paying proposition. The queen has told me this is a propitious cycle.''

"We'll all do our part," Laura said lamely, feeling more depressed all the time.

"I *know* you will, dear. You'll have to work some overtime this week. I realize that and I appreciate it. You know we can't pay you for it, but someday later in the fall we'll try to find some compensatory time off, right?''

"Right," Laura said through gritted teeth.

Judith Epperman sighed happily. "We'll just pretend our earlier little...unpleasantness...concerning all these rumors never took place. At a time like this, we all pull together.''

Outside at the desk, someone bonged the visitors' bell. "I'd better get that," Laura said.

Mrs. Epperman waved her away.

Laura found Cora Chandler's habitually dour son standing at the reception counter. Two gray-clad moving men stood beside him.

"The truck is parked at the back," Chandler told her without preamble. "You want to let them in? Then I need to settle up accounts here.''

"Sure," Laura said, recognizing one of the movers. "Hi. It's Mr. Peterson, isn't it?'' She rummaged in the desk, finding the right envelope. "Here's the key to the room. If you guys want to go on up and get started, I'll work with Mr. Chandler, here, and come up later to make sure you're doing all right.''

Peterson took the proffered heavy bronze key. "Use the back stairs and elevator?''

"Right. And if there are any questions, just dial me here at the desk."

The two movers trudged across the atrium toward the front elevator. Chandler stood glowering and silent while Laura produced the file showing Cora Chandler's apartment billings. Only the current month was outstanding. Chandler glanced over the sheet with the expression of a man sure he was being cheated, then abruptly pulled out a checkbook and scrawled a payment for the entire amount.

Laura wrote a receipt and handed it over. "I want to say again how sorry we all are, Mr. Chandler."

He shrugged, with no change of sour expression.

"I'll walk up with you," Laura said.

"Suit yourself."

It was hard to know if he was always so dour, or whether there was something for him to be angry about. In the elevator, Laura tried to find out. "I hope you know we provided the best possible security and emergency system calling, Mr. Chandler. Cora's death saddens all of us."

"Right," he said impatiently. "Don't worry. I know the score. I'm not making any waves here."

Laura tried to read his dark expression. "I don't understand."

Suddenly Chandler's ball-bearing gray eyes focused directly on her, as if he were seeing her for the first time. "Look. She could be an unpleasant old lady. She poked around in things that weren't any of her business. Except for the past six or eight months, when she was sick as hell and sort of trying to make up to people before it was too late, she was about as pleasant as sandpaper."

"Surely you're not suggesting—"

"I'm not suggesting anything. Period. She's gone. She was dying anyway, and she was starting to be in a lot of pain. Whatever happened—happened. The way I see it, somebody did her a big favor." The doors of the elevator opened. Chandler stepped out and looked sourly in both directions. "This way, right? Look, like I said, don't sweat it. These things happen. Now let's not say any more about it."

LAURA STAYED IN the Chandler room only a few minutes. The movers brought up cartons and started to wrap and pack the odds and ends of a lifetime. Chandler morosely went through drawers and tossed things into a trash container. Laura felt chilled again. Her instincts were not wrong in this thing. Cora Chandler had not died a natural death, had she? But if that were so, how could anything ever be proved when even her son seemed to be part of some conspiracy of silence?

When she went back downstairs, she was more troubled than ever, and no nearer any good idea of what to do about it.

In the still-quiet atrium, the impeccable Julius Pfeister was just struggling in from the front foyer, toting a laptop computer in one hand and clinging to his cane with the other. A white delivery truck was just pulling away from the entrance. Putting her worry aside, Laura hurried to help by taking the computer from him.

"Why, thank you, Laura." The old man smiled. His face was red and wet from the early-morning heat, although his seersucker suit and stiffly starched white shirt looked perfect.

"I'll help you to your room," Laura offered.

"Very kind indeed."

A cloud of Old Spice accompanied them to the elevators. Laura punched the button and they rode up.

"That was a really early delivery," Laura observed.

"Yes indeed, yes indeed," Pfeister said briskly. "Need to maintain a tight schedule in this business."

She had no idea what business he might mean. "Oh?"

"Yes. Computer went punk, so I called and they picked it up just now. Left me this laptop as a loaner. Repair will take a day or two."

"I guess you can't afford to fall behind on your letter-writing in the meantime."

Pfeister's smile looked superior. "I was an investments counselor before we came here. I still keep my hand in. The computer keeps me in contact with the markets and my clients via the phone lines."

Laura was pleasantly surprised. "You still have clients, then?"

"Over a million dollars so far this year."

"I've never heard you mention it before."

Pfeister chuckled. "Well, a lot of these folks here don't have much to do, you know. It might make them feel bad, knowing an old gent like me is still a power in the market."

The elevator doors sprang open. Leaning on his cane, the old man took the laptop machine from Laura. "I can handle it from here. Many thanks."

Riding back downstairs, Laura had something new to think about. She had had no idea about Pfeister's continued involvement in stocks. She realized that she had underestimated him. Now she wondered how many more residents had aspects of their lives that few suspected. They might be old but they were not necessarily simple. And Timberdale was not a simple place. Things might seldom be what they seemed.

The elevator doors slid open to the atrium. In a flurried blur of bright floral rayon, Maude Thuringer rushed out from hiding behind a *Ficus benjamina.*

"You startled me," Laura told her.

"I saw you with Mr. Pfeister. He's your prime suspect, right?" Maude's eyes snapped like windows in a slot machine.

"There aren't any suspects," Laura groaned. "I've told you—"

"Let me tell you who to watch. Ellen Smith."

"Maude, you've simply got to—"

"And if *she* didn't do it, then I'll bet dollars to doughnuts on Sue Mullins."

Despite herself, Laura stopped dead in her tracks, stunned. "*Sue Mullins?* My God, she's just a poor old kitchen worker."

"Yes, but people from the kitchen can go anywhere around here without being suspected of anything! Did you ever think of *that?*"

"So can Still Bill and his maintenance people," Laura pointed out. "And the maid service. And Kay, from the clinic. And *me.*"

Maude's mouth dropped open. She rushed to cover it with a veiny hand. "You're so right. It's like *Murder on the Orient Express.* We've got candidates all over the place." She looked crafty again. "No one is immune from suspicion, right?"

Irritated and frustrated, Laura had no idea why she said it. "No, Maude, and that includes you."

The old woman's eyes shocked wide. Then she turned and rushed off, heading for the stairs.

When Laura reached the desk, she found one of Maude's suspect list, Still Bill Mills, waiting for her.

"Just wanted to get the checklist from you," he said.

"Checklist?" Laura repeated, drawing a blank.

"Uh-haw, checklist. Miz Francie said she would leave it with you."

"Checklist for what?"

"For the luau, she said." Still Bill focused with his good eye. "Did you lose it, or what?"

"Bill, she didn't leave a checklist."

Still Bill thought about that while he rooted around in

his ear with an index finger. "Hmm. Well, I guess then the whole thing will just have to go on autoerotic pilot. I guess I can handle that. When you work around here a while you get to be ambidextrous, and besides, we've had luaus before, so it ain't like it was a new president."

Laura studied his calm, lantern-jawed expression. "You *can* get everything ready in the atrium, then, Bill?"

"Sure. Just do what we did last time. Hey. You don't look so good."

"I've had a morning," Laura admitted.

"I'm going to the kitchen for some java. You better come with me."

They walked through the atrium to the dining room. One of the early risers, Sada Hoff, had come downstairs and waved to them from the hallway. Going through the still-unlighted dining area, they entered the kitchen through swinging doors. Here lights blazed, and the large, steamy room was redolent with the aromas of fresh coffee and hot pastry. A lank college-age boy, Steve Berne, was just removing cinnamon rolls from a wall oven while two women, one youthful and the other middle-aged, arranged silvery coffee urns and utensils on rollered serving trays. Laura remembered the girl's name was Renfro. The older woman was Sue Mullins. Buxom Margaret Knott worked furiously nearby, pulling plates of fresh melons and fruit from one of the large refrigerators and placing them on another wheeled cart.

"Morning, Maggie," Still Bill called.

Mrs. Knott nodded, but kept furiously at work. "Can't visit now," she grumbled. "Running behind as usual."

"Thought we'd get something."

"Have to help yourselves. Schedule won't wait for anybody." She slammed two more plates on the cart.

Still Bill walked to the nearest coffee urn and poured two cups, handing one to Laura. Then he sauntered over to the pastries, looking over the array with great seriousness. "You got'ny doughnuts today?"

"Do you see any doughnuts?" Mrs. Knott snapped.

Still Bill sighed. "Nope. Guess I'll just have to fall back on my usual buns." He took one from the tray and morosely bit into it.

Laura carried her cup over to the carts, now almost fully prepared by the other two women. The Renfro girl gave her a quick, half-frightened smile and continued hurriedly piling food on another cart, evidently afraid of a tongue-lashing if she slowed down. Sue Mullins, large and bony-shouldered in what looked like a homemade cotton dress, paused to brush the back of a large hand across her filmy face. As usual, she summoned a bright and somehow sad smile. "Good morning."

"Good morning, Sue. Breakfast looks good today."

"The fruit is real nice. This is the best time of year for local fruit."

"Just in time for the luau later this week."

"Yes ma'am." Mullins's deeply lined face brightened. "Everyone will have such a good time. My husband loved this time of year, all the fresh fruit and vegetables."

"You're a widow, Sue?"

"He died…five years ago, now."

"I'm sorry."

Mrs. Knott sang out impatiently, "Time for lights on in the dining hall. Let's hustle. Get this stuff out there before the complaints start. Not that they won't complain anyhow. Hurry it up, hurry it up. Hubba hubba!"

Laura carried her coffee out of the kitchen and into the dining area as the lights came on and things began to bustle.

In the few minutes she had been gone from the atrium, it had come to life. The Castles were down now, and so were Jed Blake, Maude Thuringer, Judge Young, Davilla Rose, Ken Keen, the Spinkses, and the Murphys. The halls in both directions bustled as more couples and singles filed in, and the pleasant murmur of voices filled the central portion of the building. Roger Rodgers was lecturing the Buckinghams and the Clovers, and Milly Kett came slowly into view, maneuvering her walker; she spied Laura and sent her a quick, sun-bright smile.

Laura passed the Harrisons and the Wilcoxes; they were discussing Mevacor. The gist seemed to be that something had to be done about prices.

Moving on through the crowd, Laura wondered if there was any resident not taking several prescription medicines. She would have been surprised to find anyone. Sometimes it seemed that half the daily conversation centered on drugs—pain pills, heart pills, diabetes medicines, things for high blood pressure and things for low, capsules for regularity and others for diarrhea, anti-inflammatories, salves, unguents, injectables, and puffers. The specter of sickness was the one universal.

Except for their uniformly advanced ages, however, the residents might have been a gathering at a local country club or church. Most looked reasonably happy and prosperous. They were the lucky ones, people who had earned enough and saved enough to avoid loss of their independence. Timberdale did not represent an end of the line. Ahead of them might be deterioration and, for some, eventual stockpiling in a nursing home. That was a fear that haunted many of them. But for now they coped.

Mrs. Pfeister appeared at the end of the atrium. Laura, going that way, stopped to greet her.

"Thank you for helping Julie up with his computer," Mrs. Pfeister said.

"He told me about his stockbroker work," Laura replied. "I had no idea. You must be very proud of him."

The little old woman's eyes sagged. "He convinced you?"

Laura didn't get it. "Convinced?"

"I'm sure he must have told you how he's still in the stock business, and how he remains in contact with the markets via his computer?"

"Yes, of course."

"Laura," Dot Pfeister said slowly, with regret, "you should know this. There's no line to the stock markets. There's no stockbrokering going on up there."

"But I don't understand," Laura said, trying to read the woman's sad expression.

Mrs. Pfeister's thin lips quirked in the ghost of a smile. "I pay a young man fifty dollars a week to take Julius's calls on his home computer in Oklahoma City and send back quotes and replies just like New York might do."

Dismayed, Laura began to understand. "Then he doesn't really—"

"He was an important person for a long time. Sometimes a man can't just—give it up."

Laura didn't say anything.

The old woman added, "It's a harmless enough delusion, isn't it? Doesn't a person have the right to a little self-deception if it makes life more worth living? Things don't always have to be what they seem. Do they?"

EIGHT

PREPARATIONS FOR a special event like Cruise Weekend would have kept Laura hopping any time, but with Francie Blake off on her latest romantic adventure, things were crazy. Despite her gnawing worry that she was missing some ghastly clue that would make everything clear about Cora Chandler, Laura had little time for checking anything out.

Not that she knew what she might check out anyway. She felt stupid and frustrated, and maybe silly. Was she, after all, being as ridiculous as Maude about all this?

Tom called at work Tuesday, mentioning a big case in Wichita and wanting her to ask for three days off to go with him. When she explained about Cruise Weekend—she had told him about it before, but he hadn't been listening—he got that hurt tone in his voice and said he understood. When she suggested that he might try to give her more than a day's notice next time, he hung up on her.

Tom—she told herself—was the least of her worries.

On Thursday night Judith Epperman held the last Cruise planning session. It droned on and on. When Laura finally hurried out of the building after ten o'clock, she was mentally calculating how much she owed Trissie's baby-sitter, and for once wasn't thinking about her mystery or delusion or whatever it was.

Naturally that was when it happened.

It was a hot, windy, star-bright night. No one else was around the curved walkway leading to the dark side of the building. Hurrying, Laura wished she hadn't yielded to daytime habit and had parked nearer the front like everyone else.

She was halfway across the paved parking area when she heard the footstep behind her.

Fear gusting cold, she turned, groping for the little tube of Cs gas in her purse. She couldn't see anyone.

"Who's there?" she called.

One of the big evergreens rustled and then was still.

Torn between the urge to run and the need to know, Laura moved cautiously back toward the evergreen in the curved flowerbed, her little gas canister held well in front of her with her thumb on the trigger. "Come out where I can see you!" she called. Her voice quaked.

There was still no response. But *someone was there,* on the other side of the shrubs. They had been watching her— following her.

Laura's heels scraped softly on the sidewalk as she skirted the cluster of evergreens, always facing them as she tried to move around enough to see behind them. Her feet sank into the soft, bark-strewn earth of the flowerbed. Her heart was going ninety miles an hour and she felt faint. But she was *not* going to turn tail and run. This was a chance— a real chance—to learn something. The gas canister gave her enough courage…barely.

She took two more steps, eyes glued to the dark area behind the shrubs. "You might as well show yourself," she called. This time her voice faltered, and she thought, *I can't do it, this is it, I'm running for it.*

Too late.

The sound behind her came at the same instant she was starting to turn. But she was not fast enough. Something heavy and dense—a sack of something—slammed into her back, pitching her forward to hands and knees in the soft dirt and woodchips. The force of her fall drove her face into the dirt. Spitting and choking, she rolled over to try to defend herself from her attacker.

But there was no one, only a nandina bush swaying violently from being brushed by the silent, invisible attacker. Beside her on the ground was a soft, aromatic plastic bag of peat moss, the thing she had been hit with.

Whoever had hit her with it was gone.

"NOW LET'S GET this straight," Aaron Lassiter scowled, looking up from his notebook. "You drove into town and came to the courthouse to report this because you didn't want any commotion out there at Timberdale?"

"That's right," Laura said. They were in a tiny cubicle of the sheriff's department in downtown Norman, and she was nursing a Coke Lassiter had brought her from the machine in the hall. She felt silly for even being here, but she felt scared, too.

"You didn't see who it was," Lassiter confirmed, glancing over his notes.

"No."

"You got pushed down and then he fled."

"That's right."

Lassiter closed the notebook with a sigh. "If anything like this ever happens again, my advice is not to pursue the culprit the way you did. You should have gotten in your car, locked it, and gotten out of there."

"I know," Laura said. She wanted to tell him all about her suspicions in the Cora Chandler death, and how it had raced through her mind that there *was* a killer, and he had been following her, and her only chance to unmask him had been in confronting him. But it sounded so incredible, even in her thoughts, that she just kept quiet. She liked Lassiter. She didn't want him to write her off as a hysterical idiot.

"Is there anything else you can add?" Lassiter asked.

"No," she told him.

There were some minor formalities. She would need to sign a statement later. Lassiter or another officer would be out at the center in the morning to poke around.

"I suspect it was a kid, some kind of prowler," Lassiter told her as he walked her to her car. "I doubt he'll be back. But I want you to be more careful, and we'll circulate word out there that somebody has been noticed spooking around the parking lot, so everyone can be more cautious."

"Whatever you say," Laura said meekly.

Lassiter held her by the shoulders and looked down hard at her. "You're sure you're okay?"

"Yes," she lied.

Nodding with satisfaction, he put her in her car, signaled through the glass and waited until she had locked the inside locks, and then stepped back and waited until she drove away.

Why didn't I tell him all of it? Laura wondered in dismay.

Because she was sure of it: there *was* a killer, and he had just made an attempt on her life. The bag of peat moss had been heavy enough to break her neck if it had hit her just right.

Or maybe she was being crazy again, and it was just a kid, prowling, peeking in windows.

She knew no more than she had before. She was only more scared.

WHEN LASSITER APPEARED at Timberdale the next morning, Mrs. Epperman was furious.

"It was *obviously* just some teenager out for a prank," she told Laura after Lassiter had left. "You weren't harmed."

"I got knocked down," Laura pointed out.

"Yes, and you were pushed with a sack of peat moss.

Do you think a mad-dog killer would push you with a sack of *peat moss?*''

Laura didn't trust herself to say anything.

Mrs. Epperman strode up and down her office floor, orthopedic shoes clumping. All she needed was a swagger stick to complete the Patton impression. ''You know how high-schoolers like to come out here sometimes and put silly, nasty notes on windshields, or try to peek in windows. God knows I'm not condoning such nonsense, and we report every incident, but it's not like anything serious has ever taken place. Now, as to this event, I'm *certainly* not going to alarm the residents by putting up any kind of notice, as that officer suggested. We'll alert the security guard. But beyond that, there will be nothing more said about this stupid incident, do you hear me?''

Hang on. You need this job. ''Yes, Mrs. Epperman,'' Laura said.

''It was your fault for investigating a noise in the bushes anyway. So what's done is done. Now please get on with your duties. This is our big weekend, remember, and the trip to Jungle Safari leaves in less than an hour. We have to hustle and have fun.''

Laura left the office with the feeling that someone was crazy. Was she the crazy one, imagining things?

The feeling of dread was stronger in her. She hadn't imagined the attack, inept as it seemingly had been. Maybe it had been meant only as a warning. Maybe the next time—if she persisted—it would be much more serious. She didn't know what to do, and she felt utterly alone.

NINE

JUDGING BY the look of the Jungle Safari bus riders who staggered back into Timberdale Retirement Center Friday afternoon, it had been hell down there in southern Oklahoma's Arbuckle Mountains. Most of the pale, wilted oldsters headed straight for their apartments.

Laura stood at the reception desk and watched. Everyone looked so innocent. Her desire to be wrong about her suspicions made her feel almost dizzy as she mentally warred with herself. *Cruise Weekend; God, what a time to be distracted like this.*

But at least everything seemed to be arranged. Peace had even been declared by Ellen Smith; her luau painting—bright blue breakers crashing over orange candy rocks—hung on the west wall behind a thick glass panel in a frame built by the maintenance boys. Mrs. Smith had checked it out and pronounced it good. She had then thrown herself into further artistic creation, spending much of the past two days in the kitchen's walk-in freezer, where she was hacking away at some kind of ice sculpture to be unveiled later today.

Across the atrium, Still Bill Mills shakily descended a rickety wooden stepladder, having stapled up the last of the fast-disintegrating palm fronds. Still Bill was already in his islands costume, which consisted of faded pink cutoffs, dirty tennis shoes, and a yellow T-shirt from the Little Rock Riverfest. As Laura watched him, he reached behind a planter and produced what first appeared to be a batch of straw, but then, as he crammed it on his head, turned out to be what had once been a wide-brimmed straw hat. He issued some orders to the two young yard boys, who had been helping him, then ambled over to the desk.

"Palm fritters look good?" he asked.

"They look fine, Bill."

"I had to have the boys glue some of 'em together."

"You can't tell it."

He grunted with satisfaction. "Just goes to show you, there's more than one way to eat a cat."

"What's next on your list?"

"Hang the crepe paper streamers and put down the Visqueen plastic, scatter out the sandpile."

"Fine."

"Hope none of these folks has ever been in Hawaii for real. When I was there in the army during the war, it sure didn't look anything like we make this place look every year."

"No one is going to notice. I'm only concerned about getting things done in time."

"We'll make it, but I'm sure getting tuckered. Think I'll slip outside for a short break, and sneak me a smoke."

"Do you ever smoke inside here, Bill?"

He rolled his good eye sharply toward her. "Are you kidding me? The queen would have my yingyang."

"She smokes herself sometimes."

"Sure, but noblesse obligatto, you know."

Laura smiled. "Right." She wondered how she could even mildly suspect this man. Strike him from the list, she thought.

Still Bill pulled a rumpled sheet of notepaper out of his pocket and consulted it. "Oh. We got the carpets shampooed in the old Chandler unit. I think it's all cleaned now, ready to show."

"Did the cleaning get the smell of cigarette smoke out of the unit?"

Still Bill's eye rolled again. "Smoke? She never smoked. She was a fiend on smoking."

"I forgot," Laura said.

He studied her with frowning intensity. "You still worried about that?"

"About what?"

"About how she died and all?"

"No. Of course not."

He shrugged. "Okay. Miz Epperman said you'd check the unit when we were through with it."

"Okay, Bill. I'll get up there, although going into her place now that it's just a vacant unit is going to feel sad."

"Yep. I know. I miss that old lady myself. I'd known her a long time."

"She was a charter resident, right?"

"Right. Sold a grand old house near the campus in Norman to move in here. I'd known her and her husband forever. Of all the places I have ever lived, Norman is the only one."

"Bill, did Cora have enemies?"

"Land, no! Oh, she was cranky sometimes, and liked to gossip. She had tiffs with people here, but everybody has tiffs with everybody in a place like this—it goes with the territory. A lot of people that knew how sick she was, they felt terrible about it."

"Did many residents know? I didn't."

"That was how she was. She didn't complain. Some people are like that: episodic. Of course she was like the old judge too—fairly sedimentary."

"Was she rich?"

Still Bill grunted surprise. "Hardly. Of course you don't live in a place like this if you're a pauper. She had some stocks and stuff." He eyed her sharply again. "But nobody killed her for her money, if that's what you're thinking."

Brought up short, Laura feigned surprise. "Why in the world would I think something like that?"

He shrugged again. "Well, Maude is going around telling people the two of you are investigating a murder."

"Damn. It's not true, Bill. We're not investigating anything."

He brightened. "Glad to hear that. Maybe you ought to make sure Miz Smith hears it, too."

"Ellen? Why?"

"Well, she and Cora used to fuss like old hens sometimes, and they had that one blowup over the pig picture. I think Cora tried hard to bury the shovel, but everybody knows there was still some bad blood between them. If you was to have a suspect, Miz Smith would top the list. And she knows that."

"Bill," Laura said firmly, "I'm not investigating anything."

An eyebrow cocked as he reached into his shirt pocket for his cigarettes. "Folks'll be glad to hear it. Maybe they'll even stop chattering about how you got knocked down in the parking lot last night."

"They're gossiping about that, too?" Laura groaned.

"They gossip about everything," Still Bill said cheerfully, and wandered off toward the front door.

Dismayed, Laura thought about it. She saw that her fumbling efforts to look into Cora's death had been noticed everywhere, by everyone. She had made herself a center of covert attention. And a potential target?

She had to dispel the idea that she was playing detective. At the moment, the best way she could do that was to pay attention to normal business.

Checking her watch, she returned to the desk and consulted the events timetable for the afternoon and evening festivities. With a slight shudder of embarrassment, she pulled the atrium public address system microphone out of its hidden compartment. After turning on the little amplifier and adjusting the volume, she tapped the mike and was rewarded with a soft, generalized popping noise from the concealed speakers in the walls. Knowing that other speakers would respond in other areas of the complex, she bent over the notes Mrs. Epperman had ordered be read *exactly*. As she began reading them, her voice came back to her from the walls and ceiling:

"Your attention, please...everyone on the docks, your attention, please. The S.S. *Timberdale* is preparing to sail! All passengers should prepare to board the ship promptly by five o'clock this afternoon, when we will set sail for sunny Hawaii, Tahiti, and all points in the South Pacific. A native band will entertain on the poop deck. Refreshments will be served from the captain's table. Come in native costume, one and all, and enjoy the first stop on our colorful cruise of all the islands. All aboard, please, for the second annual cruise of the S.S. *Timberdale!*"

Yuck, she thought.

At this point, Mrs. Epperman's notes read: "Ring ship's bell." Laura hadn't gotten a bell. She would hear about that later, she thought glumly.

BY 4:15, THE ATRIUM seemed to be ready. Furniture had been pushed back nearer the walls, and the plastic-coated sandpile was in place with a plastic banana plant embedded in it. The first residents sifted in and stood off to one side near the dining hall, watching Still Bill's helpers fold the big ladder and knock a lamp over with it on the way out under the palm fronds. Upstairs, overlooking the scene, the Pfeisters' door opened and they came out. Julius Pfeister wore a white linen suit, white leather shoes, a crimson silk shirt with a silver ascot, and a handsome planter's hat. Mrs. Pfeister came out wearing a gorgeous red-green-blue-yellow floral muumuu and carrying a pretty mint parasol.

Pfeister transferred his cane to his left hand in order to offer his wife his right arm. With a radiant smile, she linked arms with him and they moved slowly along the upper-floor walk, he limping as usual but smiling a beatific smile. They entered the elevator. From the other direction, Mrs. Slater and Mrs. Barksdale appeared, wearing colorful cotton dresses. Ken Keen, wearing a garish Hawaiian shirt and ugly olive-drab shorts, popped out of a hallway in front of them. He more or less crouched, hands cupped and ready at his sides, a forbidden cigarette between two of his fingers. He looked silly, but he also managed to look menacing. Laura's nerves tightened. *He could be the one.*

The two elderly women executed a one-hundred-and-eighty-degree turn and headed for the stairs. Keen looked disappointed. And harmless.

Soon the front doors opened and the members of the ukelele band came in, five college boys wearing scruffy shorts and an impersonation of islander shirts and caps, and carrying their instruments. One of the T-shirts said "Oklahoma Sooners" and another said "Guns n' Roses," but otherwise they looked fine.

Laura walked over to meet them. The leader, a red-haired boy named Stan something, grinned lazily at her. "Hey, Ms. Michaels. Here we are."

"Okay, Stan," Laura told him. She nodded toward the frond-encrusted platform along the west wall. "You see where to set up, and I guess you can start playing whenever you're ready."

"That's cool."

They wandered over and started setting up. One of them had a small amplifier, and another carried a small black box with many buttons and knobs all over its control panel. There was a great deal of chair rearranging, consultation, hooking up of cables, and shuffling of feet. One of the boys hooked the black box to the amplifier along with some other things, plugged in some headphones, and began earnestly twiddling dials, which made red lights pulse on the black box's panel. Then they started opening the instrument cases.

Laura feared the worst.

They were not, strictly speaking, a ukelele band. Ordinarily they played hard rock at campus hangouts in Norman and Stillwater. Last year, however, Mrs. Epperman had offered them enough for the gig that they had dug up some Hawaiian instruments: Stan, the leader, had a Gibson guitar, but three of the others had classic wood ukes and the other had some sort of miniature acoustic guitar. Laura held her breath when they started to tune up and some very strange howling notes issued from the amp. More residents had sifted in now—wildly colored dresses, wilder shirts and trousers, a great variety of straw hats and parasols—and Laura noticed that she wasn't the only one waiting to see what kind of noise was going to come out of their shipboard combo.

Stan, however, after muttering briefly to his fellow musicians, stepped forward and strummed a soft, full chord. He had done something funny to either the guitar or the amplifier, because the sound that came out resembled the steel-guitar sound of the islands, sort of a poor man's Martin Denny. Then the other players came in, and lo and behold the ukeleles sounded like ukeleles, and from somewhere—out of the mysterious black box—came rhythmic sounds of bongos, and sometimes a waterfall or surf, and distant exotic tropical bird calls.

"Wow," someone chirped at Laura's side. "Not bad."

Laura turned to see Milly Kett standing there in the embrace of her walker, gnarled fingers clutching the support rails. She had chosen to wear a thin summer frock that cruelly exposed her neck, shoulders, and arms, and a huge floppy straw hat with plastic flowers stuck all around it. Her face glowed with happiness.

"They've improved their act," she told Laura.

"They're better than last year?" Laura said, relieved.

"My goodness, yes. Last year they *tried*, the poor dears, but they just couldn't seem to stop throwing in those one-four-five chord progressions, and sevenths with flatted ninths—all that billy-rock stuff!"

Milly Kett listened for another few moments to what sounded a lot like "Sweet Leilani," then turned to Laura with astonishment widening her eyes. "Why, I think they've even practiced. Did you hear that cute little contrapuntal minor chord progression from the boy in the ugly pants?"

Laura forgot to listen to the music. She stared.

Kett smiled up at her. "What is it, dear?"

"You know a lot about music. I didn't realize that."

"It was my business once."

"You mean you taught music in school."

"Hell no, Laura. I played piano."

"You taught piano?"

"No, dear. I *played* piano. That was in Chicago, then later in Los Angeles. I started out playing cocktail piano—you know, 'Smoke Gets in Your Eyes' and 'Poor Butterfly' and all that kind of thing. Not that there's anything wrong with it, of course, but when the war came along and a lot of boys went off to the army and I got a chance with some of the big bands, it was a wonderful break for me, believe me."

Laura was aware of the Hawaiian music continuing, more residents coming in, some guests entering under the palm fronds. But for a moment she felt eerily removed from all that as she concentrated on Milly Kett in one of those startled compartments of surprised insight that she should have already learned might come *any* time she underestimated someone here. "Big bands?" she murmured.

"Paul Whiteman for a little while," Milly said happily, watching the kids across the room play their ukes. "But I guess my first love was always swing. When I got to play with Glenn Gray and the Casa Loma orchestra, that was wonderful. And then I played for a while with Pee Wee Hunt when he left the Casa Loma orchestra and went on his own, and later—oh, my, dear, there were so many... Benny Goodman...Harry James...even Red Nichols once, when he temporarily needed a bigger group."

"My God," Laura said. "I had no idea."

Kett was pleased. A little light danced in her eyes. "Most people don't."

"Why haven't you ever played for us?"

Clinging to her walker with one hand, the small woman held up the other. It was swollen and red at the joints, and the fingers looked like the small branches of a tree, twisted in all directions. "Can't play a note anymore. It hurts, for one thing. And with these damn fingers you never know what keys you're going to hit anyway."

"I'm sorry," Laura told her.

Kett shrugged. "There are worse things, dear." Her skinny throat worked. "As I could tell you about." But then as if by sheer force of will she smiled again.

Laura hesitated. Milly Kett looked thinner, and her color was grayish. Laura's mother had been a fiend on pronouncing on people's health by observing their color; it had been gospel with her that complexion color gave away everything about a person's health. In her last months, Laura's mother had been even grayer than Milly Kett was now. *How sick are you?*

Before she could think of a way to ask, a smattering of applause around the atrium drew her attention to the doors of the dining room, where Mrs. Mullins and another kitchen helper were just rolling in the first fruit-and-punch-laden serving cart. In the center of the long cart stood a glistening ice sculpture. Laura hadn't been allowed to see Ellen's sculpture ahead of time—artistic temperament and all that—and it had been shrouded under a sheet in the walk-in freezer for almost forty-eight hours since its creation. Now, standing high in the center of the cart, it seemed to be melting at an alarming rate. Laura could not quite make out whether it was the torso of a nude woman or possibly the head of a horse.

"My, my," Milly Kett breathed. "Ellen has outdone herself this time."

"Will you excuse me, Mrs. Kett?" Laura hurried over to supervise placement of the cart, and to get a better look.

About a dozen guests had already partly encircled the cart and its gleaming chunk of ice. As Laura pushed through on one side, people on the other side of the ring were jostled to make way for Ellen Smith. Her usual cowgirl togs had been replaced by a grass skirt and crisscross red bra, but that wasn't what anyone noticed. What they noticed was that Ellen Smith was in a real rage.

Her face red and contorted by her anger, she flew at kitchen worker Sue Mullins, pounding her fists against the bigger woman's chest and actually staggering her backward. "What have you *done,* you idiot? How long have you left my ice sculpture standing out in that hot kitchen to melt?"

Mrs. Mullins desperately caught the older woman's hands, struggling to hold her. "It's just been out a few minutes—"

"You idiot! You cow! Look at it! *Look at it!* It's ruined! Oh, no! Oh I can't believe it!"

Laura tried to intervene. "It's fine, Ellen. It really is. It's beautiful, and—"

Eyes like coals, Mrs. Smith pulled free from Sue Mullins

and turned on Laura. "Shut up, you little twit! Do you think any self-respecting artist would allow something like *this* to be shown?" She stopped abruptly, whirling around again, her eyes crazy. Then her attention fixed on something on the cart—a long serving fork. With a swoop she had it in her hands and started swinging it wildly at the melting ice sculpture, pieces flying in all directions.

From somewhere, Still Bill Mills hustled forward and managed to wrestle the fork out of Smith's hands. She fought him. He cradled her gently but firmly in his arms. "Okay, Miz Smith. Okay now."

Laura moved in to help him. "Let's go into the activity room."

At the same time, Judith Epperman came out of the office. She was dressed either as hula dancer or a thatched hut. She moved in to take Laura's place. "I'll take over, Laura. Resume the party, everyone! Go ahead and have fun, no problem here! Play, you ukelele boys! Play!" Her burly arm around Ellen Smith, she led the shaking woman off toward the door to the activity room.

"It's all right, everyone," Laura announced brightly. "Here comes the punch! Nothing serious—it's all right."

People started talking all at once, and the college kids struck up "Little Grass Shack." That helped—made it seem more normal again. Laura gave the kitchen people what she hoped was a bright, confident smile, and hurried to greet some guests who had just arrived and missed the fun.

A few minutes later, with the party in full swing as if nothing had happened, she slipped out to the kitchen to find Mrs. Mullins. The big, lanky woman was feverishly putting out finger sandwiches on trays. She looked decidedly pale.

"Are you all right now?" Laura asked gently.

Mullins heaved a sigh. "Yes, ma'am. The sculpture really *was* out just a few minutes. You can ask Sally or Jim, either one, they helped me carry it out and set it up.''

''I know, Sue. It's fine. Mrs. Smith just got...crazy.''

''She's so temperamental. I feel *terrible* that she thinks we messed it up. She was so upset. Is there anything any of us might do to make her feel better?''

Laura paused, surprised. ''I'm surprised you're worried about her after she could have hurt you, Sue.''

''Oh, I don't give that a thought.''

Back in the atrium, the party had moved along. Two of the room maids had released the red, white, and blue balloons, which floated around on their long, invisible nylon tethers. Kay Svendsen, none the worse for the wear after the trip to Jungle Safari, had changed to a wildly colored islands dress and was serving punch. Ken Keen stood nearby, watching her with eyes like candy lanterns. People milled, conversation echoing through the music.

Given the moment's free time, Laura turned into the east hallway and made her way to the elevators. A quick ride up put her in the corridor that led to Cora Chandler's old apartment, ready for final cleaning inspection. Taking the pass-key from her skirt pocket, Laura reached the door and paused. For some reason she didn't want to go in again. This was Mrs. Epperman's job, really, but that wasn't why Laura felt reluctant.

The draperies had been drawn, and the darkened apartment smelled faintly musty. When Laura turned the overhead lights on, she saw that some portions of the gray carpet had not dried yet. She turned on the air-conditioning fan to the continuous ''on'' position to circulate more air.

The moment air started stirring from the pipes, she smelled the stale cigarette smoke again.

It was much stronger than it had been the night of Cora's death. Someone had been in here since, again smoking.

Wait a minute, wait a minute. Just think. Be logical.

The movers had had strict orders not to smoke in the building, and she knew they obeyed the rules. Still Bill knew better. Kay Svendsen had been by earlier, before the apartment was emptied, but Kay didn't smoke. The cleaning staff knew it was instant dismissal if they smoked in the complex. Laura couldn't think of anyone else who should have been in here.

Did that mean something sinister, or was she groping at straws again? Hell, she thought with dismay, it probably meant nothing, right? Just pay attention to business.

Slipping out of her flats, she walked gingerly around the entry and dining room, testing how wet some areas of the carpet remained. They appeared dark, but her toes felt only the slightest residual dampness. With the fans on, the last damp spots would dry quickly.

Her back turned to the open hall door, Laura slipped one of her feet into a shoe. The bright little voice behind her made her jump out of her skin.

"Looking for clues?"

Pulse crashing, Laura spun around. Staring in through the open doorway was Maude Thuringer, flowers in her hair and vivid blue slip-dress decorated with a paper lei.

"I doubt that you'll find anything now," Maude chirped. "But on the other hand you might. Where is it that the detective revisits the scene of the crime even after it's been completely redecorated and—"

"Maude," Laura said, "go to the party."

Something about her tone of voice made Maude Thuringer's eyes widen and her happy little smile die. One small hand fluttered to her throat. Then her eyes changed again, narrowed with shocking hate. "What are you hiding?" she demanded, crouching.

"*What?*"

But the old woman turned, flew out the doorway, and was gone.

Laura forced herself to take a few deep breaths while her heart settled down. For a moment she had been deeply scared. The real killer—she could not stop thinking there was a real killer—could have slipped up on her just as easily as Maude had.

TEN

THE ROUTINE official verdict in Cora Chandler's death seemed to stick with everyone but Laura, at least on the surface. Feeling totally baffled, she let the summer work load fill her days.

July ended with a heat wave and Francie Blake's return from her cruise to Alaska. She said it might be true love. By August 15, however, she persuaded Judith Epperman to give her a week's sick leave for another trip, quite a different man. *This* might be it, she told Laura. "He's the sweetest thing. A doctor. You'd adore him, darling, you really would." Francie returned on August 27, sporting a diamond engagement ring the size of a forty-watt light bulb, but by September 5 she wasn't wearing it on a regular basis.

The hot weather hung on. Laura's summer school classes ended and she surprised herself by getting a four-point average. At Timberdale she picked up three new individual clients and reorganized her groups. A resident named Molly Eastep had a slight stroke and had to leave for a nursing home, and a couple named Washington moved in. A widow named Clancy became the new resident in the old Chandler apartment. Mrs. Epperman reported a cosmic contact from Eleanor Roosevelt, but clammed up when Laura pressed for details. The Oklahoma football team beat Pittsburgh and then UCLA, and Aaron Lassiter did not call.

Laura heard nothing from her ex-husband. Trissie said Daddy was grumpy and wouldn't talk about the cheerleader, except to say Trissie shouldn't count on seeing any Cowboys games, and they were losers anyway.

October came. On the first, the official high was ninety-seven degrees, enough to depress anybody.

On the tenth, everyone in the reorganized Wednesday breakfast club was crabby. Laura had never seen them quite so hard to handle. The new members did not help.

After Stonewall Jackson tried to reorganize Ken Keen's life for him, and was told by Keen to go peddle her papers, Ellen Smith told Keen that he was nothing but a bully, and she didn't know what he was doing in the group anyway, and she didn't want him coming around her art classes anymore and trying to see up all the women's dresses. Keen told Smith that her disposition would improve if she got it a little more often. Milly Kett tried to intervene at this point, but Stonewall lost her temper and told Milly they were all tired of her goody-two-shoes act. At that point Ellen Smith jumped all over Stonewall, and Stonewall told her angrily that such behavior was one of the reasons no one liked her. Ellen Smith looked sincerely shocked.

"I think we're all a bit on edge," Laura observed. "It's the hot weather. The humidity."

"Humidity hell," Colonel Rodgers snapped. "You people are not in shape, that's what's wrong with all of you. If you would let me lead some morning calisthenics, the stamina level around here, healthwise, would be maximized in short order. Nothing like a good workout to burn off nervous tension."

Stonewall Jackson snapped, "You're free to lead workouts. You know that. We've been over that a hundred times. All you need is volunteers, and you can't get any."

Rodgers harrumphed. "Won't work on a volunteer basis. Too lazy. All of you. Your attention is directed to previous statements by this person in regard to that issue. Regular calisthenics. Ought to be mandatory morning regimen for all hands."

"Colonel," Laura interjected, "this isn't the kind of residence where we require people to do things they don't want to do.''

Rodgers drew himself up to his full, imperious height and glared down at her. "You make us eat this rotten chow three times a day. Want to play a *real* game of cards, like stud poker, required to go to our rooms. Game room off-limits for serious poker. Disgraceful. Make us look at those damned paintings of Mrs. Smith's in every hallway. Can't even hang a decent war picture anywhere. Complain when I talk in a normal tone of voice. Let people like that Chandler woman watch those commies on Public Broadcast TV with the volume turned up so loud a man can hear it next door.''

Stoney Castle said, "That's right, beat up on the dead."

"I'm not—"

"Let the poor old woman rest, can't you? She never made any noise. I was just down the hall from her, and she was always quiet as a mouse.''

"You forget, Stoney," the colonel shot back, "that I lived right next door to her. Wasn't just her deaf-ear TV. Davilla, here, was trying to teach her how to write poetry. She'd go over there to Cora's apartment night after night. Sit up till all hours sometimes, reading stuff back and forth." He screwed up his face in distaste. "'I think that I shall never see, a poem lovely as a tree.' Yah-ta-ta, yah-ta-ta, yah-ta-ta.''

"You see, Laura?" Davilla Rose whined. "It's just like I've often said. Nobody appreciates me. Everybody is mean to me.''

The colonel glared at her. "Don't get me wrong. Live and let live. That's my general order. I just wish the management felt the same. You say no calisthenics when it would be *good* for them. Then you have all these boot camp rules. Make a man sit around and listen to poetry through the walls. No consistency.''

"Surely they weren't arguing," Laura said, fishing.

"We worked on poetry," Davilla Rose said huffily. "There's nothing wrong with working on poetry. Why do people insist on picking on me?"

"*Somebody* argued with her in there more than once," the colonel insisted. "And if you ask me, I still think there was more to her death than met the eye."

No one replied. The room got painfully quiet.

Laura put on her best casual expression. "Why do you say that, Colonel?"

"For one thing," he glared, "the footsteps up and down the hall at all hours of the night. Then soft taps on her door—whispers."

"Who?" Laura asked, hearing the sharpness in her voice.

"How do I know? A man can't recognize whispers."

Ellen Smith said scornfully, "That certainly doesn't mean there was a plot against the woman."

"Two times," Rodgers said, glowering, "after she was dead and out of there—two times, in the night, I clearly heard somebody unlock that door and go in there...move around. Drawers opening and closing, closet door swinging, footsteps. Who was *that*, if everything was on the up-and-up?"

Again no one spoke. Laura felt every eye on her. She kept staring intently at the colonel, aware of the pulse in her throat. "Why didn't you tell anyone about those things at the time, Colonel?"

"I did. I told Epperman."

"Are you sure?" Laura gasped.

He sat up straighter with angry indignation. "Of course I'm sure! You think I'm losing my marbles like some people I could name around here?"

"But what did Mrs. Epperman say?"

"Said it was nothing—to mind my own business."

Laura hesitated, trying to figure out her next question. In the silence, Milly Kett's walker made a rattling sound, and she turned to see the old woman shakily getting up from her chair and into the walker's steel embrace.

"Milly, are you okay?"

The smile wavered but held. "I'm feeling a little poorly today. Nothing serious. I think I'll just go to my room and rest."

That was unusual. Milly never complained about anything. "It's almost the end of the hour anyway, everybody. Shall we call it a day?"

Ellen Smith's multiple silver bracelets jangled as she got to her feet. "Sure, Laura, unless you want to take more of our valuable time playing Sherlock Holmes."

"I don't know what you mean," Laura replied as firmly as possible.

"Right," Smith said sarcastically, and headed for the door behind Milly.

"Before we go," Colonel Rodgers said, "I want to place an item on the agenda for next time. It is imperative that we address matters of substance. I move that we schedule an in-depth discussion of the total lack of organization in the chow hall."

"I'll make a note of it," Laura said, and hurried out of the room.

She caught Milly at the elevator doors. "You're sure you're okay, Milly?"

"Yes," the old woman said with a tremulous smile. "Fine. Thank you, dear." But her color was liverish.

Worried, Laura carried her notebook and file folders down the side corridor behind the offices to the Xerox room. She had been more careful about leaving anything lying around since the notebook vanished.

After closing the door, she reached behind the old filing cabinet against the wall and located the magnetic box where she always hid the cabinet key. Unlocking the cabinet, she pulled the drawers open and made some quick file entries. It took about ten minutes. Then she stowed everything away, closed and relocked the drawers, replaced the key in its hiding place, and returned to the reception area.

There was a sheet of paper on the counter. Her name, written atop it in large, spidery handwriting, caught her eye. She picked it up.

Laura Michaels—

Stop meddling. Give it up. You have been warned.

There was no signature.

Laura looked around wildly. Her pulse thumped in her ears. A half-dozen residents stood or sat around idly toward the far end of the atrium. They looked up with interest as the clicking of her high heels signaled her approach.

"Stoney?" she said, aware that her throat was dry. "You came straight out of the session, right?"

"Yep," Stoney Castle said, eyes narrowing. "Why?"

"Did you happen to see anyone leave a note for me on the desk?"

"Didn't see a soul. We all sort of milled by there, of course. And some other folks were just coming in from a walk. Pretty thick traffic jam there for a couple of minutes. Why?"

Laura scanned the others. "Anyone else see anything?"

No one spoke. A couple of them were now watching her with the veiled, careful eyes of someone who suspects lunacy. Laura forced a smile and went back to the desk. She called the sheriff's office, but Aaron Lassiter was not in.

It was more than an hour before he returned her call.

"Timberdale Retirement Center, Mrs. Michaels speaking."

A vaguely familiar male voice said tentatively, "Laura?"

"This is Laura Michaels."

"Great. This is Salt Lassiter. I mean Aaron Lassiter. From the sheriff's office. Returning your call."

Laura looked around the atrium, seeing no one near. She had begun to calm down by now and had been second-guessing herself. "Oh, thanks for calling back, Officer Lassiter." Now what was she supposed to say?—*I found this anonymous note, obviously written by one of the old people here, and it was kind of hateful and I'm scared, poor little me.*

She said, "I, ah, just wondered if there was anything new."

He paused a long time before replying. "Are you okay? You sound nervous."

"No. I'm fine." Damned if she was going to make him think she was a hysterical female. Maybe later she could tell him, but—

"No, ma'am, there's nothing new at this end. If you mean about that old lady's death, that case closed routinely a long time ago. We sent a copy of the certificate to Mrs. Epperman out there for your files. I guess you just missed it."

"Um, yes," Laura said, still arguing with herself.

"I'm glad you called, though," Lassiter told her. "I've been meaning to call you."

That got her attention. "Oh? Why?"

"Well, they've changed my shift around, and now I get an evening off during the week once in a while. I know it's awfully short notice, but I was wondering about dinner Thursday night."

"Tomorrow night?"

"Yeah, I guess that's too short notice, right?"

Laura thought briefly about Tom, who wouldn't like it. Then she wondered if the sitter would stay over with Trissie. She decided she could work it out. Maybe if they became friends she could risk confiding in him. Besides, it sounded like fun.

She said, "I think I can work it out."

"You mean you'll go?" He sounded astonished.

"It would be about seven before I could get home from work and get a sitter for my daughter."

"Okay, great! I'll pick you up tomorrow night about seven, then."

"Good. Do you need directions to where I live?"

"I don't think so. It's in the Ravenwood Apartments, right?"

She hadn't told him that. So he had been thinking about her, too. And checking her out. She felt warm. "That's right."

"Great. I'll see you there, then." The connection broke.

"WE'RE GOING to trial in Tulsa," Tom Benson said that evening over his plate of Laura's lasagna. "Be back late Friday, I guess. I'll call when I get in."

"Use your napkin, Trissie," Laura said. "Okay, Tom, that will be just fine."

"Have we got any rolls?" Trissie asked.

"No, honey, we don't."

"It's an interesting case," Tom went on. "Mineral rights cases often are."

"What's the issue, exactly?" Laura asked.

"Oh, you wouldn't understand, Toots," he said casually. "No need to worry your pretty little head about it."

Laura sipped her coffee.

Tom patted his mouth with the napkin and reached for his wineglass. Sipped. Frowned thoughtfully. "Next time buy the Sonoma Valley white zinfandel, Laura. It's not a big wine, of course, or even great. But it has an insouciance about it. With something like lasagna, unless you were going to go all the way to a robust Italian red, something from Bolla, maybe, it would be just right. A rosé like this just doesn't quite have the clout. I thought I had explained that to you before.''

"I'll try to remember," Laura murmured.

Trissie put her pimento cheese glass down loudly. "Mom, can I have more Kool-Aid?"

"Sure, honey." Laura got up.

"Personally," Trissie said, "I prefer red Kool-Aid. Orange is okay, but this lemon is kind of yucky. Don't you agree, Mom?"

"Behave yourself," Laura said, pouring.

"What?" Tom Benson said, looking up blankly. "Did I miss something?"

A UNIFORM WAS supposed to do something for a man. But when Laura opened the door of her apartment promptly at seven Thursday evening, she decided that a pale summer suit, pretty dark blue tie, and a suntan the color of old walnut left any uniform in the dust.

"Hi," Aaron Lassiter said, his grin bright in his dark face.

"Hi," Laura said. *Wow*, she thought, *brilliant repartee.* Then she thought, *Why are we so nervous?* She said, "Come in just a sec while I get my purse."

Lassiter hove into the entryway, his broad shoulders seeming to fill it. In the small space he was much more impressive than he had been at Timberdale. He smelled nice, too, some kind of after-shave Laura didn't recognize.

Laura went into the living room, where Trissie was on the floor in front of the TV set, watching "Mister Rogers." Jill, sixteen, the baby-sitter, was curled in the chair with a schoolbook. When she saw Lassiter rumble quietly into view, her eyes widened and her curled-up legs straightened into a more graceful position at the same moment one hand flew to pat her hair.

"Girls," Laura said, getting her purse from the coffee table, "this is Mr. Lassiter. Aaron, this is my daughter, Trissie, and this is our friend, Jill."

"Wow!" Trissie said, spinning around on her hindside. "You're *big!*"

Lassiter grinned down at her. His grin looked like honey and cinnamon. "Pleased to meet you, Trissie. Hello, Jill."

"Hi," Jill breathed, just short of wriggling all over.

Lassiter glanced at the TV. "You guys watching 'Mister Rogers'?"

"It's a rerun," Trissie told him. "They tape-delay it."

"He's a pretty neat guy, isn't he?"

"Aw, I think he's kind of a woosie."

Lassiter squatted beside her on the floor. "How come?"

"Aw, he sings songs and talks to baby dolls and everything else. And he talks so soft..."

"A real man doesn't have to be loud and rough, Trissie. Sometimes it takes more guts to be soft."

Jill's eyes glazed over and a little moan escaped her parted lips.

Lassiter turned to her. "Are you in high school, Jill?"

"Yes, sir," Jill whispered, and turned candy red. "But I expect to graduate early. I'm real old for my age."

Lassiter paused as he evidently tried to figure that out. Then he grinned at her. "I'll be over there next week to do a little safety talk. Maybe we'll see each other then."

"That would be *great,*" Jill breathed.

Lassiter looked at Laura. "Ready?"

"Ready," Laura told him.

She felt very small walking to the parking lot beside him.

"You look wonderful," he told her with a big, crooked grin.

The mint sundress was new and so were the pale hose and pumps. Laura had examined herself in the bureau mirror and pronounced the outfit just right. But when he said it, she felt the startling nearness of a blush. *This is crazy.* "Thank you. So do you."

He chuckled. "Somebody told me once I clean up pretty good for what I am."

She had the impulse to ask him what he was, but didn't.

His car was a small Plymouth, three or four years old but burnished a gleaming cream, and as immaculate inside as a new car on the showroom floor. He put on his seat belt and Laura did, too.

"I thought we'd go to Picasso's, if that's okay," he told her, as they pulled away.

"That sounds wonderful."

"So how did your day go?"

The question made her pause. Was this the time to tell him about the anonymous note? She was afraid of looking silly. "I guess it was kind of routine."

"Must be interesting, though, working out there."

"My counseling groups can be."

"That kind of work must be really neat. Tell me about it."

Laura made a couple of noncommittal comments, unconsciously waiting for his eyes to glaze over the way Tom's always did when she talked about her interests. Lassiter kept quiet and paid attention. Laura found herself talking faster, the words tumbling out. She felt like she was almost babbling. *He's listening*, she thought, dazed. *My God, he's really listening to what I have to say!*

It felt pretty amazing.

Later at the restaurant, when he asked her more about some of the Timberdale residents, she dwelt on Julius Pfeister, always so smashingly turned out with his jackets and ascots. She didn't tell about the self-delusion. Then, because he really did seem interested, she told him about some of the others, Milly Kett in particular, and her evident illness.

Later, because she insisted on stopping the talk about herself, Laura managed to draw Lassiter out a bit. Quiet and diffident, he answered her questions and then slowly seemed to relax and grow more talkative, telling her about his parents and brothers and sisters, the kind of career in business he hoped to have one day after the long process of finishing his degree while working full time at the courthouse. Laura relaxed completely. When they had finally finished the last cup of coffee, she regretted it, and then was amazed to see that it was past eleven o'clock.

"Yikes, I need to get home. This is a school night for Trissie and Jill both."

They drove from the restaurant toward the apartment complex. Part of the time was spent in companionable silence. Laura liked the feeling that they didn't have to be talking every minute. There was a lot going on here that she liked.

They reached the apartment complex. Lassiter parked close to her unit and walked her to the door.

Was now the time to mention the note, her other suspicions? Looking up at him, she knew it was definitely not that time. He looked very big and gentle, and she felt small again. *Now what?* she thought. She felt fluttery inside, waiting to see what was going to happen.

"Well," Lassiter rumbled, and the smile came.

"Thank you. I had a lovely time."

He reached awkwardly for her, arms drawing around her shoulders with slow, clumsy care. She moved closer and tilted her head back for the kiss. Instead, he only pulled her close for an instant in a gentle, powerful hug. Before she could quite register her surprise, he had released her.

"Good night," he said huskily, and stepped back.

She put her key in the lock, opened it, and went inside.

Jill looked up sleepily from the couch. Trissie, however, was wide awake. "Where is he, Mom? Did you have a fun time? Why didn't you invite him in? Boy, he's a neat guy, Mom. Did he kiss you?''

"Trissie, be quiet. Here you are, Jill. Thanks a million. Would you like me to walk you across the complex?''

"Aw, Mom!'' Trissie wailed. "You're no fun *at all.*''

HE WOULD call again, and it wouldn't be another interval of months—Laura knew that. She caught herself thinking about him several times on Friday.

Why did he seem to preoccupy her so much after one date? She didn't know. Going out with him had been fun. She still couldn't quite get over how nice it had felt, some-one really listening to her. She felt he might be one of the neatest men she had ever known.

But unfortunately the date had felt a little clandestine, too. It had been so long since she had gone out with anyone besides Tom that she wasn't quite sure it was right. And yet—she argued with herself—she and Tom were not en-gaged. Was she supposed to mention Aaron to him? Keep it a secret? Not see Aaron again? Feel different?

It could, she thought, become a problem.

A WORSE PROBLEM came along first, in the dead of Friday night.

Laura was sleeping soundly when the door chimes of her apartment sounded with shattering suddenness. Rousing with shock, she looked at the luminous dial of the bedside clock: 2:21.

Clambering out of bed, she wrapped her robe around herself and padded through the darkened apartment.

"Mom?'' Trissie sounded startled, scared out of sound sleep.

"I'll answer it, sweetie. Go back to sleep.''

Flicking on the porch light, she peered out through her peephole, caught her breath, and opened the door.

Lassiter, in uniform, holding his round-rimmed hat in his hands, stared at her with eyes gone to pinpoints from the sudden glare.

"I'm sorry to bother you this way," he said.

Laura struggled to get awake and cope. She had no idea what was going on here—how to feel. "What is it?" she asked. "Do you know what *time* it is?"

He looked grim. "I could have called or let you find out in the morning. But I remembered our talk the other night. I thought maybe it would be best if you heard about it from me."

A sudden chill gusted through her. "What's happened?"

"I just heard on my radio. There's been another death out at Timberdale."

"God! Who?"

"I don't know yet. I'm heading out there. Do you want to go?"

Laura thought about Trissie. The apartment deadbolt locks were strong. "Yes, but I have to find a sitter. I can try Jill. Can you give me five or ten minutes?"

"May I wait inside till you find out?"

"Oh, hell, of course. I'm not thinking. Come in."

He stood inside the foyer while Laura went to the telephone. She felt vulnerable and odd in her thin robe and bare feet.

Jill's mother answered on the second ring, and sounded grumpy until Laura told her it was an emergency. Then she said she would walk Jill over within ten minutes.

"A deputy sheriff is here. He'll come and bring her."

"All right, then...I hope it's not too bad, Laura."

"Thanks." Laura hung up and turned to Lassiter. He had already put his hat back on. "What's her apartment number?"

Laura told him and hurried in to inform Trissie. She was shaking but she hid it from her daughter. She wondered what lay ahead now. Remembering the anonymous note, she wondered if someone else had been asking too many questions, too.

ELEVEN

Flashing blue-and-white gumball lights atop a medical emergency van made Timberdale's front entrance look like a garnish mall arcade. Aaron Lassiter spun the steering wheel of his sheriff's cruiser and stood on the brakes, skidding the vehicle to a halt behind the van. Laura was pitched forward against the restraint harness.

"Sorry." Lassiter grunted.

Laura didn't answer.

Another sheriff's cruiser and Dr. Fred Which's battered old Volvo were parked beyond the van. Laura's watch showed almost 3:00 a.m., and the rocketship ride from her apartment had been quite unlike anything she had ever experienced.

Lassiter cut the engine and hurried around to her side as she hopped out. Grasping her elbow, he propelled her firmly toward the entry, making her half run to keep up with his long strides. He was a different man on duty like this—grimly quiet and purposeful—and he almost frightened her with his competence. Under any other circumstances, she would have time to like it.

Lights in the atrium had been dimmed for the night. The only person in sight was Stacy Miller, standing behind the reception desk with tears streaking her face. Laura hurried over to her.

"Oh, Ms. Michaels, it's awful!" Stacy choked, and immediately broke down again.

Laura hurried around the counter and put her arms around the sobbing girl. "Stacy, who was it?"

"Mrs. Kett."

"Oh, shit." Another of her favorites, Laura thought. And why had she been so sure Stacy was going to name Ellen Smith?

Lassiter pressed forward with a scowl. "What room?"

"Two-eleven West," Laura said automatically. "I think I'd better stay here with Stacy a minute or two."

"Right." Lassiter strode toward the stairs.

Laura stroked Stacy's tangled hair and let her cry. When the sobs began to subside, Laura released her and led her back into Judith Epperman's office, where lights blazed, and sat her down on the couch. By the time she had brought cups of coffee from the employee lounge, Stacy was shakily under control again.

"Better now?" Laura asked gently.

Stacy hiccupped. "Y-yes. I think so."

"Tell me what happened."

Stacy stammered what she knew.

Around 1:30 a.m., Davilla Rose had been on the way back to her room after an unusually late canasta game in the Pfeisters' apartment. Milly Kett, often a member of the canasta group, had been invited to play but had declined, saying she felt ill. Walking by the Kett apartment, Davilla heard the television set blaring loudly inside, and became concerned because Milly was habitually such a quiet person. About to knock on the door to reassure herself that everything was all right, Davilla noticed that the door was ajar, and pushed it open. Seeing her friend sprawled face-down on the living-room floor, she rushed in, took a closer look, and hit the emergency call button on the wall of the dining room.

Stacy Miller, running to respond to the call, found Davilla Rose moaning hysterically over Milly Kett, who wasn't breathing and had no pulse. Davilla had called the Pfeisters, and they were already on the scene in their pajamas. By the time Stacy had called 911 and Mrs. Epperman, the Kett apartment had begun to look like the local bus station at rush hour. She still hadn't been able to restore order or get everyone back to their own rooms when Mrs. Epperman arrived thirty minutes later and screamed at her for being nine kinds of incompetent, including (a) not clearing the apartment at once, (b) not closing the hall door, (c) not calling her before she called the emergency number, and (d) not administering CPR. Apparently Judith Epperman had also theorized—once the door was locked and no potential lawsuit witnesses were in hearing—that Milly Kett might have been saved by prompt CPR, and her death might be all Stacy's fault.

"Who's up there now?" Laura asked.

"She is—Ms. Epperman, I mean—and a man from the sheriff's office, and the two paramedics, and Dr. Which."

Laura studied her expression. "Stacy, are you okay now? I really ought to get up there. But I won't leave you if you—"

Stacy shook her head violently. "I'm okay."

Laura stood. Stacy looked up, grasping her hand in an icy grip. The mascara that had started around her eyes had been carried all the way down her face and neck in uneven black rivulets. "Did I kill her?" she choked. "Was it my fault? If I had done CPR right away, like Mrs. Epperman said—"

"Stacy," Laura snapped, "Mrs. Epperman is full of shit. Forget it."

Hurrying upstairs and down the Two West corridor, she had the distinct feeling that she was being watched. She realized that she probably was. By now the Timberdale grapevine had been functioning at 110 percent efficiency, and there were probably residents peeping out from every cracked door.

The door to Milly Kett's unit, 211, stood solidly closed.

Getting a grip on herself, Laura knocked. The door opened a few inches and Lassiter glared out at her, then let her in.

Every light in the apartment was on. The first thing Laura saw was Milly Kett's chromium walker, overturned on the carpet near the door. She didn't see Milly. Her next impression was of a hell of a crowd: Mrs. Epperman to the left in the kitchen doorway, Lassiter close by in the dining room, another older man in deputy uniform standing in the living-room portal, two youthful paramedics in the furniture-choked living room, one standing and the other crouching beside something Laura couldn't see, and Dr. Fred Which just beyond them, scratching his head in puzzlement and looking down sadly at the same thing being stared at by the paramedics.

Drawn by horrified curiosity, she stepped around the walker and around a stack of bulky, glittering medical emergency equipment half blocking the portal into the living room. This let her see what everyone else was looking at, Milly herself.

They had rolled her onto her back and attempted to establish an airway. A tiny trickle of drying blood stained the collar of her pink nylon robe, and a small bit of silvery nylon tubing stuck out of a narrow slit in her throat. Bottles and vials and tubing lay all around her. She looked asleep.

The face of the color TV console in the far corner glowed, but no sound came. It had been muted. Laura caught the sharp odor of menthol or something like it. She was seized by a sudden, violent sense of déjà vu. She looked up and met Which's eyes.

He grimaced sadly. "I'm afraid she's gone, all right."

The older deputy sheriff stepped around Laura with a small camera in hand. He pointed it down at Milly. The strobe unit flashed blindingly. Milly's robe had been tossed up in her fall, and one thin, veiny bare leg was exposed to midthigh. *That isn't right,* Laura thought, *they should cover her up first.* Then she realized she wasn't thinking straight. She turned and made it into the kitchen.

Judith Epperman followed her. "Can you imagine anything worse than this?" she fumed under her breath. "More confusion and gossip, more bad vibes. And it's hard to entice new residents at this time of year anyhow. Damn!"

"How can you be talking about leases at a time like this?" Laura burst out. "Milly is *dead* in there!"

Mrs. Epperman removed her eyeglasses and let them tumble to the end of their thin gold chain on her chest. "Well, of course you're right, Laura. It must have sounded unfeeling of me. Actually, as you well know, no one loves these dear old people more than I do. It's sad. Definitely sad." She sighed. "But someone has to be practical, too, remember. It's up to you and me and the rest of the staff to have Timberdale humming along at peak efficiency. Turning a profit. Ensuring future security and happiness for the living. It may seem hard to say that, but being hard is the most Christian thing we can do for the others, don't you see." She blinked myopically.

Laura didn't quite trust herself to speak. Turning to the sink, she noticed a small plate containing the wilted remnants of a green salad, a small glass filmed by the milk that had been in it, and two delicate cups and saucers, each with a tiny bit of tea in the bottom. *Two cups of tea? Again?*

Mrs. Epperman interrupted her confused train of thought. "I want you to remain here," she said. "I wouldn't have called you out in the middle of the night, dear, but since you're already here, you might as well make yourself useful."

Laura mentally shook herself. "What do you want me to do?"

"Don't let any unauthorized people in. That stupid Stacy had let half the residents rush in. They were all over the place, jabbering like loons. It will take a week to calm them down again. If the officers ask any questions, do what you can to answer them." The large woman sighed with disgust. "I've already pointed out that the emergency call system was working and there was nothing any of us could do. They haven't said anything about Stacy's failure to initiate CPR, so we won't either. Obviously this was just another unhappy accident. We aren't liable in any way, shape, or form. That's the main thing to remember in anything we say or do: make sure no one gets any stupid ideas about filing a lawsuit against us." She sighed a second time. "It's just routine, just nature taking its course, and we're in the clear. All right? You understand our position?"

"I understand," Laura said bitterly.

Mrs. Epperman walked out of the kitchen. Laura heard her saying something soothing to the men in the other room. Then she heard the apartment door open and close.

Laura looked down into the sink. It was immaculate. She felt stupid. *What did you expect to find? More stolen flowers?*

Aaron Lassiter came in, his brow furrowed with concern. "You okay?"

"Sure," Laura lied.

"You look funny."

"She was a nice old lady. I liked her."

"Yeah," Lassiter replied glumly. "Doc says it looks like a stroke or heart failure. Just like that other one back in the summer."

Laura didn't say anything.

Lassiter went on thoughtfully, "Doc says she was real sick, just like the other one, too. Wouldn't have lived a lot longer even if she hadn't fallen down."

"Will there be an autopsy?"

"Not a full-scale one, I guess. Real close physical exam, but it looks pretty cut and dried."

Just as in the case of Cora Chandler.

"Aaron, did you notice the smell in the living room?"

"Sure did. That's weird, isn't it? That's just like the other one, too. Ben-Gay or something. There's a jar of it on the floor beside the couch. You can smell it on her, too."

Laura thought about it. She realized that she was probably jumping after conclusions every bit as wildly as Maude Thuringer might have done. Mrs. Epperman had said to play everything down.

Well, to hell with it. "Aaron, do you think you ought to have it analyzed?"

He stared, doing his John Wayne forehead. "Analyzed? That rub-on junk?"

"Yes."

"What for?"

"I don't know. It's just a coincidence, and it seems funny to me."

His frown deepened. "I suppose I could have it analyzed. But why? What are you suggesting here?"

She almost blurted out all her suspicions, but this wasn't the time, and he would surely think she was crazy. "It's just an idea," she said lamely.

He shrugged. "Okay. A lab check can't hurt anything."

Someone hammered on the apartment door. Laura hurried to open it a crack. Two more young men stood in the hall. She recognized one of them. The truck from the funeral home had already arrived.

TWELVE

LAURA WAS IN the Xerox room, kneeling in front of her filing cabinet, when the footstep scuffed behind her. She jumped a mile.

Maude Thuringer swooped in triumphantly. "You've been avoiding me. But you can't get away from me now."

Heart starting to resume its normal pace, Laura climbed to her feet. "I haven't been avoiding you, Maude."

"Foof!" Maude came into the cubbyhole and melodramatically closed the door behind her. "What are you up to, Laura Michaels? What are you really up to, with another murder on our hands?"

"We don't know anything was a murder," Laura replied mechanically.

Maude's heavy, old-fashioned knitcord dress swirled. "You know as well as I do that it's the same thing. The same modus operandi. Are you covering up for someone?"

Laura groaned and closed the filing cabinet drawer. There had been no option but to attend her all-day seminars Saturday and Sunday, even though she had gotten only two hours' sleep early Saturday morning after returning home from Timberdale. She felt strung out and exhausted. "Maude, there's no whistle to blow. Stop acting like this."

Maude held up a quivering index finger. "It's just like the other one. You know that. Female resident. Dead of night. Alone. TV set blaring. Odor of Campho-Phenique or something. Don't pretend to me you didn't notice all the similarities."

"Maude, stop it."

"The door was open this time. That's *classic*. Just like *The Adventure of the Speckled Band*."

"Wait a minute," Laura groaned. "Now you've gone too far. Just because an old Sherlock Holmes story—"

"It's the same situation. Almost exactly."

"Maude, we had to read that story in high school. You think a *snake* killed Milly Kett?"

"Of course not, you ninny. But *something* did."

"You know what the coroner's report said. Milly died of heart failure."

"Right," Maude said sotto voce, sarcasm dripping. "She's feeling too bad to play cards with her friends, but then she stays up half the night, watching some stupid TV show with the volume turned sky-high when she was always the most considerate neighbor in this place. Then she goes and opens her apartment door, and walks back into her apartment, and her walker tips over in the dining room, but she somehow flies on into the living room eight or ten feet away, where she just happens to drop dead. Everything perfectly normal. Right."

The anonymous warning note flashed in Laura's memory. She couldn't have Maude broadcasting crazy theories all over Timberdale. "Maude, for the last time, forget it. And just keep quiet!"

Maude's eyes danced with excitement. "I'm not giving up on this. I intend to keep asking questions, investigating this myself. You can't stop me."

"Maude!"

The little woman turned, snatched the door open, and fled.

Laura rubbed aching eyes. The only person who seemed to entertain suspicions similar to hers was an old lady with galloping senility. If you eliminated the anonymous note— and any of a dozen residents could have left that scrap of paper solely on the basis of generalized worry or hostility—there was no evidence.

She remembered last night, when Tom came by for a late dinner after the conclusion of her Sunday seminar. He had noticed how tired and tense she seemed, and said he wanted to hear about it. So she had told him some of it.

"Well," Tom had said, rubbing her back through her dress, "you're just tired, Chicken Little. You need to stop it."

"Stop what?" Laura asked.

"Being silly," he said, and started trying to unzip her.

His feelings had been hurt when she shoved him out the front door.

She wished she could convince herself that she was being silly.

The note taken by Stacy Miller before her arrival this morning had said the official finding would be death by natural causes. Laura's call during a seminar break yesterday had even cleared up the "mystery" of the two teacups in the sink this time: Milly had called the kitchen for a snack about 7:00 p.m., and Sue Mullins had taken up the salad, some crackers, and tea. At Milly's invitation, Mullins had stayed about twenty minutes and shared the tea with her. When she left about 7:30, Mullins said, Milly had intended to put on her robe and watch the Friday night movie.

You couldn't make anything out of any of that.

Getting to her feet with knee-cracking noises almost as serious as Maude Thuringer's, she put her file key in the magnetic holder hidden on the back of the cabinet, gathered up her folders and notebooks, and headed for the reception desk.

By MIDAFTERNOON it had become apparent that no one else intended to make a cause célèbre out of Milly Kett's death. Details of the funeral plans were posted on the bulletin board outside the mailroom adjacent to the atrium, and Laura saw many of the residents study the paper and murmur a bit, but without any signs of much anxiety. Stonewall Jackson, clipboard in hand, came by the desk and reported that her notes proved she had told Milly a hundred times to get her blood pressure checked more regularly. Davilla Rose, in the dining room, got teary-eyed and said it had been a terrible shock to her, and now the poetry group had lost still another valued member, which just proved again how bad luck dogged all her projects and made her a victim in life. Julius Pfeister touched an elegant linen handkerchief to his forehead and said he had had a busy morning—the market was extremely volatile. Ellen Smith said she had spoken to Francie Blake about preparing a large pumpkin patch mural—acrylic—for the center's upcoming Halloween party. Ken Keen, caught smoking by Laura in a back hallway, grabbed her arm and tried to get his hand under her skirt.

Back at the desk, Still Bill Mills strolled by to report that he had gotten the starling nest out of the gutters beyond the Castles' apartment. He mopped his face with his bandanna. "It's back into the nineties outside."

"I know, it's terrible."

"Of course," Still Bill observed, "if you think this is bad, you should have been around here during the Dust Bowl. Of course I wasn't either, and neither was anybody else. That's because it wasn't. The whole thing overlapped out of this part of the state, among other things. John Steinbeck didn't know that."

"You and the crew will probably have to redo the Kett apartment later in the week, Bill. Everything is to be moved out by Friday."

Still Bill's shoulders slumped. "Okey dokey."

The office hallway door swung open, and Judith Epperman, her face a storm cloud, strode into the atrium. "We need to talk, Laura." She went back inside.

Still Bill jammed his straw hat back on his head. "I'm outta here," he muttered. "She looks mad, and I hate it when people get in a quorum."

Laura went into the office.

"What are the residents saying?" Mrs. Epperman demanded.

"Nothing unusual."

"You heard the official finding? Natural causes?"

"Yes."

"And there's not a lot of morbid curiosity out there? No sentimentality? No stupid rumors, like in the Chandler case?"

Laura decided not to mention Maude. "No."

Mrs. Epperman tilted her head, thinking about that. "Well, Milly was obviously weaker...sicker. Made it easier to accept, maybe. Good. Let's keep it that way, Laura, right?"

"Right."

"Check out the Kett apartment today. No one has been in there since you locked it up the other night. Make sure no lights were left on and the air-conditioning is turned down, everything is shipshape. The family will be going up there when they arrive, and I want to be sure they don't walk into any kind of mess left by the paramedics or anything."

The idea of returning to the apartment brought back the memory of a similar visit to the Chandler unit. Something turned over in Laura's stomach. "I might have Still Bill check it out, Mrs. Epperman."

"No, I want you to do it, Laura. I would do it myself,

but I'm dreadfully busy, updating her billing files and so on.''

Laura decided she was being childish. Nodding, she started for the door.

"Laura?"

"Yes?"

"Four letters. 'Grand and festive party.'"

"Gala."

"That will work. Thanks."

THE DESK telephone call light was blinking. Laura picked it up. "Timberdale Retirement Center."

"Hi," the familiar male voice said. Aaron Lassiter.

"Hi yourself," Laura said, brightening.

"I just wanted to check in with you—make sure you're okay."

That made her feel good. "I'm fine. I sure appreciate your calling to check up on me, though."

"Yeah. Well, also I know it's short notice again, but I was wondering about maybe Friday evening."

"For?"

"They're doing *How to Succeed* down here at the campus theater this weekend. I know you've got classes to study for, and the show is a hundred years old, but I saw it once in New York and thought it was really fun. A guy just made some tickets available to me, if you wouldn't be too bored. I should have thought of it sooner, but like I said—"

"I accept," Laura said instantly.

"You *do*?"

"Did you get a report back yet on that jar of salve?"

"No, that probably won't come back before the end of the week."

After hanging up, she thought some more about the feeling of complication she was suddenly getting in her life. She thought about Aaron Lassiter as a law officer, too. It was time to tell him her worries, even if he thought she was wacko, she decided.

It was quiet in the atrium at the moment. There was nothing to be gained by delaying the visit to Milly Kett's apartment. Better to get it over with, she thought.

She went to the security box and got the master key.

THE UPSTAIRS HALLWAY was deserted. Laura fitted the master key into the deadbolt lock on 211 and turned it. The door opened silently.

Reaching inside, she turned on the dining-room lights, then stepped into the apartment and quickly closed the door behind her.

The paramedics and Dr. Which had straightened up after themselves. The furniture-packed apartment looked musty and crowded, but fine. Milly's walker had been righted, and stood just inside the living-room doorway. No lights had been left on.

The apartment felt stuffy. Laura had set the thermostat at sixty-eight during the interminable time Lassiter and the other deputy helped Dr. Which and the paramedics straighten up in the wee hours of Saturday morning, and she hadn't remembered to raise it again. Thinking that even the unseasonably hot weather outside shouldn't make the apartment this warm, she went to the thermostat to adjust it. With a small tingle of surprise, she saw that it had already been reset to eighty.

Had she turned it up when she left the other night without thinking about it? Impossible.

But Judith Epperman had said the apartment had been locked up since then.

Nerves tightening, she turned from the thermostat and crossed briskly to the living room. Flicking on the overhead lights, she raked the room with a more critical eye. She vividly remembered how everything had looked when they finished the straightening up. Everything looked the same now.

Except that the magazines—several issues of *People* and *Reader's Digest*—were now aligned at perfect ninety-degree angles to the edges of the table. The paramedics had knocked some of the magazines off the table as they gathered up all their gear the other night, and Laura had been the one who retrieved the magazines and replaced them. She had put them at a casual angle, not straight, with military precision.

Moving around the coffee table, she plopped down on the overstuffed couch and scanned the room again. She felt her pulse. Everything looked normal. She started to rise, and lightly bumped her knee on the edge of the table. Looking down, she noticed that the narrow drawer in the front of the table was slightly open, its front just jutting into view.

She pulled the drawer open. Inside she saw some playing cards in a frayed cardboard box, a clutter of grocery store coupons, and a number of scraps of yellow notebook paper with Milly Kett's large, loopy handwriting on them. She examined several. They seemed to be reminders Milly had written to herself—shopping lists, dates and times of doctor appointments, names and addresses.

Laura replaced the notes and closed the drawer. Sitting there on the too-soft couch, she reexamined her memory of early Saturday morning. She saw herself thoughtlessly fanning the magazines after picking them off the floor, then placing them back on this table at a casual angle.

The reset thermostat and rearranged magazines obviously meant someone had been in the apartment since she had locked it early Saturday.

Laura felt a chill. All of Maude Thuringer's meddling questions came back to mind. Why had the apartment door been open when Davilla Rose passed by? Why had Milly apparently unlocked it, then walked back into the other room? Why had she evidently crawled from her fallen walker to the living room, when the call button was close at hand? Why had the TV set been turned up loud enough to get Davilla's attention, when Milly Kett had always been such a quiet and private person? Why—if she had been feeling ill and was heading downstairs for help—why had the TV set been on at all?

Why—Laura remembered—had Cora Chandler been watching a TV channel she loathed, and why had there been cigarette smoke and stolen flowers in her apartment? Who had it been in the parking lot, and who had written the note?

Who had been in here?

Laura rubbed her bare arms, which were suddenly covered with goose bumps.

THIRTEEN

"ABOUT THIS WEEKEND," Tom Benson said Tuesday evening, taking a second helping of Laura's spaghetti.

Laura felt her insides tighten. "Trissie, will you pass Tom the bread, please? Thanks."

Tom took a crust of the French bread and bit into it noisily. "I mean, we haven't made any plans."

"I assumed," Laura said guardedly, "you might be busy."

"No, actually I just hadn't gotten around to it. But I was thinking, they're having that revival of *How to Succeed* at the OU theater. How about if I got us some tickets for Saturday night, after your seminar?" Tom glanced at Trissie, who was busy arranging spaghetti strands on her plate into the shape of an elephant, or maybe a horse. "It's kind of adult for you, Tris, but there's a lot of fun dancing." He crunched energetically on the bread and then added, "How about if I get you a ticket, too, and you go with us?"

Inviting Trissie to go anywhere with them was new, and surprise forced Laura to pause to readjust the answer she had been about to give.

Trissie, however, saved her the trouble. "It sounds neat," she piped up. "But I don't think Mom will want to go see it twice."

The sound of muffled bread-crunching abruptly ceased. Laura concentrated on winding her food onto her fork.

"What's she talking about?" Tom asked.

Laura had to meet his eyes. "Actually, I have plans, Tom."

His eyebrows met over his nose. "Plans?"

"Yes."

"When?"

"Friday night."

"Who with?"

Laura opened her mouth.

"No, no," he said quickly, grimacing. "Erase. It's none of my business."

"She's going with the sheriff," Trissie said happily. "But he won't be wearing his gun."

"Deputy sheriff," Laura corrected. "And Trissie, will you just hush, please, and let the big people talk?"

"Poop!" But Trissie bent over her plate and started giving the elephant a tail.

Laura braced herself. It was ridiculous to feel unfaithful, she told herself. There had never been an understanding between them. She said, "I'm sure I mentioned him to you, Tom. His name is Aaron Lassiter, and we met when he came out to Timberdale to investigate Mrs. Chandler's death."

Tom's good-looking face sagged. He did not seem angry. He looked more like a small boy confronted by an adult cruelty he could not understand. "I see I should have asked sooner."

"It's no big deal, Tom."

"I should have asked sooner. I took you for granted. I was stupid."

"You weren't stupid," Laura said quietly. She was not liking this.

He shook his head, refusing to let himself off the hook. "I'm sorry, Laura. I really am."

"Tom, it's *okay.*"

He hesitated, seeming to struggle with a turmoil of thoughts. "I know I'm not very interesting, Laura. I—"

"Oh, Tom, for heaven's sake! I'm just going to a show with the guy!"

He lapsed into silence. Uncomfortable, Laura asked Trissie about her schoolwork. *How can I talk about our relationship when I think there's a killer running loose?* Maybe he would drop it, she thought.

He didn't.

It was later, Trissie was in her room, and they were loading the dishwasher.

"We have to talk," he said dully.

Oh hell, Laura thought. "Okay," she said cheerfully. "About what?"

"We've been seeing each other a long time now, right?"

"Right."

He handed her a skillet. "We get along great."

She took it and put it in the dishwasher. "Yes, we do."

"Sooner or later we have to talk seriously. About our future."

"Tom, we agreed a long time ago that we wouldn't rush anything."

"I want to talk anyway. Maybe it's time we got a lot of things straight. Talked about commitments and plans together."

Laura poured the dishwasher soap into the door receptacle, using the time to ponder her options. She wished she could go hide. "Because I have one date with someone else?" she asked.

"No! Because...because it's time, that's all."

"Tom, I won't discuss it now."

"But I want to."

Suddenly she was awfully tired of his calling all the shots, she being the meek and reverent little acolyte. She was shocked to realize that that was how the relationship really felt to her. "No," she said.

His voice stiffened and became more hurt. "I can't stay in a relationship any longer if things aren't a lot clearer."

She put down her towel and turned to face him squarely.

Her heart had started to beat sluggishly, and yet she felt eerily calm. "Then maybe it's time we sort of took a vacation from each other, Tom."

He stared, and his eyes looked shiny. "Are you serious?"

"Yes, Tom. I am. I'm sorry."

He stood there a moment, then turned and walked straight to the door. The sound of it closing behind him made a little echoing noise in the kitchen.

Trissie came in from the other room. "Did he leave already?"

"Yes, baby," Laura said, breathing again, "he did."

Trissie's sober eyes showed she could sense that something was up. "Is he coming back?"

"No, Tris. He isn't."

IN WEDNESDAY'S breakfast club she risked asking a few questions about Milly Kett. She got nowhere. The group members watched her with narrowed, suspicious eyes as if wondering how crazy she might be.

Ellen Smith was sitting in the atrium with her sketch pad and charcoal when Laura came out of the group session. With a sibilant tinkle of silver bracelets and necklaces, the bitter-eyed old woman got to her feet and intercepted Laura halfway back to the desk.

"Finished your little soul-searching?" she cracked.

"We had a nice session, Ellen. But I wish you would come back."

"Need another crazy head to shrink? Is that it?"

"No, I was thinking of how much you contributed to the sessions."

"Ha! Right! Every group needs somebody to hate."

"Ellen, people here don't hate you."

"Ha! They envy my artistic skill. They don't like it when someone is as talented and active as I am. I know the kind of things they say behind my back. You're a goody two-shoes, but you don't realize all the mean things people say and even do around this place.''

"Like your flowers?"

Smith drew herself up stiffly. "Yes, like my flowers."

"That could have been an accident—a mistake by a maid."

"Ha!"

"And the ice sculpture. I remember how upset you were about that. But that was strictly a mistake because the kitchen was so warm, and it started to melt instantly."

"Ha!"

"Ellen, won't you consider returning to the group?"

"Not on your life. I don't need it. There's nothing wrong with me."

"We all need people to talk to sometimes, Ellen. If you don't like the group, we might consider some individual sessions. When things happen that shake us up, like a death in the family or—"

Ellen Smith's eyes flared. "Don't imply that Milly's death was like a death in the family. I didn't even like her."

The bait had been taken. "Why?" Laura asked simply.

"Because she was no friend of mine."

Laura feigned surprise. "I didn't know *anyone* had a problem with Milly."

"Well, that just goes to show you don't know as much as you think you do, Miss Smarty-Pants."

"What—"

But before Laura could start to reel in, her fish had turned and stormed across the atrium, heading for the elevators.

AARON LASSITER called Friday night exactly on time, as expected. He didn't mention the lab report, and Laura assumed it wasn't in. She decided to put any Timberdale talk on the back burner for later.

She succeeded for quite a while. Sitting beside Lassiter's broad shoulder in the campus theater, she felt the same pleasant little rush she had had other times they were together. The musical was dated but still surprisingly good—cute and fast moving, its hectic pace and choreography well suited to a college cast. She enjoyed seeing it again.

It wasn't until afterward, in the coffee shop, that she couldn't wait any longer to ask.

Lassiter looked up over his coffee. "The lab report? Yes. It came back today, as a matter of fact."

Laura's heart beat. "And?"

"Nothing."

"Nothing?" She could hardly believe it.

He smiled crookedly. "Sorry. It was just Ben-Gay."

"I see." Laura looked down at her coffee.

"What did you think they might find?"

"I don't have any idea."

"Why did you think they might find anything?"

"Maybe because I'm silly."

"I don't think you're silly. Why not tell me about it?" She studied his face. "I haven't told anybody else. Are you sure you want to hear it?"

"Try me."

Laura took a deep breath and decided she had to risk it, even if he laughed at her. She summarized the oddities she had noticed in the two deaths, and told him about someone being in the Kett apartment after the death. Finally she told him about the missing notebook, Kay Svendsen's scary experience in the hall outside Cora Chandler's apartment, what Colonel Rodgers had said about hearing voices and movement, the silent telephone call, and finally the anonymous warning note.

"Have you still got the note?" Lassiter snapped.

"Sure. It's at home."

"I want it. You should have given it to me right away."

"You think it means something real, then?" She didn't know whether to feel relieved about her sanity or more worried for her safety.

"I'll check it out with the lab boys in Oklahoma City. There might be something there. Now what in the hell *else* have you been holding back from me?"

She told him the rest of it, including the signs that an unauthorized person had been in the Kett unit. He listened with a deepening scowl. When she finished, he didn't comment.

Finally she couldn't stand it. "So what do you think?"

"I think you've told me some funny stuff, and I don't blame you for worrying about it. But I also think there's nothing in any of it that would clearly justify reopening an investigation. I'll talk to the boss. But he's going to tell me to calm down and serve my subpoenas."

"Isn't there anything I can do?" Laura demanded.

"Well, there are a few things you might try to find out, just to satisfy yourself."

"Like?"

"Like who were the beneficiaries of Mrs. Chandler's will? Of Mrs. Kett's? Who stood to gain if they died? Also, you said they were both in a card group. Did they have any other close friends in common? Any enemies besides this Mrs. Smith? What sort of things did they do together, if anything? Had either or both of them had a big blowup with any other person out there? Did anyone else have a grudge against the two of them? Besides reading, and maybe poetry, what other activities did they have in common? Did they both see the same doctor? You said they were both seriously ill, although maybe that wasn't generally known. Who did know it? How? What do they have to say about that?"

It sounded like a long and impossible list. Laura was about to say so, but Lassiter beat her to it by adding darkly,

"Did either or both of them belong to one of these organizations that disseminate information on methods of suicide, like the Hemlock Society?"

"You don't think they were suicides!"

Lassiter's forehead wrinkled. "I'm just trying to see every possibility."

"But," Laura persisted, "wouldn't poison be the only way they could have done it? And wouldn't that have shown up on the medical exam?"

"You would think so, yes. But neither of them had a full-fledged autopsy. There are drugs and things that vanish from the bloodstream pretty fast, or are hard to detect. I remember a case where it was something as obvious as strychnine, and it wasn't picked up until some later development in the case made authorities dig the body back up and run more-sophisticated tissue tests specifically for that substance."

"But if *that's* true," Laura groaned, "then there's a possibility that both Cora and Milly were poisoned somehow, and Fred Which's exam could have missed it."

Lassiter looked more glum. "It's within the realm of possibility, I suppose."

"Damn! Any other things I should be asking?"

"Sure. Did either of them have financial problems that no one has yet mentioned? Had they had any problems with their friendship in recent times? Is there *anyone* at Timberdale who would stand to gain from these accidents?" His eyebrows went up as a new idea came. "Or is there anyone out there with a grudge against Timberdale, so that they might like nothing better than some questionable deaths that might hurt the retirement center? And is there anyone else among the residents right now with a severely painful illness that's clearly terminal? Because that's the only common denominator that's obvious right now, Laura:

both these old ladies were hurting, badly, and both were dying anyway.''

"My God," Laura breathed. "How can I find out *half* of this stuff?"

"You probably can't," Lassiter said cheerfully.

"Maybe the best thing to do is just put it out of my mind."

"Maybe it is."

Laura stared at her empty coffee cup, thinking about a myriad of complications.

The waitress came by with coffeepot in hand.

"No," Lassiter told her. "Just the check, please."

Walking through the warm night humidity to his car, Laura thought, *Maybe I would have felt better if he had just laughed at me.* Because now she felt like the bet had been checked back to her, and she didn't know whether to call or fold.

As if the conversation had not taken place, Lassiter reverted to joking comments about the musical on the drive back to her apartment. Laura felt relief. When they pulled up in her lot, however, he turned to her with a serious expression, and simply stared at her for a minute.

"What?" she asked at last.

"If you do persist in trying to check some of these things out a little more," he told her, "I hope I don't have to tell you to be quiet about it."

"I know. If Mrs. Epperman thought I was, quote, stirring up trouble, unquote, she'd have my head."

"I'd hate to see you lose your job," Lassiter said, "but it's not Mrs. Epperman I'm worried about."

"What do you..." Then she understood. "Oh."

"It's real hard for me to believe there's a killer out there," he added slowly. "But there are things happening every day that are hard for me to believe."

Laura's heart pounded faster as she stared into his eyes in the dimness. "Yes. I see."

"Let's just suppose for a second that there is a killer," he went on in a calm, conversational tone as if he were discussing the show they had seen earlier. "Let's say there is, and then suppose someone—like you, say—started asking too many questions. Let's just say you're being watched."

"I'm being careful," Laura said, her voice suddenly husky.

He stared fiercely at her. "You better be."

The car's interior light flashed on briefly as he opened his door, walked around, and opened her door for her. Stars sprinkled the clear, hot, night sky overhead as they walked to her door.

As she unlocked her door, she realized how large he loomed close beside her. All the Timberdale questions suddenly faded for the moment. She looked up at him.

"Another cup of coffee?" she heard herself ask.

He paused a beat, then said regretfully, "Better not. Better get going."

"Okay." Was she glad or disappointed? She had no idea. Yes, she did. "Thanks, Aaron. I had a grand time. Really."

He reached for her. Totally uncertain about what to expect, she let him draw her into his arms. Again there was the briefest, gentlest, loveliest hug, and he was gone.

The telephone began ringing. She hurried to answer it. "Hello?"

There was silence on the line.

"Hello?"

The unknown caller broke the connection.

FOURTEEN

DR. FRED WHICH sauntered into the atrium Monday morning at his usual time, waved to Laura, and started toward the clinic. He looked surprised and pleased when Laura hurried after him, intercepting him near the elevators.

"This is a rare pleasure," Which said, removing a wilted straw hat and wiping a large, knuckly hand over his sweaty forehead. He was wearing rumpled seersucker trousers with a brown belt, a wrinkled wash-and-wear yellow-striped shirt and wide green tie, and black loafers that looked like they hadn't been polished since the early 1980s. "What's up?" he added. "Don't tell me you've reconsidered going to Dallas with me for the Texas game weekend."

Laura tried to smile, but she was so intent on her quest for answers that she suspected it came out more like a grimace. "I just wanted to ask you a couple of things about Milly Kett's death, Fred. For the files."

Which blinked, and his prominent Adam's apple went up and down several times. "Files? What files? I turned in my autopsy report to the county, and Timberdale doesn't keep medical files on residents after they're dead."

Laura had anticipated the objection and had a reply ready. "Milly was in one of my therapy groups. I'm doing the groups for school credit, as you know. I need to close out my shrink file on her, and it will round things out if I put in a couple of relevant details."

Which looked dubious, but Laura was wearing a lavender dress that she considered rather fetching, and judging by his glances at the scoop neckline, he did, too. A faint splotch of pink appeared in his sallow cheeks. "Maybe we have time for a cup of coffee," he suggested.

Laura walked with him to the employee lounge. Sue Mullins was just leaving, having put out a few breakfast rolls left over from the residents' breakfast. Laura poured coffee, and Which began eagerly destroying all the rolls within reach. Sometimes she wondered how he could be skin and bones. Maybe he only ate Timberdale leftovers.

"So what's to know?" he asked, leering a bit as she sat across the table from him in the spartan little tile room. "Or are we maybe wanting to kiss and make up, after avoiding me all summer?"

Laura made a show of pulling out her notebook and ball-point. "Fred, my case file impressions on both Milly and Cora Chandler noted their age and apparent infirmities, but I had observations in there like, 'good color, very alert, no sign of edema or diminished mental function,' et cetera, et cetera. Then both of them just up and died on me."

Which shoved in half another roll, leaving sugary syrup all over his mouth. "Well," he said with a condescending smile, "you don't have a degree in medicine, Laura."

"Are you saying you knew both of them were about to die?"

"Well…no. But they were old, and neither of them was well. I knew that. People at places like this die every day. Sad but true. Nobody lives forever."

Laura resisted the impulse to ask him what medical school course had taught him that gem of wisdom. "I guess what I'm driving at is that I'd like to put a final note in both files, saying how and when they died, and maybe adding something—if I could—about my impression as to whether the deaths were in any way stress related."

The new breakfast roll stopped halfway to the good doctor's face. He brightened. "Oh, I get it now. Make sure your files don't contain any hint that they were badly stressed out. Which would make you look bad as a therapist, since your earlier notes hadn't included any clinical observations of same. Right?''

Laura made what she devoutly hoped was a good impression of being caught in an embarrassing situation. ''I guess I'm real obvious to someone as sharp as you, Fred.''

Which reached across the table and patted her shoulder with cool, sticky fingers. ''Not to worry, honeybun. I can assure you that the deaths were not apparently in any way stress related. You may quote me if you wish.''

Laura made a show of making notes. ''Gosh, Fred, thanks a lot. So both of them died of a heart attack?''

''Heart failure,'' Which pronounced. ''Congestive heart failure was the official finding in the Chandler case. In the case of Mrs. Kett, the official verdict was probably stroke, induced by tachycardia associated with a chronic congestive heart condition.''

Laura scribbled some more. ''So the signs were clear.''

''In the absence of anything else, what else could it be?''

''I see.'' Laura looked up and batted her eyelashes at him. ''It wasn't necessary to do a complete postmortem exam, right? I mean, you didn't have to get the body opened and organs examined, or anything like that, right?''

Hints of color returned to Which's face, but the tightening of his lantern jaw showed that it wasn't pleasure color this time. ''Authorization for a fuller autopsy was not necessary in either case. The presenting evidence was incontrovertible. Look, Laura, are you implying a question of my medical judgment here? A full-bore autopsy costs the county almost two thousand dollars. You don't throw taxpayer money around when it isn't necessary. The county commissioners have made that damned clear to me.''

''Oh, I wasn't suggesting *anything*,'' Laura gasped with what she hoped was a fine show of contrite surprise. ''I'm just trying to understand, Fred, so I can make my notes accurate. Gosh, they're going to *grade* me on this down at the School of Social Work.''

"Well," Which grunted, appearing mollified, "okay, then."

"So I can say they died of natural causes because there wasn't any sign of anything else."

"Of course," Which snapped. "The existence of small anomalies to the contrary may show up in *any* examination. They mean nothing."

Laura almost failed to maintain her dumb, wide-eyed expression. Her mind went into overdrive and she felt almost feverish. *Anomalies?* She wanted badly to pursue this. But she knew she couldn't, or the good doctor would instantly know she was checking up on him. "I see," she said meekly.

Which seemed to sense that he might have let something slip. "I'm positive about my findings in both cases. We can't spend all our time chasing down little things that don't mean anything."

"Sure," Laura said blithely, getting to her feet. "Thanks a million, Fred. You've been real nice, and now I can put just enough stuff in my file-closing reports to satisfy them down there at OU. I appreciate it."

Which looked startled. "About the Texas weekend..."

"Oh, I'm so sorry, I've got a report to write. Thanks again, Fred. See ya."

Hurrying out of the lounge, Laura started back down the hallway toward the atrium, intent on relaying her information. Rounding a corner, she softly collided with Kay Svendsen, coming from the direction of the clinic.

"Oh!" Svendsen gasped, stepping back. Her tear-reddened eyes registered recognition. "Oh, Laura, I was just coming to find you." New tears burst from her eyes and she crumpled over, hands to her face. "Dammit, I feel so helpless!"

Laura put her arms around the nurse's starchy white shoulders. "Hey, what's happened?"

Kay Svendsen dug in a white linen pocket, found a tissue, and wiped her eyes. Her hands trembled. "That damn Ken Keen."

"What did he do this time?"

"I had four people in the waiting room, and had to go to the supply room for some tongue depressors and stuff, and he got in there with me through the back door somehow."

"Oh, hell, I think I know what's coming."

"First he just sort of circled around, and I managed to keep the shelving between us. The old fart wanted me to come up to his room. He's asked me that about a hundred times, no problem. But then he darted around the shelves and caught me by the arm and *hurt* me, and ripped my uniform." She held out her left arm, revealing a long tear in the material near the shoulder, and on the pale flesh of her upper arm, a set of bright red fingerprints that looked like they must have hurt. "He's so *strong*."

"How did you get away?" Laura asked sympathetically.

"I don't know." Svendsen hiccupped and dabbed her eyes with the tissue again. "I just kind of spun away and ran for it. I know he's harmless, but I get so darn tired of him pawing at me!"

"We're going to have to talk to Mrs. Epperman again," Laura said grimly. "He seems harmless enough, sure, but he could have hurt you seriously."

"I don't know what to do," Svendsen said. "If I were bigger, maybe he wouldn't panic me the way he does. I mean, I'm not big enough to fight him physically."

Laura looked down at her friend. There were not a lot of people in the world small enough that she could look down at them. The petite Kay Svendsen could have worn children's clothing, she was so tiny. "Look, let me talk to Mrs. Epperman."

"That won't help."

"Maybe it will. Maybe it has to." In the back of Laura's mind, she was seeing Keen slipping into a woman's apartment, groping for her, finding a way, when she rejected him, to make her die. The picture scared her. "It's got to stop, and now," she added.

Kay Svendsen's sweetly shaped breasts heaved in a deep breath. She seemed back in control. "Okay. If he corners me again in the meantime..."

"Kay, you're taking karate lessons. Do *whatever* it takes."

Svendsen looked startled, then hugged her impulsively and hurried back the way she had come.

Returning to the office, Laura found Mrs. Epperman had gone somewhere. She decided that Timberdale's resident caveman could wait while she followed through on her conversation with Fred Which. Looking up the number, she dialed the sheriff's office. The woman who answered the telephone said Deputy Lassiter was in, and she would transfer the call.

Stretching the phone cord to its maximum, Laura closed the door of Mrs. Epperman's office and waited.

"Lassiter."

"Aaron? Hi. It's Laura."

He sounded instantly worried. "Is everything all right?"

"Fine. Listen, you remember our conversation about the...events out here?"

"Sure. Now what?"

Laura told him about her conversation with Dr. Which.

Lassiter picked up on it at once. "Anomalies, huh? Wonder what *that* meant."

"Me, too. I didn't dare ask and get him all defensive and worried."

"Well, sure. Might not mean anything, either. Some weird medical hairsplitting—"

Laura cut in, "Can you get at those medical reports? Dig them out of the files? Whatever he was referring to, he would have had to mention them in the reports *somewhere*. Maybe they would tell us something."

Lassiter sounded dubious. "If he didn't make anything of them—"

"Aaron, he didn't *want* to make anything of them."

There was a silence. "Are you sure you want to keep on with this?"

Laura felt the urge to get apologetic, but she was damned if she would; this might *be* something. "Will you study them for me? Please?"

His sigh was audible. But then he said, "I'm not sure I'll have time today. But sure. I'll do it."

"Remember there was a third death here in the last year, too," Laura told him. "Her name was Hawes. Jane Hawes. H-a-w-e-s. Hawes."

"God," Lassiter muttered. "You're a bulldog, aren't you?"

"Hey, just check them, Aaron, okay? Do that and I'll pay for dinner next time. It's probably nothing. But humor me."

"Consider it done."

By WEDNESDAY Aaron Lassiter still had not called back. Laura went to the breakfast club meeting at a low ebb, and paradoxically it turned out to be one of the best sessions she had ever had. Colonel Roger Rodgers, confronted by Stonewall Jackson after his latest list of suggestions to "enforce better discipline" in Timberdale's social schedule, looked up blankly and said quite meekly that he suddenly realized he was wasting all his time trying to be military instead of accepting his retirement. Then, even more amazingly, Stonewall crossed the room and gave him a hug, and said they shared a common affliction: wanting to issue orders to the world. Davilla Rose wanted to read an autumn poem, and the group let her read it; no one so much as looked funny when the reading then bore an uncanny resemblance to Joyce Kilmer's "Trees."

Judge Emil Young was absent. Checking on him, Laura learned he was running a slight fever and starting on antibiotics prescribed by Dr. Which.

That evening, Trissie was watching TV, and Laura was trying to cram notes on deviant social behavior when the telephone rang. She jumped to it, thinking at once of Lassiter.

"Laura? Richard."

The flat, tinny sound of her ex-husband's voice brought her back to the present. "Hi, Richard. What's up?"

"I wanted to see if I could pick Trissie up at five-thirty instead of six Friday. We're driving to Dallas."

"Oh, sure. That's fine." Laura thought about it. "Going to the Texas game?"

"No, we've got better things to do." His smugness oozed out of the receiver. "There's a Dallas Cowboys cheerleader show, and we've got front-row seats."

Shit. "Oh."

He went on, "I might as well tell you now, Laura. We're going to be making a lot of weekend trips to Dallas from now on."

Laura recovered. "Okay, Richard, fine. As long as you get her back in time to get a good night's rest Sunday night."

There was silence for a moment, then, "Also, Laura, I think you and I really need to sit down soon and talk about the custody arrangement."

The slight feeling of unease became a distinctly scared chill. "Do we have something to discuss?"

"Yes. It looks definitely like I'm going to be getting married again pretty soon. Maybe by Thanksgiving. Cindy and I both want to have Trissie with us, part of a complete, healthy family unit."

Laura's pulse thudded and she felt slightly sick. It was her worst fear, smack in the face. "Trissie is happy with me, Richard."

"You could have reasonable visiting privileges."

"But I have custody and I like it this way. A legal fight—"

She heard his intake breath of exasperation. "There won't be any fight if you're reasonable."

"But—"

"And if you try to fight me on this, it will be the sorriest day of your life!"

"Richard—"

The connection broke.

Holding the dead instrument in her hand, Laura felt the chill become a block of ice in her stomach. She had to remind herself to breath. *You've learned a lot of coping skills. You can handle this.*

But it was just as she had imagined. His romance with the cheerleader was on again. Marriage perhaps as early as Thanksgiving, he had said. Have Trissie with them as a family unit, he had said.

It sounded so much like him—so sure, so arrogant and tunnel-sighted. She felt some of the old, impotent anger. She tried to remember that anger accomplished nothing.

She knew at once that she would not give Trissie up to live in the kind of crazy world Richard considered "normal and healthy," not unless Trissie clearly wanted it that way. Moving a few steps out of the kitchen, she was able to peer across the dining alcove and into the living room, where her daughter lay sprawled in front of the TV set, raptly reading a book while the tube blatted. Trissie looked beautiful. She also looked healthy and well adapted. *I won't let them put you in a crazyhouse, honey.*

But she knew that meant she would have to fight. Richard would go to court in an instant. All the old bitterness and animosity would be fanned back to life. It would become a competition for him, a contest to prove his masculine superiority all over again. He would stop at nothing.

Laura thought again about her shaky financial situation, and the job at Timberdale. She was back to the realization she had had earlier. She must not allow anything to threaten her job. Nonsense about the so-called mystery had to be put aside once and for all. Her whole future—Trissie's— might depend on it.

She felt let down and sad.

The telephone jangled again, startling her. She snatched it up. "Richard," she began bitterly.

"It's me," Aaron Lassiter's surprised voice cut in.

"Oh," she said, leaning her forehead against the cool wood doorframe. "Hi."

"Did you hear about the little emergency out at Timberdale a while ago?"

Laura jerked her head up. "No. What?"

"Calm down, calm down. It wasn't anything as bad as you sound."

"What was it?"

"Ambulance run. You know a gent named Keen?"

"Ken Keen? Sure. There isn't a female out there who doesn't know *him*, believe me. What happened?"

"He fell, broke his leg."

"Good grief!" She couldn't deny her sense of relief. "How did that happen?"

"I'm at the hospital emergency room. Maybe you can hear him yelling bloody murder in the background. As near as I can figure it, he tried to put some moves on that little nurse of yours out there, Miss Svendsen, and she put *her* move on *him,* only hers was some kind of karate. Knocked him on his butt.''

"And broke his leg?"

"Yep. In two places."

A giggle burst out before Laura could stop it. She knew she should feel sorry for Keen, but the picture that leaped into her mind of tiny Kay doing *The Karate Kid* act on him was too much. "I'm sorry," she said, recovering. "He *is* going to be all right?"

"I think they're going to keep him a day or two. He's going to be in a hell of a big cast."

"How is Kay?"

"Seemed upset when I last saw her, but handling it. But listen, Laura, that isn't even why I called. I need to talk to you as soon as I can get out of here. Could I possibly come by in an hour or so?"

"Sure," she said, less certain than she sounded. "What's it about?"

"I managed to spend quite a bit of time late this afternoon with those records we talked about."

Nerves tightened again. "The autopsy reports?"

"Yes, and I—"

"I'm sorry to have been so foolish," she said quickly. "All I'm doing with all this is keeping things stirred up and possibly even jeopardizing my own job out there. I see that now, and—"

"No, no," Lassiter interrupted sharply. "That's why we've got to talk, Laura. Very, very seriously."

"What do you mean?"

"You said I might just find something in those reports Dr. Which did."

"Yes?"

"I think I did."

FIFTEEN

JUDITH EPPERMAN was already in the office, and in foul temper over Ken Keen's injury, when Laura arrived Thursday morning with far grimmer things on her mind.

"It's just terrible," Mrs. Epperman fumed, pacing back and forth, her orthopedic shoes creaking on the office carpet. "Only a week and a half before our big Halloween party, and all the work we have to do to get ready for that, plus our new-resident newspaper advertising campaign due to start Sunday, and Kay Svendsen practically kills a poor old man who couldn't harm a fly!"

"I called the hospital from home this morning," Laura replied. "Ken had a peaceful night, and they plan to release him sometime this morning."

"Thank goodness for small favors. Call right away and cancel the flowers I had ordered for the hospital. Every little savings counts. Track down Still Bill and make arrangements for him to take the bus to the hospital to bring poor old Ken home where he belongs. Tell Mrs. Knott to prepare something special for him—a nice dessert tart or something."

"A tart is appropriate."

"What do you mean by that?" Mrs. Epperman bellowed.

"Nothing."

Mrs. Epperman glared, then looked down worriedly at the papers on her desk. "I've got to get through all these advertising proofs. The board of directors is breathing right down my neck, and if we don't get this place up to maximum occupancy, somebody's head is going to roll and it could be mine. You're going to have to pull your weight today. I've got to get to Oklahoma City to look over the correction copy on these ads. When Ken Keen gets back, for heaven's sake go out of your way to be nice to the old dear. Make sure he knows that Kay Svendsen has been disciplined.''

Laura looked up from her notebook. "Disciplined? What did you do to her?"

"Put a note in her personnel file. That's all, this time. Good LPNs don't grow on trees. But that's between us. With Ken Keen you can make it sound like we cut her salary and put her on formal probation. He's talking lawsuit. We've got to head that off. Try to be positive, dear, in my absence. Be cheerful. There have been times lately when you've really looked like a drag. Watch Francie, how she's always so upbeat and happy. You could learn a lot from her. That will be all for now. Get on with your work.''

Returning to the reception desk, Laura had to struggle to achieve any kind of focus on the routine. Suddenly the quiet of the atrium seemed menacing. Her skin prickled as if someone were watching her from hiding.

Was she overreacting to the information Aaron Lassiter had brought last night?

Lassiter had reached her apartment about an hour after his call. Laura allowed Trissie to stay up long enough to say hello, then scooted her off to her bath and bed. Lassiter sat glowering in the living room in front of the muted TV set until she brought coffee and sat down to face him.

"Well?" she prodded nervously.

"I got out the death certificates and Which's reports that went with them. I also found the report on that woman named Jane Hawes who died at Timberdale last winter. All three cases were identical in a number of ways. All were women. All happened in the living quarters with no one else around. All at night. In all three cases, as the cause of death, Which put down a background of chronic congestive heart failure and either a myocardial infarction—a heart attack—or some kind of embolism, or both.

"In the fine print in all three reports I noticed a couple of other things. He commented each time on—wait a minute…" Lassiter dug a small notebook out of his shirt pocket and flipped it open. Frowning, he resumed. "In each case he noted, quote, evidence of acute hypovolemic shock including drooling mouth, cyanotic extremities, and scattered bluish reticular patterns. Unquote. He also noted—get this—that Mrs. Hawes had an odor of something like Ben-Gay on her, too. In her case, the officer's notes say it looked like she had jumped out of bed and staggered around in confusion, knocking over a lamp and end table, and then collapsing while she was trying to get the sliding doors open to her third-floor deck."

Lassiter stopped, snapped the small notebook closed, and glared.

Laura studied his expression, then admitted, "I'm not sure I get it."

"I've got a pal who's a doctor," Lassiter told her. "I went to him with some questions—all hypothetical, of course. Well, the short of that conversation is that some of these findings aren't consistent with your usual heart failure, and they damned sure didn't sound like your normal stroke to him. *He* said, unless there was some injury that caused a massive loss of blood, drastically reducing the blood pressure, he would look harder at some sort of a drug reaction as the cause of these people getting disoriented, passing out, and dying from shock."

Laura rubbed the chill bumps on her arms. "If that's the case, why didn't Fred Which raise the question?"

"Nothing is sure. All three ladies *could* have died the way his reports said. Citing natural causes and closing the books is the easy way out."

"I don't know," Laura said. "Fred may be a little lazy, but—"

"He's a lurch," Lassiter cut in. "I checked on him. There were four hundred and nineteen people in his med school graduating class. You know where he ranked?"

"Bad?"

"Would you guess four-oh-eight?"

"Oh, hell."

Still scowling, Lassiter sipped his coffee. "He wouldn't want a hassle; it would create controversy for him, and he just wants to slide along. Also, it would probably piss off—oops, sorry—*irritate* the big dogs who own controlling stock in Timberdale by bringing a ton of bad publicity and hurting business."

"But the sheriff—"

"The sheriff wouldn't appreciate it, either. The last thing we need is more cases, especially when it's all so speculative."

Laura began to feel excited and horrified at the same time. "Then you think there really *might* be something."

"There might," Lassiter said grimly. "Yes."

"Are you going to the sheriff?"

"I already have."

"And?"

"He said the cases are closed and we have no evidence, so forget it."

"I can't believe that!"

Lassiter's barrel chest heaved, and his lips turned down. "I'm afraid I can."

"But you just said—"

"I've been trying to see it from your point of view. I'm reaching. But none of this amounts to a hill of beans, from a law enforcement aspect. None of it has to mean a damned thing."

"You mean we're at a dead end?"

"Officially, yes."

"That's incredible."

"We're overworked down there. We don't need iffy stuff to add to the pressure. Also, in case you didn't know it, one of our county commissioners is a major stockholder in Timberdale; so is one of our district judges; so are a couple of Norman bankers and top attorneys. Do you think we would make any of them happy if we went off chasing butterflies?"

"But," Laura protested, "if they knew there had been foul play—"

"Right. *If.* But we don't know. All we have are coincidences, and the fact that Fred Which did a half-ass job on examinations, and chose to ignore signs that something besides heart failure might have killed these folks."

Laura stared at him. In the corner of the room, her small wall clock chimed ten. "What do we do?" she asked finally.

"Well," Lassiter said glumly, "I'll go the extra mile. On my own, I'll check out wills, estate records, details printed in the newspaper obits at the time, stuff like that. But I think we've had it, and the truth is just what the official verdict has said all along in all three cases."

"Okay," Laura said, trying to convince herself he was right.

"I won't be able to do it for a few days, maybe. One of our deputies is sick and I'm going to have to work an extra shift this weekend."

"Oh," Laura murmured, aware of her disappointment. What had she been imagining would happen this weekend with Trissie out of town?

"So what I want from you," Lassiter went on, "is a promise you'll do one thing."

"What?"

"Be careful."

"Why, of course I will," she said, surprised.

"I mean it," he told her. "I mean, let's go back to looking at it from the theory that something *has* been going on out there. If—and I stress the *if*—there's been foul play, you could get too close to it. If you did, you would be in more danger than anybody. Because if somebody was actually killing old folks, it has got to be some kind of a psycho—maybe the last person you would ever suspect— and psychos will kill anybody."

Now, FINISHING HER routine paperwork, Laura started her morning rounds. In the kitchen, breakfast was almost ready and everyone was hard at work. Mrs. Knott said she had heard just about all the complaints she wanted to hear for the rest of her life, and Sue Mullins characteristically nattered on a bit about how well meaning all the residents were, and how eccentricities should be overlooked.

"If you weren't running around all the time, taking them special trays and snacks that they don't pay for, maybe you'd have more time to do all your kitchen work that you're paid to do," Mrs. Knott snarled.

Laura happened to be watching Mullins. Her face went slack with surprising pain and resentment. But instantly she squared her shoulders and refused to fight back. "Yes, ma'am."

Muttering, Mrs. Knott went back to work, and Laura got out of there.

In the clinic, she found Kay Svendsen already on duty, although no one had shown up for treatment yet. Svendsen looked pale and scared.

"I hear Romeo hobbles back from the hospital today," Laura said.

Svendsen's pretty eyes rolled. "Why do you think I look like this?"

"Kay, gosh, what happened, exactly? How did he get knocked down?"

"Easy enough. He backed me into a corner. I said to lemme go, and he didn't. I pushed, and he grabbed my breast. He *hurt* me. I guess I lost my temper and shoved him back pretty hard."

"Sort of a karate move?"

Svendsen looked grim. "Yep."

Leaving the clinic, she started back toward the atrium. The halls remained deserted. Turning a corner halfway through the wing, she heard a slight sound behind her and whirled, nerves jangling, just in time to see the movement of someone ducking out of sight in the basement staircase doorway.

Someone following her.

Without thought about anything but discovery, Laura raced back down the hall the way she had come. She jerked the metal security door open. The bare concrete landing beyond the doorway stood empty.

Below came the sounds of footsteps on bare concrete stairs.

Laura hesitated. She didn't have time to think. Sanity said to run away. But this might be her only chance to get a glimpse of whoever had been harassing her. Whoever it was, they were running. They wouldn't attack in broad daylight, would they? Scared, she plunged down the stairs as fast as she could go.

At the halfway landing there was still no one in view. She heard a door below open, scraping on the pavement, and then the unmistakable sound of someone falling, the painful gasp of breath, and then the scramble of footsteps again. She rushed on down.

Another door. This one, she knew, led into the furnace and electrical equipment basement. She jerked the metal door open.

Black in there. She felt along the rough cinder-block wall and found the light switch—flipped it on. Lights flooded the room, glinting off overhead pipes and ductwork, squat black furnaces and boilers.

At the far end of the room, someone tried to rush out of sight. But it was too late.

"Stop right there!" Laura cried.

SIXTEEN

THE FIGURE AT the far end of the room stopped dead, then slowly turned to face Laura.

"Come here," Laura ordered, feeling the first flush of intense relief and discovery.

Maude Thuringer, eyes bright with frustrated defiance, slouched past the furnaces and boilers to stand at last in front of Laura. Maude had barked her knees and hands in her fall. She was bleeding. She looked more chagrined than seriously injured.

"Maude," Laura groaned, "what are you doing, following me?"

The old woman stared at her shoes. "You're a suspect."

"A suspect? Me?" That was when the light dawned. "Are you the one who's been calling me at home, and then not talking?"

"I needed to know if you were there. If you were out, it might be a clue."

Laura had a hot flash of relief and amazement. "And you stole my notebook?"

"Of course, you ninny. I had to see what you were writing down. They could have been clues."

"And in the parking lot, Maude?"

Maude's eyes narrowed bitterly. "You weren't supposed to see me."

"That bag must have weighed thirty pounds. I'm surprised you could lift it high enough to hurt me."

"I'm stronger than I look."

"You could have really hurt me."

"I knew what I was doing," Maude replied defensively.

"I didn't hit you in the head or the neck. I just knocked you down so I could get away."

"Maude, my God! Why did you write that note?"

Maude's eyes glazed. "Note? What note?"

BACK IN THE ATRIUM, some of the earlybirds had appeared on the scene. Laura spoke to several of them; they seemed okay. Davilla Rose said her back hurt, and no one understood how bad she felt. Ellen Smith complained that the light in her apartment this time of year was terrible for working in acrylics, or anything else for that matter, and she planned to write to the board of directors about it. The old judge hobbled down, looking gray as a dish towel, and said he was fine, an obvious lie. The Castles sallied out the front door for their morning trot around the grounds.

Laura hardly noticed. Maude Thuringer's shenanigans explained much that had made her feel paranoid. But Laura was convinced Maude had not written the note. Which meant the mystery remained.

The front entry doors swung open. Ken Keen hobbled in on crutches, accompanied by his middle-aged son. Keen did not look happy. One of his pantlegs had been slit to accommodate a large white cast that extended from his ankle to his hip. A few people in the atrium glanced curiously at him, and he glared back. Everybody probably knew how he had gotten hurt.

Keen's son, a short-statured man wearing worn cotton slacks and a dark green sportshirt, stood talking to his father for a few moments. The younger man frowned and gestured, as if lecturing. The elder Keen slumped on his crutches, staring morosely at his bare toes sticking out of the cast. After a while, the younger man awkwardly patted him on the shoulder, turned, and left.

Keen turned slowly on the unfamiliar crutches and started for the elevators. The doors opened and he started

inside. But then the doors tried to close too fast. The end
of one of his crutches got caught in the crack. The doors
sprang open again. Keen dragged his crutch inside and
leaned heavily against the back wall of the car, removing
his cap to mop a thick bare arm across his forehead. He
looked dazed and confused.

The doors of the elevator closed. The indicator did not
move, meaning that the car wasn't moving. Keen had forgotten to pick a floor.

Laura hurried across the atrium and punched the button
that made the doors spring open again. Maybe she could
pour some oil on the waters here. "Having trouble, Mr.
Keen? Gosh, it's hard to manipulate those crutches and
work the elevator buttons all at once, isn't it. Are you going
to three, to your apartment? Let me help."

Keen stared at her with beaten, baffled eyes. "Three,"
he croaked.

Laura pushed the button. The doors closed. Tilting her
head back, she watched the floor indicator blink, changing
from 1 to 2.

"Thank you," Keen muttered behind her.

"Don't mention it," Laura said without thought, watching the indicator.

"But it really is sweet of you to help," Keen insisted.
Then, "You're a very sweet girl," he added huskily behind
her.

Close behind her.

Laura swung around in panicked reaction, but she wasn't
fast enough. Both crutches clattered to the elevator floor as
Keen's arms went around her. His weight and enthusiasm
slammed her back, bumping her head painfully against the
metal wall. She saw tiny yellow stars. Before she could
react, Keen was all over her—his face blurrily filling her
vision—and then she tried to duck but it was too late, and
he grabbed her by the sides of her head and jammed his

mouth against hers, trying to shove his cheesy-tasting tongue right down her throat.

Laura reacted by reflex. She shoved—hard—and brought her knee up sharply. Keen gasped in pain, half doubled over, and let go of her, staggering backward. He hit the far wall of the elevator with such force that the whole thing shook, and then he started sliding slowly to a spread-legged sitting position on the floor. He farted and his pants split.

Laura spun to the elevator control buttons. At the same instant, the elevator stopped and the little arrival bell dinged. The doors slid open. Laura jumped out, almost colliding with the two residents standing there in wait of a ride, Mrs. Oliver and Mrs. Slipp. They stared at the sprawled Keen, then at Laura, and moved back away from her as if they had just witnessed a murder.

"But I love you!" Ken Keen cried from the elevator.

Laura pushed past the women. "Excuse me, ladies." She started down the hall.

Keen's voice called pitiably, "But I can't pick up my crutches! Help me! *You've got to help me!*"

He could ride the elevator the rest of his natural life as far as Laura was concerned. She didn't know what she felt most, disgust with Keen or anger at herself for being so stupid. No matter. She kept right on walking, while behind her Keen's cries for help became shriller, and Mrs. Oliver and Mrs. Slipp decided to take the stairs.

The incident had left her shaken. Ken Keen's strength and agility had shocked her. Was he as harmless as everyone had believed, or had that instant of sheer panic in the elevator been the kind of thing that was the last emotion ever felt by Cora Chandler, or Milly Kett, or Jane Hawes?

Oh, surely not, Laura thought. But she *couldn't* be sure. Not of anything, now.

BY LUNCHTIME a normal day's routine had been established. Mrs. Epperman had not returned from Oklahoma

City. Laura had a salad and iced tea, and circulated. Ellen Smith, ajingle with Indian bracelets, arrived late, inspected the food server trays, and came to Laura's table to complain that the food wasn't hot. Colonel Rodgers, overhearing, said the military could serve hot meals in the Arctic. Stonewall Jackson looked up from her clipboard and said this wasn't the army. By the time the meal was over, Laura had decided she would pursue the last possible hints on her hidden list, Maude Thuringer or no.

She maneuvered to get a few words with Davilla Rose, who had gone to the atrium to disappear into a large, overstuffed chair and frown over her poetry notebook.

"Davilla, do you remember Mrs. Hawes?"

"Janie? Of course. We've talked about her. Poor soul."

"Was she in your poetry group?"

Davilla Rose's face screwed up in distaste. "*Janie?* My heavens, no. All she ever did was watch soap operas. She wouldn't have known a quatrain from a turnip." Davilla sighed. "Not that anyone else truly appreciates my knowledge of verse anyway."

"But Milly Kett was in your group, right?"

"Oh, yes. She was coming along nicely."

"And Mrs. Chandler?"

"Yes." Mrs. Rose blinked. "Why?"

"Don't I remember being told that Mrs. Hawes was quite ill before her death?"

"She certainly was. Cancer, I think it was." Davilla Rose's eyes screwed up. "Why?"

Laura was saved an answer by Ken Keen, hobbling out of the dining room with Maude Thuringer close beside him. Maude looked like nothing had happened, but she did have Band-Aids on both palms.

"Hey there!" Keen cried happily, and thunked toward her on the crutches.

Laura expected him to berate her for the elevator incident, but he acted like it had never happened. "There she is," he leered. "Miss America."

"Hi, Ken. Hello, Maude."

Keen adjusted the crutches in his armpits. "Damn things. Say! Have you had lunch yet?" He and Maude had eaten at the adjacent table.

"I just finished," Laura told him.

"How's the food today?"

"Not bad."

Keen turned to Maude. "Let's go try it."

She patted his arm. "You just had lunch, Kenny."

His eyebrows raised in surprise. "I did?"

"Yes."

He frowned. "Did I enjoy it?"

Laura left them there and started across the atrium. Maude pursued her, grasping her arm with icy fingers.

"Yes, Maude?"

"Don't get the wrong idea," Maude whispered. "I'm only watching him as closely as possible because he's become my prime suspect."

"Good work," Laura groaned.

Nearby, she found old Judge Young seated on one of the couches, his hands cupped on the curved handle of his cane, his head bent to his chest, softly snoring. At her approach, he raised his head and focused on her.

"Judge, don't you think you ought to go rest in your room?"

"Surrender to a small difficulty," he rumbled, "and you only exacerbate existing predilections toward passivity and further diminution of normal functioning."

At the desk, Kay Svendsen was waiting. Her eyes gleamed with hidden mischief. "Wow, you talk about *me* being rough on him."

"I guess you heard about the elevator."

"*Everybody* has heard about the elevator."

"Well, dammit, he backed me into a corner."

"Tell me about it."

"Fortunately, he seems to have forgotten it already."

"Oh," Svendsen said glumly, "he hasn't forgotten. That's just his new strategy."

"New strategy?"

"Yes. He told me a few minutes ago that he's had a change of heart—learned his lesson. He says he'll never insult a woman again."

"That's amazing," Laura said.

"Sure is. He told me he'd decided not to sue either of us. All I've got to do to seal the bargain is spend just one night with him."

Could someone like Ken Keen be a wily killer? It seemed out of the question. But she couldn't cross him off her list.

SEVENTEEN

"WELL," AARON LASSITER told Laura late Friday night on the telephone, "at least we know someone isn't stalking you—I mean anyone dangerous."

"There's still the note," Laura said, curling her bare toes under the bedsheets.

"I tend to think that was somebody's bad joke."

"I hope so."

"Try to look at it that way. Just cool it."

"Let me tell you something I thought of that I might still try."

"What is it?" He didn't sound happy.

"Maude's confession doesn't necessarily mean everything else was an accident."

"Well, sure. We can't know, but—"

"Good. Now listen. Maybe there's a pattern here that we're not seeing. Or maybe there's a psychological profile for the type of person who could do something like this— kill innocent people somehow and make it look accidental. I'm seeing my faculty adviser at school tomorrow during the lunch break, and I plan to talk about those aspects with him."

Lassiter's voice warmed. "Good idea." He paused, then added, "I wish I were there with you right now instead of in this damned courthouse."

"I wish you were, too," Laura said instantly, with feeling.

There was a silence. Her heart thudded. She looked down at herself in the rumpled nylon pajamas. A thought lanced through her mind: If he were here, she wouldn't be wearing these things. She had the one cute, sexy black negligee....

His voice broke the fantasy. "I better get back to work."

"Yeah," she said regretfully. "Good night."

After she had hung up, it was impossible to return her attention immediately to the overnight textbook assignments. Rolling out of bed, she padded barefoot through the apartment to the kitchen and got a glass of milk. Trissie's dark bedroom doorway seemed to mock her. She wondered where her daughter was right now, and what kind of custody scheme Richard might be cooking up with his cheerleader. Then she thought about Tom Benson, who had promptly gone into a sulk when she said she wouldn't have time to see him this weekend. She worried. About a lot of things.

THE LUNCH BREAK in the killing schedule of back-to-back classes for the weekend social work students started at noon and went until one-thirty. Leaving the moment the morning session adjourned, Laura hurried from the adult education center on the south end of the campus to the old, converted former fraternity house on the northeast side where most of the faculty of the school were officed. With the Sooners playing away from home, the streets near the stadium were no more busy than on a normal weekday, and she made good time. The noon carillons were still chiming in the student union clock tower a block away when she found a parking place near the ugly old brick house and hurried inside.

The office of her faculty adviser, Dr. Barnett Hodges, was on the second floor at the back. The aged wood floor squeaked as she walked down the rear hallway and entered his tiny foyer. Off in the distance someplace the carillons started playing "America the Beautiful." It was stuffy with the air-conditioning shut down for the weekend.

Laura skirted the unoccupied reception desk and tapped on Hodges's old-fashioned frosted-glass door.

"Come," a throaty voice called from inside.

Laura went into a squarish, high-ceilinged room with bookcases everywhere and a large, old-fashioned oak desk backed against the lone high window. Stacks of papers and journals made a mountain on the desk, and acrid pipe smoke blued the still air. Dr. Barnett Hodges loomed like a benign old gorilla behind the desk, sipping coffee from a red-and-white Sooners mug.

"You're late," he told Laura.

"I hurried," Laura said. "Listen. The noon chimes are still going."

Hodges cocked an ear, then frowned. "You're right," he muttered. "I *hate* it when students are right. Sit down. What did you want to talk to me about? Flunking a class? Wanting a better job? Doing some ritualistic apple polishing to start getting ready for your comps? Be quick, Laura. I want to get to WalMart."

Laura took the chair facing the professor's claw-footed old monster and put her Timberdale group and individual file folders on the edge of the pile of papers already there. "It's about my practicum at Timberdale."

"What about it?"

Laura felt reluctant to go ahead. She knew she was risking looking like a fool. No matter. "I want to find the best sources I can get that might update me real fast on abnormal psychology in gerontology."

Hodges cocked his head and glared from under his shelf of gray eyebrows. "What kind of 'abnormal'?"

"Well…it's about predictable tendencies in older people."

"You want to be more specific? We could fence here all day, and me never get to WalMart. Why don't you ask me some of the questions you want answered?"

"Okay. Is it a common tendency in some older people to get...well...destructive in their anger about their status in life?"

Magically all the curmudgeonly veneer vanished. "Sure," Hodges said quite gently. "Self-destructive tendencies are a constant minor-key concern at nursing homes and terminal-care facilities, and to a lesser extent at retirement villages. In the case of old people with painful, debilitating, or terminal illnesses, it can become a real problem, and vigilance has to be maintained on a constant basis. I have some articles on that. Also sometimes you've got the classic theoretical progression with early Alzheimer's: increased impatience, anger, tantrums without identifiable cause or specific focus—all these people have some potential for suicide. Have you got somebody out there who particularly worries you? It might be that you should make a referral to Dr. Which or somebody, see if an antidepressant is called for."

"I'm not thinking so much about the danger of suicide," Laura explained, "as I am about a person with a growing rage...someone who might just hate a lot of people...try to do *others* bodily injury."

Hodges's shaggy eyebrows twitched. "Huh. That's bad. Well, it could happen with Alzheimer's, I suppose, although usually the violence is more verbal than physical."

Laura leaned forward, not bothering to hide her concern. "If there were someone like this, doing...pranks, nasty little things, like, not long ago someone stole some cut flowers, and then there was a crazy little flare-up at a party in the atrium because a lady thought someone had done something purposely to embarrass her. If there were someone with a lot of hostility, but they were hiding it and doing really bad things in secret, how might you identify them?"

"You wouldn't," Hodges said instantly, and then sipped his coffee. "If they had any smarts at all—and people like you're describing can be *damn* clever and wily—they might look superficially like the calmest, nicest person around the place. And I don't think they'd blow up much, giving themselves away. They would be cool as pickles most of the time, getting all their hostility out by fooling people, planning the next bit of nastiness, carrying it out in secret."

Laura thought about it. "I was hoping," she admitted, "that there might be some personality giveaways or something, some tips a person might watch for. A profile."

Hodges was watching her very intently. "You're pretty worried about this."

"Yes," Laura admitted.

"You don't think this prankster might be capable of worse acts, do you?"

"I don't know."

"I know you don't know. What do you think?"

"I think…maybe there could be real trouble."

Hodges reached for an Oom-Paul pipe and began stuffing it with shag tobacco. "I hate to hear that. Have you got a specific person you're worried about—a suspect?"

"No," Laura admitted. "That's just it. I don't. That's why I was hoping for a profile."

Hodges touched a wood house match to the pipe tobacco, and a new cloud of smoke rose around him. "Not likely," he said through the smoke, fanning the match out. "If I get your drift, you're thinking about a possible problem person, somebody hiding, and maybe they're not even there. Even a really crazy mugger or killer sometimes is impossible to pick out before he cracks, runs amok. Your compensated schizophrenic can be a real bastard to identify unless he's in the midst of an episode. Think how often you read about some mad-dog murderer. People afterward say, 'Oh, he was the quietest boy, always had perfect manners.' So you just about begin to think that the quiet, reclusive ones are the ones to watch out for, and then here comes another ghastly crime, and all the people who knew the guy say things like, 'He was always angry, always flying off the handle; everybody knew he would blow up someday.' No, Laura, there's no pattern. A lot of us wish there were. We could make a million dollars, fingering crazies before they had time to act. And the world would be a lot safer place.''

Laura took a deep breath and absorbed the mild disappointment. It was really not far off what she had feared he would tell her.

Hodges added, ''But you don't think you really have a potentially dangerous person out there, surely. Not at a retirement center like Timberdale.''

Laura's courage gave out. ''No, of course not.''

Hodges leaned back in his swivel chair, which creaked dangerously. ''Not that it isn't possible, of course. Any place can be dangerous. Timberdale, as hard as it would be for most people to imagine, could be dangerous, too. Dammit, it's *hard* to grow old. Some people don't do it very well. Old people can get just as crazy as young ones can, maybe sometimes worse. As we age, we tend to become more of what we already are. Take a person who was always angry and resentful—potentially destructive—and maybe as they got old they could show their colors for the first time.''

The hairs on the back of Laura's neck stood up. She raised one hand to soothe them down again.

Hodges heaved himself out of his chair and lumbered over to the coffeemaker, where he poured another cup of his evil-looking brew. He came back to the desk and resumed his seat. Laura waited, knowing she had come to another dead end, perhaps the last.

''It may be,'' Hodges said finally, ''that something will come about in one of your group or individual sessions out there—a real hint. Could happen. Of course it may be equally likely that you're just picking up crabby vibes from crabby older people.''

"That could be," Laura said, not believing it.

"Wish I could be more help. Tell you what. I'll whomp up a short reading list for you. Something in the literature might help.''

When she left the office ten minutes later with her adviser's scrawled book list in her purse, Laura felt that another hope had just gone down the drain.

TRISSIE CAME HOME tired but bubbling Sunday night. She had a wonderful time. She babbled endlessly about her father and his cheerleader. Laura tried to be a good sport about it, but looking into her daughter's shining eyes she felt scared.

The last thing she needed when she reported for work at Timberdale Monday morning was Francie Blake with more plans for the big Halloween party. But that was what she got.

Francie had beaten her to work, a first, and rushed enthusiastically out of her office to greet Laura the moment she arrived. Gliding like a model on those ball-bearing, computer-controlled legs of hers, Francie looked like Miss America from the top of her stunning silver blond head to the soles of her pale, high-heeled pumps. Her jewelry— diamond stud earrings, diamond choker necklace, and many-faceted tennis bracelet—blazed. She was so perfectly turned out, Laura felt grungy just looking at her. Francie must have ducked today's brisk, early-morning south wind by somehow getting from her car to the office through some kind of roll-up protective tubing, Laura thought. Not a hair was out of place. Not a streak flawed her stunning full makeup, which included exotic blue shading that emphasized her gorgeous eyes. On anyone else it would have been too much. On Francie it was just right. Her pumps matched her belted teak trench dress, an Ann Taylor, which looked new. Of course on Francie everything always looked new.

"You're finally here!" Francie exclaimed as she spied Laura. "Great!"

Laura roused herself. "Morning, Francie."

"Isn't this weather lovely?" Francie enthused, moving closer through a gentle cloud of Poison. "It's so much cooler. I just love it. A break in the weather like this always cheers everyone up. That's what I've observed." She handed Laura a bright yellow sheet of paper. "Of course," she purred, "I'm not practically a psychological genius, the way you are. All I have is what I've observed, and a little common sense."

Laura looked at the paper.

HALLOWEEN PARTY

5:30—EARLY DINNER. FUN PARTY FAVORS!
6:30—GATHER IN ATRIUM. EVERYONE COME IN CUTE
      COSTUMES!
      BOB FOR APPLES!
      PIN THE TAIL ON THE DONKEY!
      CANDY AND TREATS FOR ALL TRICK-OR-
      TREATERS!
      SPECIAL SURPRISES!
7:00—TALENT SHOW BEGINS!
8:30—REFRESHMENTS! SOCIAL HOUR!
9:00—MIX AND MINGLE! BINGO IN ACTIVITY RM. #1!
10:30—PARTY ENDS.

She looked up at Francie. "What are the special surprises?"

Francie made a pretty pout. "I thought you might help me out with that."

"What do you mean, help you out?"

"Well, I don't exactly have that part worked out yet."

"You mean you don't know what the surprises are going to be?"

"Well...yes, more or less." Then Francie brightened. "But everything else is all planned out. Still Bill is taking everyone into the city to a costume shop I've contacted. Those who don't already have costumes will be able to rent them. They'll get a special senior citizens' rate, and the man there says he'll come by next weekend and pick everything up so we won't have to worry about that. And you don't need to worry about that part where it says bobbing for apples. I mean, we wouldn't want them *really* trying to bob for apples. They might drown themselves, poor dears. We'll have the apples sitting in a barrel filled with tissue paper, and there will be strings tied around the apples, and all they have to do is bend down and get a string between their teeth and pull the apples out that way. Someone will supervise the pin the tail on the donkey, too, to make sure nobody gets stuck with a pin." Francie stopped and stared, big eyes snapping rapidly. "Doesn't it sound **great?**"

"Yes, Francie, great. I—"

"What costume are you going to wear? I'm coming as Marie Antoinette. I thought of going as Scarlett, but ooh, this dress is *so* darling." Francie's pretty eyes danced. "I just hope no one thinks the décolletage is too much. What are you going to wear, Laura?"

"I haven't thought about it yet. As an employee, I thought I might just wear my normal—"

"Oh *no!* You *can't!* Everyone has to be in costume, that's the *rule.*" Francie put a crimson-tipped finger in the corner of her adorable mouth. "What could you wear...let me see...was there anything down there at the costume shop that would be *you?*" She raised her finger and beamed. "I've got it! I saw a perfectly *precious* Cinderella costume. It would be perfect for you, so sweet and whole-some.''

"I'll think about it," Laura said through powdered tooth enamel.

"I think we ought to have everything looking just precious for Halloween." Francie waved both hands, describing arcs of incandescence with her jewelry. "We need to have cute rustic baskets all around, with dried ears of corn and lots of pretty colorful gourds in them, and of course *loads* of pretty potted mums, and some dried corn shucks if you can get Still Bill to put them up for us." Francie made her beautiful eyes open rounder. "Pumpkins, of course—lots of precious little punkies, not carved or anything, all around, and at least six of the biggest, scariest, mean old jack-o'-lanterns we can find." Francie formed a little-girl oval with her pink lips, acting cute and scared. "Oooh! It will be neat! Scary! Then, just before the talent night part of the program, we can bob for the apples. We want to have lots of cider, and make sure the naughty colonel doesn't spike it." Francie wriggled from head to toe. "Oooh! Isn't this going to be *fun?*"

"I'm sure," Laura said, trying to muster a smile of some kind.

"We *have* to promote the talent show part of things, Laura. Participation was way down last month. We need more acts Wednesday night. Will you help me encourage more residents and staff to perform? You can use your psychology on them."

"I have a preliminary talent show list. Mr. Selvey has already signed up to do his magic tricks. Sada Hoff and Davilla Rose will do poetry readings. Colonel Rodgers will play his mandolin. Maude Thuringer wants to play the piano. Fred Which—''

"Oh, no," Francie Blake moaned. "Isn't there *any* way we can keep Maudie from playing the piano again?"

"We need acts," Laura pointed out.

"I know, Laura, I *know*. But she's so ghastly. And she only knows one piece. Isn't there some discreet way you can explain to her that people might be getting tired of 'Columbia, the Gem of the Ocean'?"

"I'll talk to her. Maybe she has time to learn something else. Something by Sousa, maybe."

Francie's head jerked, making curls bobble. "Sousa? Who's that? A resident?"

"No."

Francie scowled. Then her shoulders slumped. "Oh, I get it! You're *joking*. Ha."

Laura consulted her list. "I don't have any other talent show names so far."

"What about staff? Where are the staff people?"

"I don't have any yet."

"Laura! My goodness, it's *imperative* to have staff people. This talent show is special, more than just part of a fun evening. It's a chance for residents and staff to come together."

"I don't know who we can get," Laura replied, "since Mrs. Knott said she didn't ever want to sing again, and Mrs. Mullins broke her flute."

"Well, look around. Talk to the nurses. Check up on the maintenance staff and housekeeping. My goodness, everyone has *some* kind of talent." Francie stopped and her beautiful, selfish eyes narrowed. "And you can motivate by leading, of course."

"Me?" Laura squeaked. "How?"

"Perform. Take part. Demonstrate one of your talents."

"I don't have any talents."

"Of course you do. You're much too modest. I've heard you humming around the office sometimes. You have a beautiful voice. You can sing."

"No. No way. I can't carry a tune—"

Laura got no further than that, because she suddenly became aware that Francie had entirely lost interest in whatever she might have to say. Laura's back was to the reception desk, which put the atrium and the front entry foyer behind her. Francie, facing her, had looked over Laura at someone who had just entered out of Laura's vision.

"My God," Francie breathed. "Is he beautiful, or what?"

Laura turned. Aaron Lassiter had just walked in.

Now what? Laura wondered.

EIGHTEEN

DARKLY HANDSOME in his deputy's uniform, Lassiter removed his Mountie-style hat in one of his characteristically wonderful, slow masculine movements, spied Laura, and started across the atrium toward the desk.

"Who *is* he?" Francie whispered, sleeking one hand over the tummy-spanning tautness of her dress.

Before Laura could reply, Lassiter reached the counter, his slow grin widening. "Hi," he said, as if she were the only person in the room, or the world for that matter. "I was hoping for a word with you."

Francie cleared her throat.

Laura told Lassiter, "I think you must be a mind reader."

"Oh? How come?"

"There's something I want to talk to you about, too. I saw my professor."

"Okay, great."

Francie cleared her throat again. "Laura?"

Since she wouldn't be put off, Laura introduced her. Lassiter looked down at her with his washboard forehead and tentative smile. She extended her hand, making a big diamond ring glitter. Her smile threatened sunburn. "I'm just *so* pleased to make your acquaintance, Deputy Lassiter. My goodness, I can't imagine why we haven't met before."

"How do you do, Miss, uh…"

"Oh, you can just call me Francie. Please do. And your first name is…?"

"Aaron," Lassiter said, holding her hand.

Francie jacked up her smile several megawatts. "I love

biblical names, don't you, Laura? Aaron, gracious me. Here I am, clinging to your hand like a silly puss. You're so sweet not to laugh at me.''

Lassiter got his hand loose and turned back to Laura. "Since we both have something we want to talk about, is there somewhere here where we could grab a cup of coffee?"

"Sure," Laura said. "We have a little employee lounge."

"But oh, gee," Francie purred. "The desk has to be attended, Laura. Isn't that a shame."

"I'll take the portable intercom phone," Laura replied sweetly.

"Oh, good. Then all three of us will be free to go." Francie linked her arm through Lassiter's. "You don't mind if we stroll on ahead, do you, honey?"

"Oh, of course not," Laura snapped, dragging out the portable telephone. *Right.*

By the time she had the master phone and calling pad set up, Francie and Lassiter were halfway across the atrium on their way to the lounge. Laura ran to catch up.

"Which is why I just dearly love my job here," Francie was cooing. "I believe that each of us should give back a part of our life to society, and I feel like that's what I'm doing here. Do y'all see what I mean?"

"I—yes," Lassiter said. He appeared slightly dazed.

"What a silly question." Francie smiled. "Of course you see what I mean. A dunce could see you're a sensitive, caring gentleman."

She was good, Laura thought disgustedly, you had to give her that. Any woman could instantly see through the sweetsy-cutesy-flirty act, but men were such idiots; they never saw through anything. Lassiter's ears were pink, she noticed. She had never seen his ears so pink. Of course she had never seen him with Francie clinging all over him, either.

Francie gushed, "I'm sure all the residents would feel *so* much more secure and nice if you visited frequently. You *must* promise me you'll come see us more often." Francie was getting breathless.

"I'll, uh, sure consider that," Lassiter mumbled.

They crossed the atrium and started down the corridor toward the employee lounge. Francie continued the panzer attack. "Tell me, Aaron...it *is* okay if I call you Aaron?"

"My friends do," Lassiter told her.

"Then I will, too, because I just feel we're going to be great friends, don't you? Tell me, Aaron, are you an expert on automobile security systems?"

Lassiter looked puzzled. "I've seen a few."

They reached the closed door to the lounge. Laura pulled it open. Francie glided in first, turning on the overhead light, Lassiter following her. Laura propped the door open. Her teeth ached.

There was no one else in the small, tile-floored room. Still Bill Mills's crew had waxed the floor, and the chairs still sat inverted on the round Formica-topped table. But someone had been in recently; traces of cigarette smoke hung in the air. The refrigerator thrummed along. The kitchen staff had started coffee and brought in some doughnuts.

"Sit down and I'll take care of everything," Francie announced, going to the counter. She opened one of the upper cabinet doors and reached up for cups. They were within easy reach because she was not a small girl, but she went on tiptoes anyway, fetchingly stretching everything considerably more than necessary. Laura fleetingly considered mayhem with a butcher knife, but helped Lassiter take the chairs off the table instead.

"There," Francie sighed, seating herself between them

after finishing the obviously difficult job of delivering three cups. "Well, I won't stay another *minute* and disturb you. I know you have some business you need to discuss. But the reason I asked about alarm systems, Aaron, is that I have what the salesman *said* was a very fine system on my car outside. But honest to Pete, I'm just so helpless and *dumb* when it comes to things designed for a man. Sometimes for no reason I can imagine, the siren seems to go off all by itself. It drives me wild." She poured coffee. "Do you take sugar?"

Lassiter was staring at her like a crusader in sight of the Holy Grail. "Uh...what?"

Francie arched her back and leaned closer. Her pink lips curled around the word: "Sugar?"

"Oh." He shook himself. "No. Thanks."

"About the alarm..."

Lassiter frowned with the effort it obviously took for him to pay attention to business. "Well...uh...sometimes alarms do just go off that way. It's probably okay."

Francie's full lips pouted. "I'm just so helpless with things like this. I don't know what to do." Abruptly she turned sideways in her chair to face Lassiter, and crossed her legs. *Bombs away.* "When you leave here, Aaron, do you suppose..." She stopped and prettily put red fingertips to her forehead. "I'm almost embarrassed to ask."

"What?" Lassiter grunted, befuddled.

"Well, do you think...would it be too *awful* of me..." She put fingers over her eyes in a fine show of embarrassment. "I won't ask."

"What?" Lassiter mumbled.

Francie looked up, giving him the full eye battery. "Well, I was thinking, if someone like you...who's so smart about such things and all...if you might just take a quick *peek* at my dumb little alarm system and see if I'm doing something wrong."

"Well," Lassiter said, "I could look. I don't know if I can tell anything."

"Oh, I don't know how I'll ever thank you."

Clearly perplexed, Lassiter tore his eyes away from her legs and looked at Laura. "I'm sorry I didn't call earlier."

"You must be busy all the time," Francie gushed. "Law enforcement work must be so exciting. Of course Laura is busy, too. She has her work here and her little classes at OU on the weekends, and of course her child. Did you know Laura has a child?"

"Sure," Lassiter said. "Trissie is a neat kid."

Francie drooped a little at that.

Laura felt a little better, and decided she wouldn't let Francie's presence stall her curiosity. "You have some news?"

"It isn't much, but I thought it might interest you." Lassiter glanced questioningly at Francie. She pretended not to notice, and sipped her coffee with no apparent intention of leaving them alone. Lassiter scowled and turned back to Laura. "I was talking to a friend over at the hospital. She happened to mention that she noticed Mrs. Kett's death recently. It turns out she knew the lady because Mrs. Kett was having some radiation treatments for cancer over there, and they didn't think she had much longer to live."

Laura sustained a distant but decided shock. "I knew Cora Chandler had some kind of cancer. I knew Millie was sick, too, but I didn't know about the radiation treatments."

Lassiter nodded glumly. "I guess she kept it pretty secret. She was in pretty bad shape. But my friend said the doctors kept checking her real good, and they thought she had six or eight months to live, maximum." He scowled. "One thing they check most carefully is a patient's heart during radiation or chemo treatments. Her heart tested solid as a rock."

Laura forgot Francie Blake for a moment. She even forgot to be irritated. "It doesn't make sense."

"Another thing," Lassiter added.

"Yes?"

"You've got a resident here named Young? Emil Young?"

"The judge? Yes. He's our oldest resident."

Lassiter nodded grimly. "They're treating him, too."

Francie cut in, puzzled. "Laura? What *is* all this morbid talk about sicknesses and deaths? My goodness. I thought *all* of us understood that it's part of our professional obligation to be upbeat, sunny, and optimistic. Mrs. Epperman talks about that all the time."

Ignoring her, Laura told Lassiter, "I didn't know about the judge, either. No wonder he's so weak from this chest cold he has."

"Laura," Francie broke in again, "my goodness. If Mrs. Epperman knew this kind of talk was going around, she'd have a fit. Honestly. Honey, you've got to put this kind of morbid stuff out of your mind. Those people are dead, and this is the week of the Halloween party. It's up to us to have *fun*."

Laura looked into Francie's beautiful eyes. There was no one home in there. "I guess you're right, Francie. We won't talk about it anymore." She grinned at Lassiter. "Right?"

He picked up. "Right." He drank his coffee straight down and replaced the cup in the saucer. "That Halloween party is Wednesday night of this week?"

"Yes."

"I've got Wednesday off. But you'll be out here that evening, right?"

"Until pretty late, I'm afraid," Laura admitted.

The washboard displayed again. "Well, what I was

thinking is…maybe I could just come out here and join you for some of it?''

Laura didn't know if he wanted to be near her to protect her from something, or just wanted to be near her. The request gave her such a nice warm feeling that she didn't care. ''It hadn't occurred to me—'' she began.

''What a grand idea!'' Francie cried, digging her talons into his arm. ''How *sweet* of you to suggest that. Of course we'd *love* to have you, wouldn't we, Laura? Aaron! You must be here by six o'clock. Can you be here by six? Wear a costume…no. Just wear your uniform. That will be *exciting*. Will you honor me by sitting at my table at dinner? You, too, of course, Laura. Then—''

Laura's cordless phone started flashing. That meant someone at the front desk had pressed the ''service'' button. She got up quickly, spilling droplets of her coffee on the tabletop.

''Oh, you poor thing,'' Francie crooned, jumping to her feet. ''You just rush right along. I'll clean that up for you.''

Laura hesitated, looking down at Lassiter. He looked up at her, but didn't seem sure he wanted to move. *Damn, damn, damn.* Laura turned and hurried out of the lounge.

The visitor at the desk was a brother, here to see Mrs. Henderson. Laura directed him. By the time she returned to the desk, Lassiter and Francie Blake were just coming back from the lounge.

''I'll just get my car keys out of the locker and be right back,'' Francie told him with an adoring look as they reached the desk. She darted into the inner office area.

Lassiter watched her go. He seemed dazed.

''Goddamn,'' he muttered. ''What a great-looking woman.''

Then he started, colored, and turned quickly to Laura. ''What I meant was, she *is* sort of fairly good-looking, if you like that type.''

"Right," Laura said sarcastically.

Forehead gullied, Lassiter hung in there. "You said when I first came in that you had something you wanted to tell me, too?"

"Maybe," Laura snapped, "you don't have time."

He stiffened. "If I didn't have time, I wouldn't ask. What are you mad about? Get to the point."

"Oh, I'm sure I'd better hurry right along," Laura shot back, so mad she couldn't see straight. "It wouldn't do if I delayed your going out to admire Francie's *car*."

"What's *with* you all of a sudden?"

He looked so offended and confused that her anger collapsed as fast as it had come. "Nothing," she told him. "I think I'm just tired." She told him about Dr. Hodges saying old people could develop hidden craziness, but how he couldn't suggest an identifying profile.

"Don't let it get you down," Lassiter told her.

She managed a smile. "Easy for you to say, buster."

"What can I do to help?"

"What do you mean?"

"I mean, you feel bad. What do you need from me?"

He meant it. It was astonishing. *What did she need from him?* Instantly, for just a split second, she thought how it might be to wake up in the night and have the bed warm and safe, with this man's bulk solid and close beside her. The times with Tom—the few times in the spring and summer, which had ceased to happen sort of by unspoken mutual recognition of something that had changed in their relationship—had never filled her with any real sense of security or belonging. They had been nice, and not much more. She had almost convinced herself that safety... familiarity...was enough. But this instant's imagining herself with Lassiter was infinitely better than reality had ever been with Tom.

She was shaken by this realization. But he was watching

her with those big, caring eyes. She had to say something. "I guess I don't need anything," she said slowly.

He accepted it. "Okay. Look, I'll still check those wills and things when I get time. And you continue keeping your eyes open. This business about all the victims having cancer sort of bugs me. But don't let it wear you down, okay? We can just—" He stopped suddenly, looking over her. "Shit," he muttered.

"What?" Laura said.

"Here comes Miss America again."

NINETEEN

"HERE I AM!" Francie cried, rushing out of the office corridor and grabbing a death-grip on Lassiter's arm. "But I just feel so *awful,* Aaron, asking you to do this for me. Sometimes I'm just so helpless and dumb. I don't think men like you realize how hard it is for girls who don't have a man in their life to advise them on stuff like this."

"No problem," Lassiter mumbled, and was dragged toward the front doors at the far end of the atrium. He managed a wave, and then turned to whatever Francie was babbling as she rushed him onward.

Biting her lip, Laura looked down at the Halloween party notes left on the counter. Preoccupied by the news Lassiter had just brought, she noticed for the first time that Francie had attached a second sheet to her copy of the party announcement. She turned to that page. Under the heading "Laura's Assignments" was a list of things Laura was to do to prepare for the party Wednesday night.

Head buzzing, she read. It seemed that she was to coordinate the bus trip to Norman for residents still needing costumes. She was also to double-check on the snacks and food, make certain all atrium decorations were ready in time, plan the order of presentation for the talent show acts, arrange the late refreshments, assign staff to greet family visitors, and get someone to handle the guest book.

Wondering what Francie planned to do besides look cute, Laura looked up in time to see someone else hurrying across the atrium: Maude Thuringer, with mud all over her feet and legs.

Laura hurried to intercept her. "Maude!"

The little woman stopped and turned with the look of a child caught stealing candy. "What?"

"You've got mud all over yourself. Now what have you been doing?"

Maude looked down at herself. "I had to climb into the hall planter upstairs to overhear a conversation."

Laura gathered up her client folders and notebooks. "I've got to go put these away. While I'm doing that, I want you to report to the clinic and have Doctor Which check out your medicine levels."

"I won't do it! You think I'm crazy!"

"Do you want to me to tell people about how you broke into that locked apartment after Milly Kett died, and all the other stuff?"

Maude's mouth fell open. "I never broke into her apartment."

"Oh, come on, Maude. First you deny writing me that note, and now this. You admitted everything else. 'Fess up."

"I didn't break into any apartment. I didn't write a note. I swear it!"

Laura studied the old woman's face. Her instincts told her something she didn't want to realize: Maude was telling the truth.

Which meant only one thing: There was someone else.

"Go to the clinic," Laura said woodenly.

"Oh, all right," Maude said, and slumped off, pouting.

New suspicions filling her mind, Laura carried her papers to the Xerox room. She wondered what had made her think that reviewing them at home would help clarify anything. Every time she thought some aspect of the situation had been cleared up, something else happened to set her back.

If Maude Thuringer hadn't gotten into the Kett unit, then who had? If she really hadn't written the note, who else was involved?

The Xerox room door was unlocked as usual. She pushed it open and went in.

Someone had left the overhead light on, and there was stale cigarette smoke in the air. The Xerox machine had been used recently, and the lid left standing open.

That was when Laura noticed that all four drawers of her cabinet stood open an inch or so.

Tingling with shock, she knelt to pull the bottom drawer all the way out. Her heart began to beat faster. The folders she hadn't taken home had been pulled out and jumbled.

She quickly opened the other drawers, verifying her sinking sensation.

Somebody had gone through everything.

Flipping through the folders that had been left in the bottom drawer, she tried to tell if anything had been removed. Everything seemed to be here, but it had all been riffled.

Laura knelt in front of the cabinet, feeling sick. She realized that almost anyone could have done this. Residents sometimes sneaked back here to make unauthorized free copies. Several staff members used the machine regularly for legitimate business. The location of the room at the remote end of a side service corridor made it possible to come and go at almost any time of day without being observed by anyone. Thinking about it now, Laura also realized that she had no way of knowing how many people might have seen her in here at some time or another—might have watched her take the key from behind the cabinet, and thus know how to retrieve it to get into the files on their own.

Locking up, Laura hurried to the clinic. She found Kay Svendsen alone.

"Hi, Laura. You look pale. Are you sick?"

"Kay, has Maude been by?"

"She's in with Fred now. Why?"

"Nothing. I need to talk to her. Glad you opened up early."

"I needed to check on Judge Young. I had a call at home. Mrs. Mullins, from the kitchen staff, took him his dinner last night and thought I ought to have a look at him first thing."

Laura remembered what she had learned about his cancer treatments. "He's worse?"

"I can't tell. I don't think so. Still that chest cold. I'm going to ask Fred to look in on him later."

"Keep me informed, will you?"

"Sure."

"Oh, Kay? You use the Xerox machine a lot on a regular basis, don't you?"

"Sure. Every day at least a couple of times, duping patient files, and so on. Why?"

"On any of your trips into the Xerox room, have you ever noticed anybody muddling around my file cabinet in there?"

"Nobody in particular. Mrs. Epperman, of course. Francie. Mrs. Mullins runs off new recipes in there sometimes. Mr. Pfeister is always in there with some of his stocks and bonds transactions, letters, all kinds of things. I've caught Davilla Rose in there a few times, running copies of what I strongly suspect are dirty poems. But nobody unusual, if that's what you mean. Why?"

Before Laura could reply, the examining room door opened and Maude Thuringer came out with Dr. Which behind her. "You'll be fine," he was telling her.

Maude saw Laura. "There. You see? He says I'm fine."

Laura simply blurted it out. "Maude, have you been in my files?"

The old woman looked truly shocked. "No!"

Laura studied her closely. Again she had that strong, sinking feeling that Maude was telling the absolute truth.

She wished devoutly that she felt otherwise.

LEAVING THE CLINIC, Laura headed for the central kitchen. Maybe nothing had been taken from the filing cabinet, but that made no difference. There was someone else at work here besides Maude.

Someone, she thought, must have realized that she was screening residents and trying to build case files on those who saw her individually or attended a group. The intruder had wanted badly to know what she had collected—wanted it badly enough to be obvious about the intrusion and alert her to the fact that her files were no longer safe. It was almost as if someone were saying, Catch me if you can.

On the way to the kitchen she passed housekeeping, where she found two maids on duty. Laura checked over their cleaning schedules with them. Then she went on to the kitchen, where she found the staff bustling around to get breakfast to the dining room.

"Can we talk, Mrs. Knott?" she asked apologetically.

"I'm real busy," the big woman complained, shoveling pancakes onto platters.

"I just need to make sure we're all set for the Halloween dinner and party snacks Wednesday night."

Mrs. Knott gave her a fierce look and stopped what she was doing to stalk across the kitchen to a clipboard on a nail on the far wall. She jerked it down and waved it under Laura's nose. "We're about as ready as we're going to be! Did you *see* some of the balderdash that sex kitten thought she could get us to prepare on a moment's notice?"

"I haven't seen the menu," Laura said, stepping back a pace.

Knott waved the board again. "Pumpkin ice cream. Pumpkin *ice cream?* Who ever heard of pumpkin ice cream? And did you see this part down here? She wants cupcakes with orange icing and black *what* on them?"

Laura studied the list Mrs. Knott shoved at her. "Masks," she said. "It looks like it says black masks."

"How," Knott bellowed, "do you put *masks on a cup-cake?*"

"I don't think she means real masks, Mrs. Knott. I think she must mean to use black cake icing, and paint little Lone Ranger masks on the orange icing on top."

"I can't do that! What makes her think I can do that? Doing that would take all afternoon, and half those people can't focus close enough to see something like that anyway." Mrs. Knott bent over Francie Blake's list again. "And look at this! Am I reading right? *Pumpkinburgers?*"

"It looks like she attached a recipe."

"I can't do pumpkinburgers! I *won't* do pumpkinburgers! That girl is going to be the death of me. Why doesn't she just stay in her office, plucking her eyebrows or admiring herself in the mirror? Every time she does work, she ruins my entire week."

"Mrs. Knott, I'm sorry, no kidding."

Sue Mullins, working nearby, smiled sweetly. "We can manage. We always do."

"*You're* not responsible for last-minute screwups," Mrs. Knott grunted.

"Sorry, guys," Laura said, and headed for the door.

Mrs. Knott called after her, "Will you tell Mrs. Epper-man I would like to have an appointment with her when she comes in?"

Laura turned back. "Sure will. Do you want to talk to Francie, too, about this menu?"

"About what? About pumpkinburgers and Lone Ranger cupcakes? I'll be damned if I'll even discuss it with that little stripper."

Laura retreated.

By the time she returned to the front desk, some two dozen residents had shown up. Some were scattered around the atrium, having quiet conversations as usual, and others had filtered into the dining area, where lights now glowed for the breakfast hour. It was all perfectly calm, perfectly normal. But the file break-in had reignited all the fears. She felt suspicions again of everyone.

She was still trying to think logically, and not getting very far, when the front doors swung open and Still Bill Mills came in. Clad in bib overalls and a sweatshirt, with heavy boots, he had a fishing pole and tackle box in his hands. He came to the counter and put his gear on the floor. "Back from fishing this morning. Got kind of cold. Think I'll go home and take me a hot shower, then change, be back in an hour or two. I just wanted to check with you first."

Laura managed to wrestle her mind into the routine. "Bill, I haven't seen any sign of work yet on the talent platform, and we'll need to rent some extra folding chairs."

Still Bill scanned the atrium with his good eye. "Plenty of time. We've got it all laid out on the work schedule."

"This is Monday. The party is day after tomorrow."

"I know, I know. Rome wasn't burned in a day, you know."

Laura gave up. "Did you catch any fish?"

"No, but then I didn't expect to. I never do, or seldom. But when I'm tense and all, fishing is my favoritism. It's probably except for football my number one primate. I find it real relaxtionary."

Laura watched Ellen Smith cross the far doorway to the dining room. Once, she thought, Stonewall Jackson would have been her candidate for genuine crazy if someone had asked. But Ellen Smith...there had been that furious scene about the melting ice sculpture, for one thing....

"Miz Michaels? Hello?"

"What? Oh, I'm sorry, Bill. I got distracted for a minute."

Still Bill nodded and picked up his gear. "Don't worry about the stuff for talent night. Don't you realize I'll have it all A-number-one, since I'm personally performing this time?"

Laura studied his lantern-jawed, stubble-bearded face to see if he was kidding. He wasn't. "What are you doing, Bill?"

"My harmonica, of course. I've never had any ineptitude for anything else, musicalwise."

"But you've never performed here, have you?"

His face twisted like he had tasted something sour. "Nope, and I sure wouldn't this time, but Miz Blake said we're real short of talent for this show. I like to watch the people. They have fun. If my blowing will give them some fun, why, who am I to hang back?"

Laura continued to watch the constant play of feeling across his beat-up, expressive face. "You really like all these people, don't you, Bill. I mean, it isn't just a job."

"I like 'em. Or I wouldn't be here."

She decided she had to take the chance. "Bill, if there was ever anything unusual going on around here, and I needed you to help me in some way to straighten it out, would you help me?"

He turned both eyes to her. "Why, surely I would."

"And not mention it to anyone else."

"Not if you said no. Say, you know, this place has been *different* since you came to work here, and I like it. I surely do. Mrs. Epperman is okay, but she is what you might call a...uh...you know, a dogmatic. Miz Blake is cute as a bug's ear, but she don't relate to the people the way you do naturally, even with all her giggling and prancing and posing around. So if you want help, Miz Michaels, on anything, you just say the word. I'm your man."

Laura knew she was taking a risk. The feeling of paranoia was so strong now that she wasn't even sure she could trust this man, although her every instinct said he was entirely trustworthy. But she had to trust someone. "Bill, someone broke into my filing cabinet in the Xerox room."

Still Bill jerked and stared hard at her. "You're kidding me."

"I wish I were."

"Somebody broke into your cabinet?"

"They used my hidden key."

Still Bill shook his head. "That makes me sick. Sometimes I wonder what the world is coming to. Durned old fools, meddle in everything. I mean, it's not like you was some stranger, or an advert. Why, you've been here long enough now, a lot of us think of you like a permanent fixation."

"You've never seen anybody messing around near my files, have you?"

"No, I sure haven't. Of course I don't go in there too much. I avoid that machine all the time, if not most. Them machines give off ultraviolent rays, I heard. I shun 'em."

"It was a long shot anyway. Thanks, Bill. But listen, if you happen to hear anybody mention anything about my files, or about my counseling sessions, just let me know, on the QT, okay?"

"Okay. Sure. I sure will." He frowned again and scratched his head. "I'll try to think back, too. If there's anything I might have noticed that I didn't think about. Now and again something will happen, you know, that when you look back on it later, knowing other stuff, you wonder if at the time you didn't have partial hypnosis."

"Bill."

"Yessum."

"I'd appreciate it very, very much if you didn't mention this to anyone."

"I won't. My lips are sewed."

"I really appreciate it."

Still Bill awkwardly patted her arm. "Hey, I can tell you're upset. Try and stay calm. Whatever made somebody look in your files, I'll bet we can catch 'em at it the next time. I'll think about that, too. If somebody is out to give you a hard time, we'll catch 'em at it one way or t'other. There's always more than one way to eat a cat."

"Thanks, Bill."

He rummaged in his shirt pocket, came up with a crumpled cigarette, stuck it between his lips, and turned toward the doors. "Don't mention it."

Watching him shamble away, Laura wondered how valuable an ally he might be. She knew that his cockeyed appearance and malapropisms led most people to dismiss him as an oaf. In some worlds he might have been. But he had been here since the start of Timberdale; she had seen him easily deal with people problems that would have taxed the ingenuity of a psychologist, and how he juggled all his jobs—enough for five employees—was beyond her. He was a priceless asset, and far from as dumb as he often seemed. It felt good to have him on her side.

But then she had another unwelcome thought. Still Bill Mills could not be eliminated entirely from any mental list she might make of possible suspects. He had access, he could go anywhere without being questioned, he was a smoker, and he was intelligent enough to fool people if he wished.

She wished she hadn't thought of it.

WITH ALL HER suspicions alive again, Laura had reviewed her own profile of a theoretical killer. She was not sure it helped, but as it assumed clearer shape in her thoughts, maybe more would become apparent.

The culprit, if he or she existed, was either a resident or staff member of Timberdale. That person knew the residents and knew the layout of the physical plant, including room assignments. He—maybe it was a she, but Laura would say he in her thoughts—could move around the complex without drawing undue attention to himself. He was a smoker. He was intelligent and wily, capable of hatching and repeatedly carrying out a means of murder that no one would suspect. He was methodical, cautious, and ruthless, although his motive for killing was obscure. He was probably compulsive and obsessive, given to the repetition of meaningless activities and personal rituals. He probably had little sense of right or wrong, and could justify anything, be it burglary or murder. He might be a mercy killer, focusing on people who were known to have terminal illnesses that could become painful in the extreme. Given this kind of thought process, he would undoubtedly be ready to kill again if need be, and would also feel justified in taking out anyone he suspected of having the potential to catch him. Whatever his motives, he could not have gone undetected this long if he did not have a deceptive routine exterior, probably a quiet, self-effacing, and friendly manner, perhaps even an inordinately religious or philanthropic aspect to his personality so no one could ever suspect him of anything evil.

Which was all well and good, but it didn't narrow the Timberdale population very much. Laura could think of about forty residents who might be considered candidates.

By this time, breakfast was well under way. But a walk through the dining room confirmed that Judge Emil Young had not come down. Remembering a day when another resident didn't come down, Laura dialed his room number with fingers that felt like ice.

A woman's voice answered. "Yes?"

Laura recognized the voice instantly: Ellen Smith. "I'm sorry, Ellen. This is Laura at the desk. I meant to dial Judge Young."

"This is his room," Smith said, sounding crabby as usual.

Laura was more puzzled. "What, uh...is the judge all right?"

"I just walked back upstairs with him from the clinic. He's feeling poorly."

"Is Dr. Which coming to see him?"

"Yes, but Kay said his lungs are clear. He's just run down. He's going to take it easy. I called the kitchen and Mrs. Mullins is going to bring him up a tray."

"Are you going to stay with him awhile?"

"Do I look like Florence Nightingale?"

"I think I'll come up and tell him hello."

"Suit yourself." Ellen Smith abruptly hung up.

THE JUDGE'S DOOR, solid oak like all the others at the far end of Two West, was solidly closed. Laura pressed the button beside the knob and heard the chime sound inside. There was no response at first, but then Mrs. Mullins opened the door to her.

"Hi, Sue. How is he feeling?"

Mrs. Mullins's expression changed to the sad, complaining expression that Laura had begun to expect from her. "Not well, Ms. Michaels. He's in bed. I just brought his breakfast."

"I'll just say hello to him and make sure he doesn't need anything."

The large, bony woman looked dubious. "I shouldn't stay, if I were you. He's quite low."

Laura nodded and brushed by her to walk through the dining room and to the bedroom door.

The old judge was propped up in his bed with several pillows. A kitchen tray had been arranged across his knees, and he was sitting there asleep, his cereal, fruit, toast, and coffee untouched.

"Judge?" Laura said softly.

The old man's rheumy eyes slowly opened. His head turned slowly. "Hello," he muttered. Then he straightened slightly. "Fine morning."

Laura went into the bedroom. "We heard you were under the weather. I just wanted to see if there's anything you need."

"No, no. I have no reason for complaint. This is a temporary indisposition, which, while causing a modicum of discomfort, will I am sure soon abate."

Laura studied him closely. His color seemed more normal, and there was the slightest twinkle in his tired eyes. "You look a little better."

The old man smiled at that. "A scintilla of improvement, yes. I am greatly encouraged, and planning a splendid appearance at the Halloween festivities Wednesday night."

Grinning, Laura looked at Sue Mullins and saw her responsive flush of pleasure. He *did* seem better.

The judge rumbled, "No need for you to entertain a moment's disquietude, I assure you."

"You let us know immediately if there's anything you need," Laura told him.

"Indubitably." The judge lowered his chin slowly back onto his chest.

Laura backed out of the bedroom and met Mrs. Mullins in the hall. The gaunt woman smiled wanly. "He's so strong. I think he's going to get better."

"I do, too," Laura agreed. "We sure need to keep a close eye on him."

"Don't worry. All of us will. I'll stay with him now during his meal."

Laura gave the woman a quick hug of appreciation and hurried back downstairs. The poor old judge, she thought. A terminal illness people were not supposed to know about, and now a turn for the worse. Just like Cora Chandler, facing a lingering death. Just like—

She stopped on the staircase as the thought crystallized.

Was it possible that terminal illness was a trigger for someone here?

If that was so, then the judge had just become the next likely target.

TWENTY

"WHAT HAVE you done so far?" Aaron Lassiter asked grimly that afternoon when Laura tracked him down on the telephone.

Laura looked up from her desk, making sure none of the visiting residents around the atrium were in hearing range. She said in a low tone, "He's definitely a little stronger, but Fred Which says he isn't out of the woods yet by any means."

"Won't he put the judge in the hospital?"

"I tried to convince him to do that. The judge argued against it. His hospitalization insurance is maxed out for the year already. Fred was reluctant anyway. He's been catching it from the hospital about iffy Medicare cases and unpaid bills."

Lassiter's voice over the telephone got an edge to it. "Isn't there someplace else to send him?"

"*Where,* Aaron? I mean, just tell me where."

Pause. Then, "Of course if he's better—even if your theory is correct—he may be safe."

"Maybe so," Laura agreed uncertainly. "Anyway, we're okay for a night or two."

"How's that?"

"I arranged for our nurse, Kay Svendsen, to stay over and sleep on the couch in his living room."

Lassiter sounded astonished. "Old Blood-and-Guts approved of that?"

"She doesn't know about it."

"*What?*"

"Nobody knows about it," Laura admitted. "I worked

it out with Kay. She doesn't know the real reason. She thinks I'm concerned about his health and a possible downturn in the night."

"How," Lassiter's voice asked in amazement, "do you keep it from the dictator?"

"We just don't tell her."

"How did you explain that to this nurse?"

"I didn't," Laura admitted lamely. "Look, Kay thinks she owes me one. She got the impression somehow that I saved her job when she knocked our elderly lothario down and broke his leg. I didn't really do that much. I just—well, that doesn't matter. I let Kay think that. She figures she's repaying me this way."

Lassiter's sigh was audible. "What do you do if he's the same tomorrow? And the day after that? And the day after that?"

"He'll either get better, and maybe not be a likely target, or he'll get worse and have to go to the hospital," Laura replied. As she spoke, she knew how flimsy it all was.

TUESDAY MORNING:

"Is he any better, Fred?"

Dr. Fred Which frowned and diddled the stethoscope hanging around his neck. "The same, I would say."

"Should he be admitted now?"

"I can't justify it. Laura. We'll just take it a day at a time—wait and see."

TUESDAY AFTERNOON:

"Sure," Kay Svendsen said glumly. "I intended all along to stay with him again tonight. But this could be a chronic condition now, Laura. We can't do this stopgap care much longer. He's just going to have to have a practical nurse of his own."

"We'll talk to him about that," Laura promised. "But can you help just this one more night, Kay? Please?"

"Sure," Svendsen repeated. "But then we're going to have to make other arrangements. As much as I love the old guy, I can't keep this up."

TUESDAY EVENING:

Sitting in Laura's kitchen, Aaron Lassiter shook his head slowly back and forth over his coffee cup. "There's no way we could assign a man to guard his door. My God, Laura, there's no proof of anything. We don't have that kind of manpower anyway."

"I don't know why I even mentioned it," Laura admitted. "I've even thought about the possibility of hiring an off-duty policeman or something."

"Who would pay for that?"

"I don't know."

"What the hell would people out there think?"

"I don't know."

"How could you explain it?"

"I don't *know*."

Lassiter looked at his watch with an expression of regret. "I've got to get going."

Laura walked him to the apartment door.

"What," she asked, "if I'm right? What if he gets worse, and it attracts the killer, and there's another murder?"

"Then maybe *then*, somehow, we can take action," Lassiter said glumly.

"After he's *dead*? That's insane."

His lips quirked in a humorless smile. "That's the way the system works, almost all the time."

"Oh, my God."

He gave her a quick, unhappy hug. "Just hope you're imagining things."

"That's all?"

"Well, I'll be there tomorrow night, anyway. Maybe by then something will have changed."

"Like what?"

"I don't know."

"Aaron, am I being crazy?"

Lassiter did not smile. "I don't know."

WEDNESDAY MORNING:

"Hi, Laura. Say, you look cuter than anything this morning!"

"You're sweet, Fred. About the judge—"

"Today's the big party day, right? Getting excited about everything Francie has set up for the costume gala and all, are you?"

"Sure, Fred, about the judge—"

"Oh, yes, the judge. I was just up there, Laura."

"And?"

"I hate to tell you this, but I think some of the congestion is deepening. I've increased the antibiotics, but it's just hard to tell. I intend to keep a close eye on him. If he goes any further downhill, he goes into the hospital whether he wants to go or not."

"Will you make that decision today?"

"Unless he takes a decided turn for the worse, I'll try to give it another day or two. But anyone could look at him this morning and see that yesterday's progress was temporary. I'm concerned about him."

"Then why not just put him in the hospital now?"

Which smiled condescendingly and patted her shoulder. "Honeybunch, you have to understand these senior citizens. If I ordered him into the hospital now, after all our earlier discussions about it, he would be *sure* I thought he was at death's door; the fear itself might be enough to make him far, far worse. Believe me. I know what I'm doing."

Laura walked away, her fear increased.

She needed to make other arrangements for people to keep a close eye on the judge now. Mentally she scanned her own schedule, and how often she might be able to look in on him. Sue Mullins was sure to be willing to help, maybe Stacy Miller could be bribed into looking in on him a few times in the night, Kay would surely check him late before going home and then first thing every morning, perhaps Still Bill and even Francie could become part of an irregularly timed schedule of frequent drop-ins.

They wouldn't have to know there even was a schedule, or about the growing fear that made Laura wish she could make it continuous, around the clock.

What more can I do? She didn't know. Deep inside she felt frantic. Maybe it was all a fantasy and the judge was perfectly safe. She wanted to believe that. She tried. She couldn't.

TWENTY-ONE

STILL BILL MILLS and two of his college boys were still arranging piles of corn shucks around the pumpkins in the atrium when the first Timberdale resident appeared in costume at 4:45 Wednesday afternoon. Standing nervously near the office area, Laura couldn't figure out who it was.

The small man, wearing a Victorian-style brown suit with a cutaway coat and vest, derby hat, and gray spats, hopped out of the west elevator and hurried across the carpeted area toward Laura. A giant handlebar mustache, not glued on quite straight, obscured his mouth and nose, where pince-nez eyeglasses perched precariously. He had a silver-headed walking stick in one hand and a five-inch magnifying glass in the other.

"Laura," he chirped. "Where's your costume? We have to talk."

"Good Lord," Laura groaned. "Maude, I would have never recognized you."

"Right," Maude Thuringer said excitedly, trying to adjust her mustache without effect. "You know who I am?"

"You mean who you're supposed to be? No."

"Oh, come on. Isn't it obvious?" Maude whipped the magnifying glass up to her eye, making it appear the size of a basketball. "*Now* who am I?"

Laura didn't have a clue.

"Hercule Poirot," Maude cried. "Who else? Where's your costume?"

"It's back in the office. I'll put it on in a little while."

Maude grabbed her arm and pulled her down closer for a conspiratorial whisper. "Isn't this *great*? If there's a killer in our midst, a costume party is *exactly* the place where he'll strike again. It always happens that way. I heard Francie tell the Castles that some highway patrol trooper has a hot crush on her, and he's coming tonight in uniform. That will be good. He can help us crack the case. Have you heard anything about that?''

"I think," Laura murmured, "it's a deputy sheriff."

"Great! Even better! Now Laura, listen carefully. My list of suspects has been narrowed. You're off of it now, you'll be happy to know."

"Maude, I can't begin to thank you enough. Now—"

"There are plenty without you. We've got Ellen, Stonewall, Davilla, Ken Keen—he's back on it again, I reconsidered—Kay Svendsen, Still Bill, Sue Mullins, and maybe somebody else. We have got to keep an eye out tonight. When Francie's boyfriend gets here, do you want to fill him in, or shall I?"

"Maybe I ought to do that," Laura replied.

The front doors of the atrium puffed open, and an astounding spectacle rolled in: a two-ton fairy godmother, all in sparkly white, with a broad hooped skirt, tinsel halo, tiny white plastic wings, and either a Star Wars sword or magic wand of poor design. The red-framed glasses on a chain gave her away. It was Judith Epperman.

"Yikes!" Maude Thuringer exclaimed. "I'd better circulate. Keep your eyes open. If you see a clue, raise both hands. I'll respond by scratching my head like this. Got it? Good. Isn't this great?" With that, she turned and rushed across the atrium toward the dining room, where the kitchen staff had started putting out small, lighted plastic pumpkins and what looked like candy apples.

The fairy godmother marched over. "Laura, why aren't you in costume? Still Bill is behind schedule. Isn't there supposed to be a large lighted pumpkin in the foyer? When are they going to get the microphone and amplifier on the stage for the talent show?''

''I've been busy, but I'll put it on in a minute,'' Laura said.

''What? What?''

''You asked about my costume.''

''Drat your costume! Why are we so behind schedule?''

''We're almost ready. I just talked to Still Bill.''

''What about the kitchen?'' Mrs. Epperman slammed her plastic wand against the edge of the counter. ''Drat! Why doesn't *anything* get done around here unless I supervise it myself?'' She flew off toward the dining area.

Laura went to the telephone and dialed the clinic number. Kay Svendsen answered promptly.

''I just wanted to make sure you looked in on the judge,'' Laura said.

''Yes, and I don't think he's feeling any better, but he was getting dressed. He says he intends to come down for the dinner part of the party, at least.''

''He's still running a fever?''

''A degree or so, yes, but I don't think he's contagious, and he insists on coming down.''

Laura nodded. If the judge put in an appearance, maybe it would give the impression that he was better than he was. ''I'll try to keep an eye on him while he's down here.''

''I'm going back up in a while and walk down with him,'' Svendsen said. ''I'll stick close, too. He really is pretty weak. If he isn't better by tomorrow, I'm going to talk him into going to the hospital if I have to break one of his legs, too.''

''Well, gosh, Kay, we all know you're good at that sort of stuff.''

Svendsen snorted and hung up.

Turning from the telephone, Laura saw the maintenance crew removing their ladders and brushing up around their "pumpkin patches." Still Bill Mills caught her gaze and sent her an okay signal, thumb and index finger forming a circle. She glanced at the clock. Time to climb into costume.

She had put her things in Mrs. Epperman's office. Collecting them, she went down the inside corridor to the female staff rest room and quickly changed. Intent on avoiding Francie's Cinderella suggestion at all costs, she had gone to another costume shop. They hadn't had a lot left in her rental price range. What she had gotten was a Pocahontas outfit, or possibly the mascot of some obscure college. The fake buckskin dress itched. It fit fairly well except that it was slightly large in the bust and slightly tight in the rear end. The skirt caught her at midthigh, but that was okay; the moccasins surprisingly flattered her legs in the dark panty hose, and if she was going to have any chance against Marie Antoinette tonight, she needed all the help she could get.

Bright plastic beads around her neck completed the outfit. After running a brush through her hair and touching up her lipstick, she inspected herself in the mirror. The costume looked just a little like what Ellen Smith wore every day. But not bad, everything considered.

After taking her normal clothes to the office, she returned to the atrium and found it a different place, transformed by the magical arrival of many of the residents. Their voices echoed softly around the vastness of the space, and the variety of costumes made for a welter of color and interest.

A few wore only masks. Laura instantly identified the people behind Vanna White and Ronald Reagan; their matching Nike sweats gave away the Castles. Nearby, Stonewall Jackson was wearing a Mickey Mouse mask and ears, but her clipboard gave her away. Ken Keen had decked himself out in cowboy regalia, complete with Lone Ranger mask, ten-gallon hat, and a big plastic six-shooter that looked frighteningly real, but he hadn't found a way to camouflage his heavy white leg cast and crutches. As more residents and guests streamed in, Laura counted three ghosts in sheets, two football players, two Hulk Hogans, and two Bert Lahr Cowardly Lions. She saw a witch, a riverboat gambler, a nurse, a Superman, and a host of 1920s costumes. The Pfeisters came by, he in a grand twenties-style suit and straw skimmer, she in a little beaded dress and dark velvet cloche.

"You look great," Laura told them.

"You know who we are?" Dot Pfeister asked, clinging to her husband's arm. "Jay Gatsby. And Daisy."

Julius Pfeister nodded, neck wattles bobbing. "You look splendid too, Laura. That's a splendid Daisy Mae outfit."

Still Bill Mills reappeared, this time in his costume: Mr. Greenjeans, but with a Howdy Doody falseface. Another witch showed up, and two Darth Vaders, slinking along in their black cloaks and shiny black cardboard helmets.

In a little while the bell sounded softly for the beginning of the evening meal, and the colorful entourage began moving that way. Laura joined them and was almost having a good time for the moment, but then the front doors opened and Francie Blake made her entrance. Heads turned. Conversations stopped. Possibly a few old male hearts stopped momentarily, too. *Oh no,* Laura thought, totally defeated.

Francie looked like a *Playboy* cover shot. Her empire gown might or might not have been authentic, but it had never seen the inside of a rental costume shop. It would have caused a stampede of fashion photographers at an Academy Awards function: pristine white, alive with tiny seed pearls, it flowed and glowed as Francie glided into the atrium, diamonds blazing on a neckline that plunged to Dallas. A tiny sky-blue mask over Francie's eyes only emphasized their glow. In full makeup, her hair cascading to her shoulders in elegant ringlets, she was so stunning—such a

dream out of a romantic storybook—that even Laura
gasped.

That was when Laura saw the figure who came in immediately behind this vision: a tall, handsome man in a
deputy sheriff's uniform, no mask of any kind hiding the
addled look in his eyes. Aaron Lassiter looked like he had
been to the mountain and had his vision, and it was a good,
a life-changing, experience.

Laura turned and headed for the dining room, holding
her head high. Her stupid costume brushed her legs, making
them itch.

The Pfeisters and an unidentified Bart Simpson had taken
their food to a corner table. Laura grabbed a pork chop and
baked apple and joined them. Snow White waved from an
adjacent table. Darth Vader sat down nearby, removed his
plastic helmet, and became a sweaty Ellen Smith. Kay
Svendsen, *her* Darth Vader helmet in hand, entered with
Judge Emil Young, unsteady but gamely hanging on to her
arm.

Marie Antoinette, or the good fairy, or the supreme sex
goddess, or whatever she was supposed to be, moved magically from table to table, dragging Aaron Lassiter in her
glorious wake, making introductions, batting her eyelashes,
clinging to his arm, and telling everyone how darling they
looked. Lassiter spied Laura and shot her a despairing look.
Laura was aware of how intensely glad she was to see him
for two entirely different reasons. But seeing him so dazed
in Francie's clutches made her almost gag on her pork
chop.

TWENTY-TWO

"WHY DIDN'T YOU save me a seat at your table?" Aaron Lassiter muttered in Laura's ear as they watched the party-goers take their seats for the talent show.

"You were busy," Laura said bitterly.

"I couldn't help it that we happened to drive in at the same time. What was I supposed to do? Drive around the block until she had gone inside?"

Laura felt like a pimply teenager about to burst into tears at her first prom. "Please don't touch me. This dumb dress itches."

Up on the platform arranged for the talent, Mr. Green-jeans was tapping the microphone to make sure everything was ready. The wide-body fairy godmother lurched around, directing people to chairs. Aaron Lassiter exhaled loudly, dejectedly. "I better get over there near the door, where we agreed I'd watch."

"Okay," Laura said, all the wind going out of her sails. "Thanks. I feel a lot better with you here."

"I wish I felt like you did," Lassiter said, and stomped away.

Judge Young, still hanging on to Kay Svendsen, limped over. "I feel a bit debilitated," he wheezed. "I could stay, but I think it would be wiser for me to call it a night."

Laura noticed his clammy pallor and, worse, his failure to be polysyllabic. He was feeling bad, all right. "You were great to come down at all, judge."

"I'm taking him up," Kay Svendsen said, "and then I'm getting out of this Vader outfit. I'm burning up under this cloak."

"Coming back down then?"

"Yes."

Judge Young gave her a sad smile. "Sorry to miss the rest of the fun."

On impulse, Laura leaned forward and gave him a hug, then watched him move slowly toward the back of the atrium with Kay Svendsen helping him. The old man looked worse, and Laura wondered if they could wait until Friday to insist that he check into the hospital.

A smattering of applause drew her attention back to the platform.

Incandescent in the spotlight, Francie Blake tripped prettily onto the small wooden platform. She grasped the microphone stand and turned up her smile another five thousand watts. She was a vision.

"Hi, there, everybody! Isn't this *fun?*"

The cowboy applauded enthusiastically, and the ghosts and lions joined in.

"Okay!" Francie bubbled. "Now let's get this show under way! For our first great act this evening we have a rare treat for all of you. You all know him, but I bet most of you didn't know he's a musician, as well as a caregiver. Here he is, playing his accordion, our own terrific doctor, Dr. Fred Which!"

A smattering of surprised applause greeted Dr. Which, in red plaid summer shirt and jeans, bolting out of the front alcove where he had been hiding with his oversize accordion. Strapped to his front, the instrument looked heavy enough to pitch the good doctor over on his face. He made it onto the platform, however, where Francie effusively draped herself over the gleaming squeeze box to aim a kiss in the general direction of his chin.

Already shiny with nervous perspiration, the doctor unsnapped the straps that held the accordion closed, drew the bellows partway open, and launched into his first number.

It wasn't Dick Contino, but it was the right song: "Lady of Spain." To Laura's surprise, it wasn't half bad.

From her place near the elevators, she could study the faces of the residents in the crowd. She couldn't see more than half of them because of the masks. The Darth Vader costumes must be the most uncomfortable ones in the house, because another of the Vaders, Stella Northington, had vanished for a while and come back in normal clothes, leaving only one archvillain left. Ellen Smith was not a quitter, and she sat near the back with her shiny black helmet stubbornly covering her head. Vanna White and Ronald Reagan were holding hands. The woman behind Davilla Rose in the fourth row kept bobbing to the right and then to the left, trying to see the stage around Davilla's tall, black, peaked hat. Colonel Roger Rodgers, in a Confederate colonel's uniform, sat ramrod straight. The Castles discreetly went out the back way, heading for the rest rooms where they would get into their square-dance costumes; they were next on the talent list.

Continuing her scan, Laura spotted Lassiter where he had stationed himself in the shadows of the entryway. Francie had found him, too, and stood close beside him, talons dug into his bare arm. Lassiter seemed to be having trouble keeping his eyes away from Francie's cleavage. An idea came to Laura's mind, but she realized instantly that it wouldn't work: using an AK-47 at this range, she would not only take out Aaron but also probably half the people in the atrium. Now, a hunting rifle with a telescopic sight....

The violence of her own jealousy surprised Laura, especially given all the more serious things she had to worry about. She tried to ignore it. First things first, she told herself, and don't let yourself get in an uproar. After all, you didn't know him that well yet. No one is perfect. He must have faults. Just because he's tall and dark and handsome and quiet and careful and intelligent and sensitive, and likes Trissie, he *must* have faults.

And right now Laura had to stay focused on her worry, and her plan for coping with it.

The applause was so sustained for Dr. Which's accordion that Francie Blake tripped prettily onto the stage, gave him another effusive hug, and asked him to do an encore. Everybody seemed to like the idea. The doctor, red-faced with pleasure, mopped his brow and threw himself into another golden oldie, "Roll Out the Barrel." He was only as far as "we'll have the blues on the run," however, when it began to become apparent that he had strenuously rehearsed only one piece, and his encore was going to be something of a struggle.

Two minutes later, the Castles reappeared at the back of the atrium. She was wearing multiple short petticoats and a short, bright orange square-dancing skirt. He was in western clothes, too, a thin-cut plaid shirt that just managed to stretch over his little potbelly, bright blue jeans, and straw hat. Their white dancing shoes matched. They sidled along the wall to where Laura was standing.

"You guys look great."

Both of them looked nervous and apprehensive. "I don't know why we let ourselves be talked into this," Mrs. Castle fretted. "What if they laugh at us?"

"They're not going to laugh at you."

"The platform is too small. We can't do all our steps."

"Well, you could dance on the floor in front of the platform."

"No," Mrs. Castle moaned. "They couldn't see us."

"We'll be fine," Stoney said. "If we don't throw up."

Mrs. Castle didn't think it was funny. "You're sure the music will play fine through the sound system, Laura?"

"It worked fine when we tested it," Laura assured her. "Now, don't you worry."

Mrs. Castle looked down at her flowered white blouse. She had ribbons in her hair and around her wrists. "I *may* throw up."

Laura patted her arm and got out of there.

Onstage, Dr. Which struggled to the labored conclusion of his barrel rolling. The applause this time was considerably less enthusiastic. Francie Blake reappeared and gushed thanks, saying how wonderful he was, what a good sport, how he could always go on professional tour if he tired of being a doctor. The doctor left the stage to another mild round of called-for applause.

"And now," Francie's voice cried through the PA system, "we all know what fun square dancing can be! Well, we have a wonderful treat for you in that regard."

The Castles appeared onstage. Laura ducked behind the reception desk and knelt in front of the control panel for the sound system. The Castles' tape recorder was all set up. Mrs. Epperman bustled over. Her fairy godmother stuff stuck into Laura's back as she leaned close to make sure all the controls got adjusted correctly. Laura snapped on the switches for the wall speakers in the atrium, then pressed the recorder's "play" button. The country music started just fine, and the Castles began to do-si-do.

Mrs. Epperman breathed a sigh. "Look at them. Aren't they just too precious for words?"

Laura watched. The Castles whirled and turned, tapping vigorously.

"Now, are all the snackie-poos ready for intermission, Laura?"

"I'm sure they are. I talked to Mrs. Knott less than an hour ago."

"Go make sure, Laura, will you please?"

Laura grimly obeyed. She was greeted in the kitchen by dense, steamy warmth, bright overhead lights, and a bustle of activity. Mrs. Knott was still arranging fruit trays, and three other women were putting them on carts, putting ice in punch, laying out row upon row of cupcakes, and lighting small orange candles.

"We doing okay?" Laura asked.

Mrs. Knott churned past her on the way to the walk-in freezer. "Looks like it, unless Tweetie Pie wants to make more changes."

Laura grinned at Sue Mullins, busy with the cupcakes. "None that I've heard about yet. Those look nice, Sue."

The lank woman nodded nervously. "I just wish I could have gotten the little icing masks nicer."

"They look just like the Lone Ranger. Don't worry about it."

Mrs. Knott churned back with a bucket of ice. "If you didn't vanish so often to go somewhere and smoke, Sue, maybe you could get all your work done on time."

"I'm hurrying," Sue Mullins replied fretfully.

Mrs. Knott glared at Laura. "If they call for this stuff to be brought out a minute before nine o'clock, I'm resigning!"

That made everything seem normal. Laura nodded and left. In the hall just outside, she encountered Kay Svendsen, back from Judge Young's room and again in her nurse's uniform.

"He okay?"

Svendsen looked worried. "Yes, but he shouldn't have come down earlier. He's really a lot weaker. I asked Still Bill to go up and adjust the ventilation a little, get more air in there."

Laura felt a quick stab of suspicious worry, followed by

guilt that she could be so paranoid. "I'm going up myself," she said.

Taking the stairs up to the second floor, she hurried down the hall, shoes whispering on the thick carpet. At Judge Young's door she tapped sharply, rather than sounding the interior chimes. Still Bill Mills opened up.

"Hi, Bill. Everything okay?"

"Yep. I got more air flow out of the louvres. He's asleep."

Intense relief. "Okay. Good."

"Almost my turn downstairs, is it?"

"Two or three more acts, then yours."

Still Bill sighed and removed a harmonica from his shirt pocket. "I don't know how I ever let myself get talked into this."

Laura grinned at him. "You'll wow them, Mr. Green-jeans."

"Well, I ain't all that bad. I been playing this thing a long time. Almost forty years."

"You're probably great."

"Well, I ain't great, but when I start something, I stick to it. I have never been one for premature withdrawal."

"Were you just leaving?"

"Yep. Don't want to miss my turn down there."

"Okay. I think I might stay here a few minutes to make sure everything is all right. I'll lock up when I come down."

"Want me to come back up right after?"

"I don't think that's necessary, Bill. I'll get Kay to come up later and check his vital signs again. If he doesn't seem fine, I guess we can always ask Dr. Which to send for an ambulance."

Still Bill nodded and left. Laura closed and locked the door behind him. Heading for the judge's bedroom, she was aware of the deep silence in the apartment, and how quiet it was in the entire wing with everyone downstairs for talent night.

Only a small table lamp lit the bedroom. The judge slept propped on two pillows in his rumpled bed. He snored gently. A wrinkled copy of the day's newspaper lay on the floor beside the bedside chair.

Laura watched the judge. His breathing was slow and steady, but with rasps in it. With his teeth out and his skimpy hair uncombed, in repose, he looked far older than he ever had when he sat in the atrium, leaning stolidly on his cane, sometimes dozing. In sleep he looked ancient, and very weak and vulnerable. Laura felt a rush of admiration for him. It was his spirit that held him together when he was awake; pride kept his facial muscles tight, and his intelligence and courage kept a light in his eyes except at times like this. Without his spirit shining through, he looked far weaker than he would have let anyone observe.

Suddenly a sound came from the other room: a faint rattling at the door. Startled, Laura sat up straight, heart thudding. The sound came again—a soft tapping sound at the apartment door.

Telling herself she was being melodramatic, Laura took a few deep breaths as she hurried to the door. Sue Mullins stood there, staring wide-eyed with surprise over the covered tray in her hands. "I didn't know if anybody would answer the door or not. I brought a snack for the poor judge, since he had to leave early."

"That was very thoughtful of you, Sue. Here. I'll take it. He's sleeping."

Mullins handed over the tray. "I guess I'd better hurry back. Mrs. Knott will have cats if she misses me. Thanks a lot."

"Thank you, Sue." Laura backed into the room and

closed and relocked the door. Leaving the tray on the dining-room table, she checked the judge again and found him sleeping peacefully, as before. How nice it would be, she thought, if everyone was as concerned as the Sue Mullinses of the world. And if there weren't crazies.

The judge continued to doze. He wouldn't hear anyone tapping or ringing at his door, wanting in. Maybe that made him safer than Cora or Milly had been. Laura had to believe that.

She checked her watch and then crept out of the apartment, double-locked the door, and hurried downstairs.

BY 10:00 O'CLOCK the talent show had begun to run disastrously long, and a few of the older residents had toddled off.

"I *knew* this would happen," Mrs. Epperman fumed. "I hate to say it, Laura, but this is all your fault. The final timetable was your responsibility. We can't all just sit back and expect poor little Francie to take care of *everything*. I'd better check on the punch myself. Sometimes I feel all alone in this operation."

Onstage, Davilla Rose doddered up to the microphone to do her poetry reading. Her peaked hat was badly askew. In the audience, a few grimaces were exchanged. Davilla always read, usually the same "original" poems.

Laura scanned the crowd, which had begun to thin out. Darth Vader still sat stubbornly in the back row. The Castles had gone. Pluto and Donald Duck, and one of the Hulk Hogans, were just trying to sneak out. Most of the others remained, including both Cowardly Lions.

Near the elevators, Aaron Lassiter remained at his position; Laura saw that he had his handi-talkie in one hand and Francie Blake in the other. More accurately, Lassiter seemed to be talking on his handi, and Francie seemed to be massaging his free arm. Laura thought about hand grenades.

Kay Svendsen reappeared. She had gone up to check again on the judge. She sent Laura an OK sign and sat down near Vader.

Davilla Rose's voice quavered over the sound system with the beginning of her readings: "I saw him once before/ As he passed close by my door,/ And then he came again/ With wit and might and main...." Nobody had ever accused her of being original.

Across the room, a frowning Aaron Lassiter finished talking on his handi-talkie, said something to Francie, and started around the periphery of the area, headed for Laura. Seeing his worried look, she went to meet him halfway, in the first-floor conversation area near the side hallway.

"Babe," he said morosely, "I've got to leave for a little while."

"Is anyone going with you?" Laura blurted, her worst fear getting out before she could muzzle it.

He looked puzzled. "What? No. I just had a call on my radio. There's been a bad wreck out on seventy-seven and they need me to help direct traffic until the ambulance and wreckers get there. I'll be back as soon as I can, okay?"

"Okay," Laura said, disappointed.

He headed for the front doors. Laura turned to go back the way she had come. Dr. Which was sitting in the end chair on the second row, and he signaled her as she started past. She slipped over and bent to hear what he had to say.

"Great show," he whispered, smiling.

"Thanks."

"Do you think it might be running a little long?"

Laura maintained her smile. "Gee, that hadn't occurred to me."

"I'm going to bug out shortly. I'll come by in the morning and look in on the judge again. But I think he's around the corner on this one. I've asked Kay to look in on him once more about midnight, just before she checks out for the night.''

"Okay, Fred, I appreciate it.''

The doctor shook his head. "I hope the old guy appreciates all the friends he has around here. You looking in on him...Bill Mills...Kay Svendsen, of course...Mrs. What's-her-name from the kitchen...Ellen Smith. I'll tell you what, the judge is getting checked almost as often here as he would at many hospitals.''

"I just hope he's all right, Fred.''

Which's Adam's apple plunked up and down again. "Say, you look tired and worried, babe. What time do you get off tonight? Want me to wait, and maybe come by your place for a late drink or something?''

"Another time, maybe, Fred, okay?''

Which sighed.

Laura headed back toward the reception desk. Mrs. Epperman stood behind the counter, still glowering. Not feeling ready for more chewing out, Laura veered away and headed for the women's staff rest room.

The cool, silent tile room was vacant and felt like a blessed refuge. Someone had been smoking, and the odor was faintly unpleasant, but Laura ignored it. She bent over a washbasin and wet a paper towel under the cold tap, squeezed it damp, and patted it on her face. She had the start of a headache, and her skin felt hot. Damn, her Indian maiden costume itched! Her reflection in the mirror looked flushed. Too much running around, she thought.

The door of the rest room opened behind her, and in the big mirror she saw Marie Antoinette. Marie readjusted her décolletage, which she had very nearly come out of entirely, and wrinkled her pretty little nose. "Pew! Someone has been smoking in here again. If it's that darned Sue Mullins and I catch her, I'll kill her.'' She hurried to the bowl beside Laura's, turned on the cold water until it gushed, then plunged both hands and wrists under the flow. A dew of hectic perspiration honeyed her upper lip. ''I'm about to burn up!''

''Well, you've been awfully busy, Francie. I noticed.''

Francie's heavily mascara'd eyes rolled her way, then back. ''It's the pressure. I've worked so hard on this party with practically no help from anyone. I *do* so want everything to turn out right tonight.''

''I bet you do,'' Laura said.

''Aaron had to run to a little auto accident.''

''Yes. I know.''

''But he promised to hurry right back.''

''Yes. I know.''

''God, he's the most exciting man I've met in *years*. Honestly! I mean, I thought Jeffrey was exciting, but Aaron puts *everyone* in the shade.''

Laura patted her face dry and got out of there. Walking to the back of the atrium area, she scanned the scene. Nothing seemed changed, except that Ellen Smith seemed to have given up and left.

On the platform, Davilla Rose was still reading. ''And so on that night, so late and dreary,/ While I labored, so tired, so weary…''

Laura glanced at her watch and decided she had time to look in on Judge Young one more time, just to be sure. She went to the elevator, found it waiting, and rode up to Two. Padding down the hallway again, she heard the faint smattering of applause from below. She was tired and strung out, and would be glad when this night was over.

Reaching Judge Young's door, she inserted the master

key and unlocked it. She stepped inside, walked quickly into the bedroom, and cried out.

Darth Vader stood at the judge's bedside.

THE JUDGE was still propped up, still asleep. On the far side of the bed, staring out of his ugly black plastic mask, Darth Vader took a half step backward in surprise. His big black plastic gloves had been tossed on the edge of the judge's bed; in one startlingly pale, thin hand that protruded from the tubular sleeve of his padded black jacket, Vader had a glittering medical instrument—a disposable hypodermic syringe. In his other hand—a woman's elderly, veiny hand—was a small glass vial of cloudy liquid.

"Ellen?" Laura gasped.

The plastic mask had a metallic mouthpiece in it that simulated Vader's mechanical sound. The person inside it issued an unrecognizable bark. "Go *away!*"

"Like hell I will!" Laura shot back, starting to recover from the initial shock. The emergency call button was right there beside her on the wall. She slammed her hand down on it, sending the signal.

Vader raised pale, skinny hands in front of his eyes and jabbed the needle of the syringe into the rubber cap on top of the small, evil-looking vial. The movement stirred the liquid in the medical container, making it cloudier.

"Stop it!" Laura said, and looked around for a weapon.

Her outcry made Judge Young start violently. His eyes opened. He stared in uncomprehending surprise at the figure looming over him. Vader retracted the plunger on the syringe, sucking fluid into its barrel. As Laura stared, transfixed for an instant by the sheer unreal terror of it, Vader shoved the vial into a cloak pocket and bent toward the judge.

The judge tried to roll to the other side of his bed. "Wait," he pleaded thickly.

Where the hell were the people responding to the emergency call? Maybe, with the party in progress, nobody would see the flashing light.

Which would be far too late. In another few seconds, Laura realized, this nightmare would see Vader plunge the needle into the judge's arm. Whatever the fluid was, Laura felt sure of one thing: it would kill the old man.

Frantic, she edged farther into the room.

"Stop!" Vader rasped.

Laura stopped. There had to be something in here she could use as a weapon, but the best thing—the table lamp—was on the far side of the bed, with Vader directly in the way.

"Don't do this," she pleaded. "You mustn't do this. Whatever you've done in the past, we can get you help. People are on the way now."

Judge Young rolled terrified eyes toward her. "What is all this? What are you doing here? Why—" He stopped, suddenly overcome by a paroxysm of violent coughing that doubled him over.

Vader reached down for his bare, skinny arm, needle poised.

Talk wasn't going to do it. Laura grabbed the straight chair inside the doorway. Swinging it over her head, she rushed around the foot of the bed, intent on braining Vader with it.

Vader looked up, jerking back. *"No!"* the metallic voice rasped, sounding masculine.

Laura swung. The weight was more than she could handle well. Vader moved to the side with shocking quickness, and the chair whistled past his helmet, a clean miss. The chair's weight carried Laura forward off-balance and she went to one knee. The chair hit the end table lamp, knocking it against the wall in a shower of glass and electrical sparks. Laura tried to recover—she let go of the chair and whirled to her feet, seeing Vader coming at her—but she was not fast enough. Vader slammed against her, knocking her against the side of the bed and then to the floor with an impact that knocked her breath out of her. Then—*my God, this is as bad as any nightmare*—Vader was right on top of her, his breath a harsh, metallic rasp through the mouthpiece of the mask, steel-cold hands at her throat, and sheer panic gave her the strength to tear the hands away, pound futilely at the slick black plastic of the helmet, shove Vader to the side, where he tumbled onto his side, his helmet coming off in the fall.

Laura, scrambling to her knees, saw the helmet roll away and first caught sight of the swatch of tumbled gray hair, then the lantern jaw, and finally the full face, eyes alight with craziness.

Sue Mullins staggered to her feet and faced her.

"*You?*" Laura groaned in recognition.

Mullins clawed at the broken table lamp on the carpet. Her eyes looked totally crazed. She brought the lamp up in a vicious swing. Laura saw what was coming and tried to duck back, but this time she was far too slow. The judge yelled hoarsely. The heavy lamp base slammed into Laura's skull. There was a distant, hollow, clanging sound that echoed and reverberated through her head. *Just like a bell,* Laura thought dazedly. *Just like they say sometimes in sports on TV: "He got his bell rung."*

How funny. How very, very funny.

Then she knew nothing.

TWENTY-THREE

IT WAS A FUNNY, dreamlike state. Laura drifted in it, seeing puffy pink clouds and occasionally hearing voices. At first it seemed the voices were loud and agitated, and then there was a time when she didn't know anything again, and then gentle hands pressed her face and hands, and the voices were distant, and she was being moved somewhere. Like when she was in labor, maybe, and already woozy? But that made no sense. She drifted and felt peaceful, and then she began to be aware of a pulsing headache, and more voices, closer and more real, and gratingly insistent.

"There she comes. She's coming out of it now, I think."

"Oh, the poor thing, the poor thing! And to think I doubted her!"

"Laura?" Gentle fingers brushed her face. "Laura? Are you awake?"

Laura opened her eyes. The first thing she saw was the face of Dr. Which, staring soberly down at her from very close. It was his hand brushing her temple. Then she moved her eyes and became violently disoriented for an instant. *My fairy godmother? And she looks like that?*

*Oh, wait a minute...*memory flooded back and she started thinking a little clearer. Blinking, she looked again. It was Mrs. Epperman standing there, plastic wings askew, her face twisted and tear-streaked.

Laura took a deep breath. It hurt, but not too much. She looked around. She was on the couch in Mrs. Epperman's office, and the clock on the wall said 2:05.

She jerked violently awake. "Judge Young—" She tried to sit up.

Dr. Fred Which gently but firmly forced her shoulders back down. "Take it easy. You're all right. Everything is all right."

Laura's head swam as memory flooded back. "Sue Mullins—"

"It's okay, it's okay! Take it easy."

She gave up and sank back onto the couch cushion. "What happened? What day is it? What—"

"It's a little past two in the morning," Which told her. "You've had a little trip to la-la land. How do you feel?"

Mrs. Epperman gushed, "Oh, you poor thing! We've been so—"

"Hang on a minute, please," Which cut in gently. "Laura, do you know where you are?"

Laura looked around. The limited movement made her head hurt worse. "Sure. I'm in her office, downstairs. But Sue Mullins—"

"It's *okay,* Laura." Which continued to hold her shoulders down. "Let's not get up too fast. Your brain has been rattled a bit."

"What happened? You said the judge is all right?"

"He's fine. No worse, except for being shaky. Both of you had a bad scare. But people got to the room before she could get the insulin into him."

"Insulin?" Laura repeated incredulously. She still felt woozy and disoriented. "That's what it was?"

Which's young face tightened. "A particularly fast-acting type. God knows where she got it. Maybe somebody around here uses the injection method and she stole it from their apartment. It doesn't matter. For somebody like the poor old judge, it would have been lethal enough, and it would take a hell of a sophisticated chemical analysis to uncover any hint afterward."

Laura stared at him, fighting the pained confusion to try to read his expression. "Afterward?"

The doctor frowned. "Laura. What year is this?"

"Aw, gosh, Doc, ask me a hard one."

"Who's the president of the United States?"

"If I said George Washington, would you lock me up?"

Which smiled. "I think you're going to be just fine."

"May I sit up?"

"You can try."

With him helping her raise her shoulders, she sat up. The room went around a few times and somebody with a hammer started banging behind her eyes.

"Okay?"

"Sure," she lied. She looked around. Mrs. Epperman, her tinsel halo off-center, frowned in concern. Back near the closed office door, Still Bill Mills stood silent, pale as parchment.

Dr. Which said, "You're going to the emergency room in a few minutes. I want some X-rays just to be sure your skull isn't cracked, and a CAT scan as well."

"I think I'm okay."

"I do, too, but humor me."

Mrs. Epperman plumped down on the sofa beside her. "Laura, my poor dear girl! Maude Thuringer has told us how you were suspicious long ago! And no one would listen to you. It's horrible. If you had just shared your thoughts with me, perhaps none of this would have happened. I hate to say it at a time like this, but really, it's all your own fault! If we hadn't responded swiftly to the emergency call, you might be dead, and the judge as well. Bill, here, is a hero."

Laura looked back at Still Bill. "What happened?"

He scratched his head. "Well, I saw people running and all, so I went too. When I got to the judge's room, you was out cold on the floor and Miz Epperman, here, and Nurse Svendsen was rassling with Miz Mullins. I tell you what, she was about to get the best of both of them, the way she was swinging that chair. So I had my trusty Crescent wrench in my back pocket, and about the time she whacked Miz Svendsen alongside the head with the chair, I let *her* have it with the wrench." Still Bill looked pleased with himself. "That ended that fight."

Which asked, "What did she hit you with, Laura?"

"The lamp," Laura told him.

Still Bill sighed. "I guess that poor woman was violent right from the first, but nobody could see through the dogmatism."

"Where is she now?"

"She's in the back. Your boyfriend is with her, and a couple of the other boys just got here from Norman. They're fixing to carrying her off to the jailhouse."

Dr. Which asked sharply, "Is the sheriff out there, too?"

"Yessum, he is."

The doctor stood. "I want to talk to him. She's a sick woman. I don't want her taken to the county jail. She needs to go straight to the security ward at the state hospital."

Still Bill shoved his bony hands into his pockets. "Well, if you want my advice, I don't have any. But I think you better hurry, because they were fixing to load her up when I left."

Which gave Laura a hard look. "Stay put till I get back."

"No," Laura said, struggling dizzily to get to her feet. "I want to see her before they take her away."

"You're not well enough. I forbid it."

"Fred," Laura cried, "don't you understand *anything?* I have to see her."

THE SHERIFF, Aaron Lassiter, and a beefy deputy Laura had never seen before stood waiting in the barren concrete staircase foyer at the back of the building. Standing between them was a shrunken, disheveled figure Laura almost didn't recognize until she raised havoc-filled eyes.

Lassiter moved fractionally toward Laura's side and grasped her hand in his. She realized that her hands were like ice.

The sheriff shuffled his boots in obvious discomfort. "Here she is, Ms. Michaels."

Laura faced Sue Mullins, seeing the pain and confusion—the madness.

"Suffering," Sue Mullins said in a mechanical tone. Her eyes glazed. "Must end suffering."

Laura had to know. She felt driven. "After Milly was...gone...did you go back in her room?"

"Yes."

"Why?"

"Earring. Lost."

"And you got in my files, too. Why did you do that?"

"See what you knew."

"Were you going to kill me, too, Sue? Is that it?"

The woman's eyes widened and her jaw fell. "Why would I do that? I *like* you! That's why I slipped that note onto your desk—to keep you away."

Laura's control broke. She reached out, sympathy overwhelming her. "Sue, if any of us had guessed you were so ill—"

"Bitch!" Sue Mullins screamed shockingly. "Don' touch me! I'm not the sick one! They are! And now they'l have to suffer!"

The sheriff and his deputy moved with surprising quickness and caught the woman's clawlike hands before they could tear at Laura's eyes.

IT WAS MORE THAN an hour before things calmed down Back in the offices, Laura had a cup of coffee and a sho of whisky that Judith Epperman produced from somewhere in her desk. The whisky had such a calming effect tha Laura didn't bother to wonder why her boss had it at work

Mrs. Epperman insisted on murmuring more apologies and compliments. Francie Blake fluttered in and fluttered out. Mrs. Knott, from the kitchen crew, and Joe Bradley, from maintenance, looked in worriedly and wanted to gossip; Mrs. Epperman scolded them away for "tiring the poor, heroic girl." Then the office door opened again and Aaron Lassiter, hair standing on end and eyes emitting X-rays, came in. Dr. Which was right behind him.

His forehead filled with wrinkles of concern, Lassiter came back and plopped down on the couch beside Laura and grabbed one of her hands between his big, comfy paws. "Are you okay?"

"Sure," she told him, feeling the rush. "Except for a headache."

His eyes went to the bandage on her forehead. "It's all swollen."

"I heal fast. Honest."

Lassiter glanced at Mrs. Epperman. "The doctor and I need to talk to Laura alone."

Mrs. Epperman looked startled, but left, closing the door behind her.

Dr. Which sat on one of the straight chairs. "Sue Mullins said a lot of other things after we got you away, Laura. She wasn't making a lot of sense. A lot of hysterical talk about her mother and how she suffered from cancer, and how a sister of hers lingered for years with some debilitating disease. I'm no shrink. That's your department. But I think she must be truly crazy. She was babbling about how she did everyone a favor by putting them out of their misery."

Laura shuddered. "She talked to me once about her mother's illness. It was clear then that she had more than the normal sense of horror about it. I didn't see how bad she was. Maybe I should have."

"She fooled a lot of people. I think everyone in the world has probably met someone in their life who was like that—borderline crazy, maybe, capable of terrible acts. Most of them just never get ignited. Sue Mullins did."

Laura shuddered. "She put the needle in the top of the vial. The stuff inside was cloudy."

Which nodded. "Right. Suspended zinc, an additive used to cloud the insulin when it's been mixed thoroughly. If you hadn't stopped her, she would have given the old judge enough to kill a horse."

"Instantly?"

"Very quick. Given a huge dose like that, the patient's blood sugar plummets. Within minutes he's into insulin shock. In somebody as old and weak as Judge Young, that means bingo, you're out of here. Permanently."

Laura turned to Lassiter. "Did she kill the others this way? With insulin?"

"No."

"How, then?"

"She wasn't entirely clear, but she said enough. Nitroglycerin."

"Nitroglycerin?" Puzzled, Laura looked at Which.

"For the heart," Which cut in. "Put a pill under your tongue, and almost instantly it dilates the blood vessels, which relieves pressure on the heart." He frowned. "Or you can also apply it as a salve."

Laura turned back to Lassiter. "I don't get it."

Lassiter held her hand. "The doc and I have already talked about it. In an older person—especially one who's already weak—a quick application of two percent nitro can very easily drop the blood pressure to an unacceptable level. There have been cases where even healthy people just stroked out after nitro."

Laura's skin crawled. "She gave them nitroglycerin that dropped their blood pressure so fast that they died?"

"Shock. Yes."

"No one could have detected it," Which said defensively.

Lassiter shot him a look of pure disgust, but then turned back to Laura. "There's going to have to be a search of her house, maybe even exhumation of a body, and then who knows what we can prove in court? But she said enough when I was back there to give us an awfully good idea of what she must have done those other times. We've got her."

"Injected them with nitroglycerin," Laura said wonderingly, trying to see the picture.

"Not an injection. Not with the last two, anyway. Maybe she just got in a hurry this time—tried a new method."

"But what was the old method?"

"Remember when Cora Chandler was found? And Milly Kett too? The jar of some aromatic patent-medicine salve on the table?"

"Ben-Gay," Laura said.

"I think," Which said, "that stuff was damned little Ben-Gay and a hell of a lot of two percent nitro. Enough Ben-Gay in the jar to mask what it really was, which was nitro salve. You rub it in and it goes to work."

"But we had the one jar analyzed."

"Here's a theory," Lassiter said. "We just finished talking about it with the sheriff. What we think is, Mrs. Mullins talked her way into an apartment somehow. You remember the cut flowers you found in the garbage disposer? What if Sue Mullins appears at your door late at night, with a 'present'—a vase she just stole—or a bouquet of flowers? You invite her in. She's nice. You talk. She asks how you're feeling and you say kind of achy. So she produces a jar of Ben-Gay out of her purse, and says it always works, go ahead, rub some in. She's so nice, she convinces you. You rub it into your arms and shoulders while she sits there, still visiting with you. But it's not Ben-Gay. What it is is two percent nitro with just enough Ben-Gay in it to fool you. You absorb a hell of a dose of nitro through your hands and where you're rubbing. Your blood pressure, according to what Fred tells me, goes through the floor.''

Fred Which nodded, even more pale. ''Your bp can simply go nearly flat. It's fast and possibly lethal.''

''But—'' Laura began to protest.

''Then Mrs. Mullins switches jars—takes her doctored jar of Ben-Gay, and puts a real one in its place to explain the odor on the victim. Then she gets out of there.''

''And,'' Which added, ''the victim, unattended, dies.''

Laura thought about it and shuddered. ''It makes sense.''

''No one could ever guess,'' Which insisted. ''*No one.*''

Lassiter looked up sharply, his jaw tight with controlled anger. ''Especially,'' he snapped, ''if they weren't really working very hard at their job.''

''See here, I resent that.''

''Screw yourself.'' Lassiter put his arms around Laura in a protective gesture.

Closing her eyes, Laura leaned against his chest. That felt good—safe and warm and nice. Inside she was quaking. ''I was so scared!''

''Yeah, but it's okay now, babe,'' he said in his deep, gentle voice. ''It's over.''

That was when something slipped inside Laura, and the tears came.

WHEN SHE wobbled out of the office on Lassiter's arm about an hour later, she saw that a few sticky-eyed residents still clung to chairs around the atrium. Their eyes followed her mutely, filled with worry and concern. Some of them would need to talk about this, she thought. After the things Mrs. Epperman had just said in the office, she suspected there would be no problem setting up additional group and individual talk sessions to meet their needs.

Lassiter guided Laura toward the front doors, his strong arm helping support her. She had gotten dizzy all over again just from the effort of wobbling to the rest room and putting on her normal clothes.

As they neared the door, the clatter of high heels on tile sounded sharply behind them. Turning, they were confronted by Francie Blake, pale and gorgeous in capri pants, a pink sweater, and four-inch spikes.

Francie rushed to Laura and gave her a brief, perfumy hug. "You're a heroine. A real heroine. We're all so proud of you, and happy you're going to be okay."

"Thanks," Laura said. "I—"

But Francie had already turned to Lassiter. "You're going to drive poor Laura home now?"

"Yes," Lassiter told her. "After an X-ray."

"That's wonderful," Francie told him. "It's just what you should do. Then, when you're finished with that, will you please come by my place for a little while?" She gave him a smile that was supposed to be disingenuous. "I'll make coffee. I know it's awfully late, and I actually had very little to do with all this...but I think I must be having some kind of...reaction." She hugged herself and shivered prettily. "I'm *scared*. I really, really am. If you could come by, just for a few minutes?" She stopped, eyelashes batting.

"Miss Blake," Lassiter said, "I really would like that."

"Oh, good! I'll—"

"But," Lassiter cut in, "I don't see how I can."

"Oh?" Francie looked surprised and crestfallen. "Because...?"

"I don't think it's right," Lassiter told her, scowling. "I believe in strict observance of being engaged, and all."

Francie frowned, then beamed. "Oh, *that*." She held up her hand that bore the huge rock. "This is nothing. I'm not really engaged. This ring is just a...a sort of *friendship* ring. My goodness, I'm not engaged at all."

"I didn't mean you," Lassiter told her.

She stared. So did Laura.

Lassiter said, "I meant me."

"You?" Francie gasped. "Engaged?"

"You are?" Laura added in dismay.

"Well," Lassiter said, turning to her. "Maybe not quite yet. But I'd like to be. I mean...what I'm trying to say is...if you'll have me. Or at least—man, I'm screwing this up. But when I thought you'd been badly hurt tonight, it made me see...what I'm *trying* to say is, about us being...uh...regular with one another...I mean, in the olden days they would have called it going steady, or if you were in a sorority, being pinned."

"Aaron," Laura said, flooded by warm, sparkly tingles of pleasure and astonishment, "are you saying what I think you're saying?"

"I think so," he said, and frowned furiously with embarrassment.

Francie Blake made a moaning sound and turned to rush off, killer legs moving swiftly over the tiles. Lassiter's brow furrowed mightily as he watched her go. Then he turned back to Laura.

"So what do you think?" he asked nervously.

Laura almost laughed and almost cried. "My gosh, Aaron, we don't know each other well enough to be engaged."

He glared. "Maybe later?"

Laura stopped talking and stared up into his troubled, uncertain eyes. This, she thought, was the most incredible development of all.

She was going to have to consider this from a lot of angles. But she thought she already knew what the answer...one day...would be.

A LOVE DIE FOR

CHRISTINE T. JORGENSEN
A Stella the Stargazer Mystery

First Time in Paperback

MURDER IN THE STARS

Jane Smith quits her boring job, ditches her faithless boyfriend and employs her unique talents to become Stella the Stargazer. Now she's offering horoscope advice for the lovelorn in a Denver newspaper.

The ink is barely dry on her first column offering advice to a lost soul looking for "a love to die for" when she stumbles upon the body of the owner of her favorite lingerie shop—stabbed to death with a pair of scissors.

Add a police detective she *almost* liked before he accused her of murder, toss in her own uncanny sixth sense and an expressive pet chameleon, and her future is a bit unpredictable...especially with a killer gazing at Stella.

"Stella's quirky humor, human frailties...will endear her to many readers."
—*Publishers Weekly*

Available in March at your favorite retail stores.

CRIMINALS ALWAYS HAVE SOMETHING TO HIDE—BUT THE ENJOYMENT YOU'LL GET OUT OF A WORLDWIDE MYSTERY NOVEL IS NO SECRET....

With Worldwide Mystery on the case, we've taken the mystery out of finding something good to read every month.

Worldwide Mystery is guaranteed to have suspense buffs and chill seekers of all persuasions in eager pursuit of each new exciting title!

Worldwide Mystery novels—crimes worth investigating...

EAST BEACH
RON ELY

First Time in Paperback

A Jake Sands Mystery

KILLER SERVE

Jake Sands has given up the high-risk life to seek obscurity after the murder of his wife and child. He now lives in gorgeous and upscale Santa Barbara—spending days in heaven and learning to live life after hell. Routine is his one constant: running, breakfast at his favorite coffee shop and conversations with his favorite waitress, Julie Price.

So when Julie is murdered, Jake can't leave it alone. Outfitting himself in neon shorts and wraparound shades, he hits the volleyball scene to hunt for a killer. And he discovers a game as volatile as a missing forty-million-dollar lottery ticket—in a world where the high score wins...and losers pay a deadly price.

"A plot that packs action and logic"   *—L.A. Times*

Available in February at your favorite retail stores.